ICE WATER IN HELL DEMOCRACY

By
Marvin E. Fox

ISBN 978-0-9896905-6-0

TABLE OF CONTENTS

The Mysterious Bubble

A destructive bubble of water inundated the Beltway of Washington, DC, on October third at 12:38 a.m. The President, Vice President, and the President's Cabinet, along with many politicians and bureaucrats, were lost in the surprise inundation.

Horror and disbelief stunned the nation as news of the unprecedented disaster spread across the land. A large bubble of water appeared mysteriously in the central capital area. Rising like a ghostly storm surge, the water peaked at the varying rooftop levels of the major buildings in the center of the city and then slowly curved to ground level as it reached the outer limits of its power inside the Beltway.

Mediacrats, journalists, meteorologists, government officials, and concerned experts in many fields hurried to the sight of the devastation. They quickly formed the expected crisis committees and attempted to explain the strange looking pile of water. The city is not ordinarily in danger from tidal waves, and the outlying areas suffered no related or unusual problems. Washington, DC's weather was balmy and pleasant as the strange upsurge of water rose to its most destructive level and quickly receded. No storms were reported near the Capital. Satellite images showed no occurrence of strange weather in the Atlantic Ocean near the nation's East Coast.

The consulted experts were unwilling to go on record with an explanation for the devilish bunch of water. The sighting, by an unnamed source, known only to the television media, of a large oceanic waterspout entering the city after traveling up the Potomac River was discarded. No additional observers who saw the waterspout could be found. The area is too busy for a waterspout of that size to have passed without having been seen by many people during daylight hours.

Only one credible suggestion was reported to the experts. The suggestion came from Cliff Barket, Jackson Hole, Wyoming's local weatherman. Mr. Barket suggested an earthquake had, somehow, instantaneously released huge amounts of ground water into central Washington, DC. The appropriate obligatory government committee discounted this, one credible theory. No evidence of earthquake activity had been recorded. The strange pile of water disappeared as quickly and as mysteriously as it had appeared.

The only progress made by the large group of mystified experts was to change the name of the disastrous inundation from tidal wave to "bubble wave." The confused experts concluded, there was virtually no tide or storm involved. Further, the volume of water at its greatest impact was shaped more like an irregular bubble than a wave. To date, no closure on this mystery has been forthcoming. The experts usually available to explain strange occurrences at the drop of a hat are not returning phone calls.

Eyewitnesses to the tidal wave, renamed bubble wave were as mystified as the experts. They said, "The water came and the water went."

Archie Strickland, a tourist in the city from Waynesville, Illinois, one of the many survivors who were nearly drowned in the bubble of water, reported, "The bubble of water came from nowhere. It covered me and everything else for a few seconds and then just disappeared. The giant flushing sound was terrible to hear."

Clarice Peebuble, a local psychic, made a few waves when she announced that her Master of the World psychic contact had informed her that the entire presidential administration had been sucked out of Washington and taken to a secret location in the Himalayan Mountains to receive Master of the world consultation and training. She declared, "The entire group will return after three years training. Under the care of her Masters of World they would become a super-evolved group of humans with enough information and newly inculcated dedication to solve all of the national problems." Some people believed Clarice might have been onto something until they considered how many national problems the wetly departed had solved in the past. Only a few were willing to believe a few Masters of the World could teach that bunch to solve a problem in only three years.

Herald Fogbreathe, the administration's ultra left-wing consultant for ultra right-wing conspiracies, accused the ultra right-wing fundamentalist of using that means to rid themselves of fair-minded politicians, and Fogbreathe demanded an immediate investigation. The Justice Department investigation bogged down as soon as it started. Half of the Justice Department had disappeared with the bubble, and the other half pleaded organization problems.

Herald Fogbreathe was then appointed by an unnamed survivor to establish an investigatory panel of respectable, non-partisan, and honest people to make an unbiased report on the situation. In order to identify the guilty people on the right, the investigators needed to know who was on the left. The investigators would then eliminate those on the left from their investigation and concentrate their efforts on the right. Investigator Fogbreathe's investigators could find no one willing to admit to ever having been anything but middle-of-the road American, and there was no government record of left-wing or right-wing people. Herald Fogbreathe had his own list of right-wingers, but he couldn't surrender it to the investigation for perusal by the investigators. Some of the supposed right-wingers on Herald's list had disappeared in what Herald thought was a left-wing bubble.

The investigators could only conclude, for the purposes of their investigation, that everyone surviving the bubble of water in Washington, D.C., was a middle-of-the-road American. The Fogbreathe investigation failed for the lack of a definition for ultra right-wingers. Besides that, City officials admitted that there was no way for one person or any group to pile up that much water in the center of the city and get it back out in less than a minute without leaving most of it behind.

The many theories bandied about solved nothing about the mystery. The wave rose and dissipated as quickly as a motion to impose a special tax on congressional pay. It engulfed the rooftops of Washington's public buildings in seconds and disappeared as quickly. It has been opined by some of the unnamed experts that the rapidity of the bubble's disappearance caused the giant flushing sound mentioned by Archie Strickland, and had nothing to do with any flushing action suggested by unidentified ultra right-wingers.

Oblivious to the disaster hanging over their heads, the Congressmen and Gentle Ladies of both Houses had been busy with the difficult effort of designing a tax bill to protect the American economy from being inundated with money from a projected small wave of the surplus green stuff headed in its direction.

The general public was in stark disbelief about any suspected surplus of money coming from Washington that would benefit people who actually paid taxes. Nevertheless, Congress was in heated debate. Each caucus was wrestling with the different aspects of the core issues and how to deflect any possible incoming money into the most politically advantageous government programs.

The Progressive Caucus favored faking a financial calamity to force the American people to think the government needed the money to save them from disaster. The progressives intended to claim that the money was becoming available due to a disastrous oversight by Republicans, who had failed to respect the needs of the poor for universal medical care. Since the progressives were to blame for spreading the surplus money claim, they knew it was only a ploy used to advance their agenda. They intended to offer legislation that would overcome the financial calamity and change the American government forever.

The moderates favored just taxing the surplus out of existence. They thought it was a safe bet that the American taxpayers would not blame politicians calling themselves moderates for taking money from the people before the people had received it.

The conservatives preferred to let the money land in the hands of each citizen and allow the economy to grow so the money would benefit the people and government. Conservatives were in the minority and had no chance of getting their legislation passed.

The liberals, being the better poker players among the anointed, decided to wait and see if the plan by the progressives had enough feet on the ground to work. If the progressive plan seemed to rise in political stature, they would hold out for everything they could get before giving it their support. If it didn't work, they could claim they didn't know any of the progressives personally and blame any problems that arose on the Republicans.

The horrible bubble of water washed the proposed tax bull and many of the debating Gentlemen and Gentle Ladies away.

To date, no bodies of the wetly departed have been found. The inability of rescue crews to discover the bodies of the famous and the infamous, the unknown and the notorious, further deepened the mystery of the bizarre occurrence. The process of disappearances by bubble was further complicated by the lack of tourists and ordinary working people being swept away or drowned when the bubble of water made its mysterious appearance and exit.

Worry about the future of the nation drove the Mediacrats into a frenzy of interviews. The usual heavy breathing, hand wringing, gloom and doom experts were exhaustively consulted. The long-suffering experts stopped wringing their hands long enough to come to a unanimous conclusion: the vast majority of American people might possibly be hit right between the eyes with their own gratuitous and undeserved tax-free earnings. There just wasn't enough time to allow government rescue efforts to save the poor, beleaguered taxpayers from spending the small oncoming spurt of individual wealth.

The Mediacrats' experts feared the untaxed money would simply remain free to drift uncontrolled through the economy. The federal government had suffered a total break down of its tax collecting agencies caused by the loss of key personnel and many computers damaged by the unexpected flood. The experts feared the terrible loss left the unfortunate and unprotected American taxpayers, unschooled in the art of redistributing their own wealth, prey to their own ignorant opinions about how to spend earned money they were breathlessly waiting to give to tax collectors.

The Mediacrats' concerns for the welfare of the fifty states was nearly as intense as that of the bureaucrats' worries for the future of DC. How would the states know how to remain in operation without the federal government telling them how to spend the federal tax money? Taxes collected from the citizens of their states, reduced to a more manageable amount by the federal bureaucracy, and then returned to the states' governments from Washington. What would happen to sensitivity training and diversity indoctrination? Would political correctness become a thing of the past? Would people indoctrinated with political correctness need psychological counseling after the demise of so many politically correct leaders? If so, how much? Who would regulate the size of toilets? How could the leaders of the sovereign states hold up under the stress of so many never before experienced burdens? Would state governments wither and grind to a halt without the regulation imposed by the lost leaders they had elected to represent them? The problems were too many and too complicated for the collection of Mediacrats and hand wringing experts to properly enumerate. They all agreed on one thing—disaster was just around the corner for every state. Well, every state except Alaska, Texas, and probably a bunch of other states that don't give a damn if anyone disappeared from Washington, D.C., anyhow.

One surviving Mediacrat magnanimously offered to take over the government himself. He, he asserted, was the only survivor left in the country who had sufficient national stature and diversity training, a Washington residence, and enough time inside the Beltway to understand the big picture in American culture. He made his magnanimous offer with some urgency because he had seen flying saucers in the air over Washington as the bubble of water disappeared. He wondered if the strange bubble of water might be the prelude to interplanetary war. The guy from Waynesville, Illinois, said there were no flying saucers, just some automobile hubcaps thrown in the air by the bubble exhausting its power as it left.

The D.C. pundits considered Waynesville, Illinois, to be too far from the outer curb of the Beltway for Archie to be a reliable source of information. They didn't know if Archie knew hubcaps from spaceships, but they were unwilling to take a chance on anyone but one of their own to know the difference.

There was a rush by Mediacrats to accept their brother Mediacrat's offer. If the nation had any luck left, he and his fellow Mediacrats would still be standing there in their wet shoes waiting confirmation for his presidential bid or the next outgoing bubble—whichever came first.

The disaster, while local, had far-reaching affects. The most pressing, far-reaching problem was for those taken away by the water. The bubble of water caused a rather large number of politicians, spinmeisters, lobbyists, lawyers, Mediacrats, and bureaucrats to attempt to get into Heaven at one time, about forty thousand or so, mostly Democrats. The Washington, D.C., inhabitants are mostly Democrats, as we all know. This was no problem for Heaven, of course, but for the participant hopeful entrants into Heaven, it did raise some problems.

The Statesmen Hear the Judgment

The crowd of political applicants entered the Domain of Eternal Judgment as one group. Some were a little breathless from the experience but none felt seriously damaged.

The highest court of all courts was unperturbed by such a large crowd. It was prepared for both the illustrious and the simple among them. Somehow those who were saved, and those who were unsaved had entered through different doors into neighboring chambers. A short railing anyone could have stepped over separated them, but there was no crossover traffic.

The two groups were present before different judgment benches at the same time. The group of those destined for Heaven was rather small, and they appeared saddened by their experience but hopeful. Saddened, perhaps, because they understood they were sinners and needed the mercy of God to save them. They were uncertain it would be forthcoming. They were still hopeful, because God allows all of his people a little hope.

The large group on its way to Hell was lively to the point of boisterousness. Its members appeared confident of their salvation. A few of them waved to the unfamiliar judge of the other group as if saying, "Look, I'm over here."

They laughed, smiled, and talked among themselves, telling each other how good it would be to live in Heaven. Some of them remarked, only to each other, of course, that they would be available for government work, ready to supervise and regulate the many problems certain to occur in such a large population over such a wide area as Heaven. They thought their expertise in regulating the progress of the never-solved national problems in Washington made them ideal for the job. They paid only scant attention to the small group they thought were on their way to Hell. Perhaps the same way they treated them in pre-bubble days.

A few angels, one for each of the people in the small group of saved people, passed among the group and whispered something to each of them. The angels took each by the arm, led each out of the hall of judgment, exiting through a large golden door with ruby handles. As the golden door swung open, the sound of quiet, dignified laughter, the clink of wine glasses, and some quiet clapping of hands could be heard.

The large group clucked, expressed their sorrow, but thought, "What can one expect for a group of people so wrong in life?" Some thought Hell might not be such a bad place. It sounded like they were having a party in there.

The court became darker and appeared less friendly as the judge for the saved souls left the Court. The Hell bent ones quickly regained their composure, smiled, and returned their attention to their friends. Each of them expected to be informed of the good things he would soon be given in the joyful afterlife.

The Bailiff stepped forward and would have asked for all to rise, but all he would have asked were already standing. The Gray Angel Bailiff paused to consider the situation, and then announced, "The High Court of all Courts number 666 is now in session." The judge, bedecked in a flowing, black robe and wearing what appeared to be a black doily on his head entered the court. The Bailiff, in a loud voice, announced, "Judge Carl Bullman presiding."

Judge Bullman surveyed the crowd and then made a brief opening statement. "You were removed from your positions and brought to this place to prevent a revolution most of you knowingly, others as uncaring accessories, would have brought about. The revolutionary effort you were engaged in was the culmination of a several decades-long effort by leftist politicians. Your purpose was to gain complete control of your political party while establishing a shadow government within the departments of government that were necessary to your revolution. You had successfully accomplished that task! The revolution you were then poised to complete would have changed the Republic of the United States into a socialist based fraudulent democracy of the United States. As a result of those actions, each of you has been convicted and found to be lacking in truth, honesty, and fidelity to your duties. You have consistently failed to obey some of the basic principles established by your creator.

"The proceedings in this court are not based on the constitutional laws of the Republic of the United States. All present in this court have understood those laws very well and violated them thoroughly. This court is governed by the laws of the Creator, and many of those laws are included in the Constitution of the Republic of the United States.

"This hearing is being conducted to give each person, in the body of the whole body of the convicted, an opportunity to oppose the sentence to Hell already pronounced against each of you. Those who accept help will be able to change their sentences in varying degrees, depending on the severity of the sentence against the individual. This is the only chance you will have to mitigate the sentence against you. I suggest you take advantage of it. All who have reason to believe your sentence is unfair, in part or in total, may speak as he or she desires. Unless just cause can be shown that an imposed sentence should be considered unfair, the original sentence on that individual will be carried out."

Calling it a stunned silence doesn't frame the scene correctly. A dreadful numbing sensation fell on each of the forty thousand in the crowd. They had gone from believing they were a shoo in for Heaven to being previously and without their knowledge convicted of crimes they had not been allowed to enter a plea for and without trail were already sentenced to Hell. It was just too much for most of them to deal with on an instantaneous basis. Who could blame them for being out of sorts?

Out of sorts it was—wet shod, clammy clothed, angry, mean mouthed, out of sorts. Everyone began yelling at once, and no one could understand what anyone else was saying. Each of them screamed loud enough to drown out his neighbor. The whole forty thousand of them loudly, and simultaneous expressed their conviction that they had been railroaded, were mad as hell, and refused to take it any more.

Judge Bullman stepped into the avalanche of screaming opprobrium, banged his gavel, and shouted, "I will have quiet in this Court." The accused weren't in a good enough mood to make being quiet easy enough to get by banging a gavel no one heard, or a shout no one listened to. Their protests had begun with an angry explosion of voices that became louder with each shouted syllable.

Judge Bullman knew how to handle the noisy situation with the enraged politicians. He didn't get upset or call for help. He pressed a button under his judge's bench. A noise like all the banshee's that ever screamed began screaming at once came from the ceiling. The whole forty thousand people crouched as though they were about to be nuked.

Judge Bullman let go of the button and once again addressed the accused. "Now that I have your attention, I will acquaint you with the bureaucratic process to be followed by anyone wishing to represent himself. First, will each of you who wish to oppose his sentence raise his hand?"

All forty thousand hands went up. There were no exceptions. That came as no shock. All were delivered to the gate of Hell in the same bubble of water. All of them had been where the bubble of water would be because they were chosen to be at that place at that time to be delivered to the Court of Hell. If they had been given time to take a good look at each other, they would have discovered everyone in the assembled crowd was deeply involved with government work in one fashion or another. Most of them knew several or many others who were in the same business. There were no average citizens in the Court.

Judge Bullman looked down from his bench and said, "All of you have chosen to oppose the sentence against you. I suggest each of you approach the problem of your defense as an individual. The best chance you have to reduce your sentence in some fashion is to seek the help of the Court on an individual basis. Your sentences are a reflection of your performance as individual living people. You can't change your past performance, but you might make some gain by looking at your past life realistically within the framework of what you should have been doing instead of what you were doing."

Judge Bullman continued, "This Court is providing two documents for each of you. The first document is small and consists of the charges you have been convicted of. The second is a large volume and informs each of the accused of the incidents in his life that supports his conviction. The second document lists each separate incident of the charges against you and the motivations you had for performing in the manner you did.

"A large area has been provided for you to study this information. You will be allowed to formulate whatever defense you wish to present. Again, you may present any defense you think is best, but for this procedure, individual defenses are recommended rather than a group defense. The Bailiff will have a station just inside the large room you are to occupy. He or his staff will assist you in any way they can. You may request your documents from him. Please follow the Bailiff to the preparation area."

The soggy group followed the Bailiff, a Gray Angel seven feet tall with large wings folded behind him, to a large room with a huge empty area in the center. The room had adequate seating and worktables for all of them. Tables and chairs surrounded a large, empty area at the center of the huge room. At the far end of the room was a stage with a podium for any who wished to use it. Their clothing dried immediately upon entering the room, and that made them a little more comfortable.

As the large group began milling around the room, recognizing friends and associates, they became many smaller groups engaged in conversations about their predicament. They were still in denial about what had happened to them. Denial caused confusion about their situation, and none of them were ready to follow Judge Bullman's directions on their own behalf.

President Clint Comingal and Vice President Gordon Patsy were the first to attempt to get a handle on the problem. They gathered the Presidents Cabinet and the six Supreme Court judges near the back of the room to discuss the best approach for their defense. Nearly everyone else had formed small groups nearer the stage. There was little privacy in that part of the room. P. Comingal broke the silence. "All right! Here we are! Do any of you have at least the beginnings of an idea about how we should mount a defense?"

After a long silence, Judge Calvin Bolton said, "Why not just do what Judge Bullman said, get the two documents provided by the court, study them, and see if we can make individual deals? We've already been convicted, and according to the judge, all we can do is lower our sentences through the action of the Court."

"If we can lower our sentences," retorted Supreme Court Judge Alan Coffin, "we may be able to reverse them entirely. I'm not planning on a change from too hot to still too hot. I want my own—and of course all of you and our subordinates—sentences changed from here, to out of here."

Senator "Big" Sam Pilfry had been watching the high-profile defendants and had trailed along behind them to see what they were up to. Sam figured he knew when the coffee was about to perk. To no one in particular, he said, "I know every one of those guys, and they take nothing lying down."

Big Sam interjected himself into the group and the conversation. "So far, it's no good," he remarked. "We don't know who's here yet. We don't know what kind of defense will suit us best. I ain't taking no judge's word on the best way to go down in his court. I think we need to take a poll of who is here and how we can use all of us to get the best deal for most of us."

Judge Alan Coffin made his recommendation. "Maybe we should begin by getting the charges from the Bailiff. We need to see what we have been convicted of. There may be something in the charges to allow us a defense. If Sam wants to take a poll, let him take the poll."

VP Patsy reasoned, "We can't get all of the charges, they're for each individual. We'll need an agreement from everyone to see all of the charges at one time."

P. Comingal thought for a minute or so, before he entered the breech. "I'll try to convince everyone that we should look at a collective defense before we look at individual defenses. That's the only way we can get all of the charges. We'll check the charges for validity. If we can do better for ourselves individually, we'll go that way. If a collective defense is best for us, we'll go that way."

The power brokers in the small group agreed with the premise of look before you leap. Comingal and his group headed for the front of the room and the podium.

P. Comingal, surrounded by his usual staff, went to the podium on the stage and addressed the assembly of the convicted. "If we could have quiet please." Everyone became quiet as their leader spoke. "I and my staff have been kicking around our situation, and I think we have the beginnings of a plan to help all of us out of this situation. We have decided to look at all of the charges against us in order to have a better understanding of the possibilities of a collective defense. Since all of the charges are in individual packages, we need your cooperation to get them on a collective basis.

"There are about forty thousand of us; it will take a rather large crew to filter and assemble the information we need. I'm going to select a number of trustworthy individuals to do the difficult work of inspecting the charges against us. The group will include our most trusted lawyers. This, of course, will include our Party's most prestigious constitutional lawyer, Mr. Flim Flamm. Mr. Flim Flamm will be supervised by one of our Supreme Court justices, the Honorable Alan Coffin. Every word of the information on individuals will be treated with the utmost confidentiality.

"I suggest all of us who think this is a bad plan go to the Bailiff, ask for their personal documents, and make the best individual defense they can. Those of us who do not share in your personal decision wish you the best of luck. We, ourselves, wish to study both sides of that street before we allow an unfamiliar judge to force us to walk into Hell on it. Do any of you have questions?"

A voice from the crowd asked, "Who is leading this team of experts on Heavenly law, and who is going to be on the team?"

"I will lead the team," P. Comingal admitted. "My Cabinet, six Supreme

Court justices, and Sen. "Big" Sam Pilfry will be on it. I intend to include James Cornball, who is really great at clarifying party positions, to join us for public relations purposes. We will be the core members of the team. Of course, there will be many others brought into the process as convenience or necessity requires. Most of you, standing right here in this group, will be instrumental in creating our defense. We feel your pain! We will be glad for the comments and suggestions from those who feel they have something to offer, but aren't directly involved in the team effort."

Elfie Spiel, from the Department of Transportation, said, "That sounds to me like the whole crew that got us into this mess. What makes you think we want a leader who was drowned by God?"

"You were also drowned by God," P. Comingal answered testily. "If you know someone who wasn't, send him up."

Elfie was mad because she, in her opinion, had died young, and she wasn't about to take the blame herself. She retorted, "Your whole administration was inundated with scandals and one bubble of water. You couldn't build a defense if they let you put land mines around it. We're all here because of you and your lousy administration."

James Cornball, the king of the spinmeisters, had heard his name mentioned favorably by P. Comingal and felt he had to defend the honor of his mentor. He yelled at Elfie, "You ain't no Democrat. You ain't no team player. Only plan you got is a lot of bad-mouth accusations. Comingal is the best man we could have. Ain't nothin' he can't get us out of. He's the slickest thing I've ever seen."

Milton Branch, who had been bubbled while he was in town from his post in a National Park, came to Elfie's rescue. "Cornball, you're the biggest motor mouth east of the Rocky Mountains. If you ever had to think before you talked, you wouldn't be able to say a word. Comingal, what public did you intend to turn this loudmouth spinmeister loose on? We're the only ones here, and we aren't the public."

P. Comingal knew he had to get through all of the petty objections before he could find the best defensive posture for himself. He decided to control the damage by hurrying the process along. He said, "I know there are many objections to what we are trying to do. Some of you will not be able to understand our message. Those who object to what we are working so very hard to do—for all of us—should seek your own counsel and your own defense as you choose. This team is the best we can get. They are the most capable among us. I have a great deal of confidence in their ability to find a happy solution to this unhappy problem that was forced on us by circumstances beyond our control."

Elfie Spiel, Milton Branch, and a few others left the main group to find a place in the back of the room where they could discuss the calamity without the help of the high-powered plotters at the other end of the room. After their worried discussions, they went to the Bailiff and requested the personal documents mentioned by Judge Bullman. After reading their past histories, they returned to the Bailiff to be ushered into a different part of the court. What happened to them? None of the others knew.

The Plan

Most of the Mediacrats, spinmeisters, lobbyists, lawyers, and the politicians who had so recently reached statesman rank, stayed to see what kind of plan Clint Comingal would come up with to reverse the sentence of fire and brimstone on them. None of them had very much faith in their ability to use their own personal history to slick their way out of it by themselves. They had watched P. Comingal skinny his way out of many very serious messes, and they had a shaky kind of hope in his ability to pull it off—one more time.

P. Comingal continued speaking from the podium. He smiled, spread his hands for silence, and then said, " Those among our group of friends who refused to understand our message are gone. That's probably best for all of us. They would have, almost certainly, damaged our defense at some critical point. We wouldn't want that.

"At this early point in the progress of the problem, I don't know what kind of defense we should apply to our situation. We need to ask the court for a list of the alleged crimes and incriminating charges against us as a collective group, and we need your permission to get the list from the Court. We need to examine the charges for validity. We need to categorize them for seriousness. We need to compile them for the sake of defensive continuity. We must then decide on the best possible method of presenting our defense, keeping in mind our individual and personal needs for that defense. No one will be forgotten. None of the allegations against any of us can be ignored. We are in this as a team, and as a team we will prevail; no team member will be left behind."

P. Comingal sent Supreme Court Justice Nance Herefor to the Bailiff to request the hoped-for single list of charges on the group as a whole. The Bailiff told Judge Herefor, "Each of you was charged separately, and the charges are in individual files. Court 666 has no list of charges on the group as one body."

Judge Herefor was dumbfounded by the Bailiff's brutally abrupt statement, and he couldn't force the Bailiff to budge an inch. Judge Herefor had to accept what he could get. He returned to the group for help to move the massive amount of material. He would need many hands to wheel the many carts it would take to transport the files from the Bailiff's station to the front of the room near the stage, and he asked those he approached first for that help.

On arriving below the stage with the files, Judge Herefor reported, "All of the files are predicated on individual defenses, and there is no list of charges on the group as a whole. We must deal with the charges as the Court issued them. If they are to be compiled, we will have to compile them ourselves."

P. Comingal was incensed. "We requested one trial for all of us, but the judge has sent us forty thousand different individual documents. That is unacceptable! How can we be expected to mount a common defense with all of these entirely individual charges against us?"

"That's right, Chief," the unhelpful Patsy agreed.

P. Comingal decided a clarification of procedures was necessary. He ordered VP Patsy, "You go to the Bailiff and explain this to him; we are mounting a collective defense. We would appreciate it if the judge could, possibly, see his way clear to give us a consolidated document with a compilation of charges on the entire group without repetitions, instead of forty thousand documents. Forty thousand documents are undoubtedly replete with repetitions of the accusations on this same group."

VP Patsy dutifully walked through the long room to the bailiff's station. Addressing the intimidating looking Bailiff, Patsy fearfully reported, "The President isn't pleased with the separate files of accusations. He, with all due respect to the Court, requests one document for all of us without repetition of the charges."

The Bailiff looked down on the hapless Patsy, and without going anywhere or consulting anyone, he abruptly replied, "The Court respectfully replies that the files you were given are the only files there are. You must use the files the Court made available for your defense in the form the Court provided."

VP Patsy returned to P. Comingal, telling him, "The judge is intractable on the form of the accusations. The Bailiff said we have to use the ones we have."

P. Comingal unruffled his feathers and took an undaunted look at what he had at hand. He said, "Nance, find my file in that mess. I'll look at my own file to see how the others are arranged."

Nance Herefor went through the files arranged in alphabetical order. He found P. Comingal's and handed it to the President. P. Comingal looked at his file without comment or change of expression for a short time. Without a word spoken to anyone, he decided he had to spread the blame. An attempt for him to face the Court alone and try to talk his way out of the charges against himself would be the last act of a doomed man.

P. Comingal stuffed his personal charge file into his coat pocket as he said, "We'll need some privacy to go over such a large volume of information. There is more privacy toward the back of the room. We can spread it all out on the tables. Flamm, you, Herefor, and Bolton take a bunch of those lawyers to the back of the room and begin the effort to look at the charges. Fortunately, there are plenty of lawyers in the group."

P. Comingal returned to the podium and addressed the accused to announce the necessity for him to assign a "best hope" control group for the defense team. He gave the large group a confident smile before he said, "We're going to need some supervision for this defense. If they are willing, I want the following people on the supervisory team. I want my Cabinet members, the VP, the Supreme Court Justices Alan Coffin and Nance Herefor, along with Calvin Bolton and the other three justices. I also want our constitutional lawyer, Mr. Flim Flamm, and I think we need James Cornball to even the team out."

The dissenting voice of Ray Blather, a well-known Mediacrat, said, "How can there be a well-rounded team when there isn't one journalist on the supervisory team? Who will be the people's representative?

P. Comingal didn't want to hear it, but he knew he had to give in or start a war with a bunch of loud, disappointed Mediacrats. He replied, "I'm sorry, these are difficult procedures, and I hope you will pardon my oversight. Of course, the press should be represented. After all, we have all been painted with the same brush. Ray, we'll be glad to have you on the team as the people's representative."

"Big" Sam Pilfry hadn't heard his name called for a position on the core team. He sure wasn't going to let Comingal's crew make his decisions for him. Some of the other members of Congress had approached Big Sam with the same fears Sam had. Sam bellowed, "You don't have any members of Congress on that supervisory team. I, personally, don't think it can function without legislative support. I think the whole thing will collapse without congressional direction to keep it steered on the proper course."

P. Comingal realized simplification had its limits, and he didn't want to antagonize the newly designated statesmen among them. He once again conceded defeat. "Sam, you know I would never make a move without the support of Congress. Will you join the team to represent all of the congressmen?"

"Sam replied, "I'll do the very best I can for all of my fellow congressmen."

That wasn't good enough for the Republic Party representative Berl Crickford. Berl demanded, "We Republicans want to be represented. We want a bipartisan effort. If it isn't bipartisan, all of us Republicans are walking out and making our own defense."

P. Comingal knew that the minority in the group were members of the Republic Party. He didn't care about them personally, but he didn't want to go up against Judge Bullman backed by only Democrats; it might look too one sided. He capitulated once more. "Berl, you know I have always favored bipartisan efforts. Of course you are welcome on the team as the bipartisan representative."

Comingal looked for a few seconds at the Chicago bunch for a demand for representation he expected from them. Only a few of them were actually from Chicago, but the total number in the group was more than a thousand. Their tall leader gave Comingal his usual cardboard smile and remained silent. P. Comingal guessed his silence meant they were expecting, or planning, for a crisis to occur so their demands would have to be overwhelmingly accepted to defuse the crisis. Comingal felt he knew them pretty well and believed he would know how to deal with them when they made their move.

While Comingal's team of experts and the massive crowd were in discussion and rumination about their situation, lawyer Flim Flamm, the six

Supreme Court justices and a couple hundred of the bubbled lawyers had gone to the back of the room. The legal team charged into the pile of charges to find some means of reversing the sentence of hellfire on themselves.

Defense Preparations

P. Comingal, followed by V.P. Patsy, wandered through the accused, attempting to form a consensus for his unspoken spread-the-blame approach to his own defense. At each stop, he repeated, "A common defense based on our uncommon devotion to duty is our best chance to beat this problem. My plan will be far superior to an individual defense each of us could make for himself."

Meanwhile, back at the workstations, the six Supreme Court judges, lawyer Flim Flamm, joined by a growing number of expensive lawyers and various levels of officials, had removed some of the charge files. Their cursory examination of the files convinced them they could make one composite file that would adequately represent all of the charges. It seemed the group, although being individually charged had generally been into the same sort of skullduggery. They thought there were a large number of individual peccadilloes which were still necessary to be considered, but the charges the lawyers thought were the main problems would make a reasonably short list, maybe one page, maybe more.

P. Comingal, seconded by VP Patsy, was pleased. Both thought the court would find a one-page compiled list, or maybe more, would be acceptable. Why they thought that before they asked the Court was anybody's guess, especially since Comingal had managed to hide his own file in his jacket pocket where it couldn't be examined by the team or included in the team's compiled list of charges that would later be presented to the court.

The next order of business for the team was to actually compile the list of charges. They tentatively decided that they might, possibly, be able to reduce the list of charges to a more manageable number. When completed, they could present the compiled list to the body of the whole body of the accused and obtain a democratic agreement from a majority of the accused. If the body of the whole body of the accused rejected the list, it was back to the old drawing board for a new try.

P. Comingal, VP Patsy, four Supreme Court justices, sixty-two congressmen, lawyer Flim Flamm, many trusted legal and advisory aides, and those from the body of the whole body of the accused who could not be put off from interfering in the process were now on the team. The new personnel insisted on joining because they felt their personal interests were too much at stake for them to remain uninvolved in an obvious future-threatening process. Comingal realized he had no authority to actually exclude anyone, so a larger team of about eight hundred committed blame spreaders were now working on the collective defense team. The swelling of the team was a problem, but Comingal felt it was still small enough for him to maintain a self-advantageous control.

Because of the clearly intense activity of the team, P. Comingal felt something had to be said to the forty thousand accused. Many of those left out of the process had begun to fidget. Their lack of involvement in compiling the charges had produced, in the minds of the fidgeting benchwarmers, a growing fear of an uncertain outcome.

Comingal mounted the stage once again and pivoted slowly as he inspected the panorama of faces around him. He gave his State of the Defense speech. "We are making great strides toward a solution. Due to the complicated nature of the task before us, we have had to call on the most expert among us to fatten up the work force to more certainly conclude this procedure to the satisfaction of all of us who have been wrongfully accused. This is a bipartisan effort; we now have nearly one hundred Republicans on the team. All of the Republic Party team members are excellent men of good character, and the new additions in all cases have been made to expedite the process."

Comingal patted his personal charge book hidden in the inside breast pocket of his jacket as he continued. "Painstaking consideration of each of our problems is guaranteed. We have all the time we want. Utilizing our time correctly will surely bring us the success we seek. We still have a long way to go, but I can see the light brightening at the end of our tunnel."

VP Patsy felt he had to do or say something. Not being able to think of anything to say, he dutifully raised his left hand and made a V with the first two fingers while giving all present the benefit of his most courageous smile.

During the wait for the team to compile its list of accusations, P. Comingal became curious about the qualifications of the judge assigned to their case. More knowledge of the presiding judge might bring out some hidden information the team could use during its defense in court. He spoke of his curiosity to VP Patsy, and they decided to approach the Bailiff for whatever historical information the two of them could discover about the judge's prior experience on the bench.

P. Comingal and VP Patsy confidently approached the strange looking Bailiff. The Bailiff was very tall and fierce looking. He appeared to be a male, but he was also obviously missing the major male components that would have been obvious in a naked male from earth. V.P. Patsy decided the Bailiff was wearing a skintight suit that hid everything, and the suit was somehow the same gray color as his skin, making his clothing invisible to the naked eye.

P. Comingal opened the conversation. "Judge Bullman must have been a very famous judge in the United States at some time. I confess, I've never heard of a Judge Carl Bullman. Can you give us any information on him?"

"There is no secret about that," the Bailiff barked. "I'll be glad to give you all of the information I have on Judge Bullman. He lived in the United States from the year of our lord 1845 until 1913. He was a devout man, honest in all of his dealings, truthful to all who spoke with him, and he was a man of sound judgment."

P. Comingal inquired further, "What were his duties during that time?"

"He had no judicial duties," the Bailiff reported, "He was a plumber."

Comingal and Patsy could barely hide their astonishment. Comingal recovered first and asked, "Isn't it rather irregular for a plumber to be presiding over an important court?"

"It isn't at all irregular," the Bailiff explained. "Work here is apportioned according to aptitude and the desire for that particular work. Work is not assigned on the basis of one's particular vocation in his former life."

The discussion with the Bailiff left P. Comingal in a quandary. He didn't know if he should be happy the judge was a plumber or fearful because the judge was a plumber. On one hand, a plumber might be easier for a group of determined and intelligent legal minds to bend to their advantage. On the other hand, a plumber might not be as understanding of the methods used by a group of determined lawyers and politicians to manage the outcome of the activities in his court. He pondered the possibilities as he and Patsy returned to check on the progress of the group's problem.

On their return, they found a heated debate going on among the team members about charges that appeared to be very serious and charges that seemed so unimportant they appeared to be mere peccadilloes. Those who thought they could brush the unimportant peccadilloes aside finally won the debate. The list of charges, minus the assumed peccadilloes, was finally produced and given to P. Comingal.

Supreme Court Justice Calvin Bolton handed P. Comingal the list and explained, "Almost all of the charges from the accusation files are on the list. The deletions are charges the team felt might, possibly, be overlooked by the court. A few more charges were deleted due to the infrequency of their appearance and, as the team considered them, the negligible importance of the alleged infractions to the team as a collective group. If the Court refuses to overlook those charges, we felt it was better to sacrifice a few of us than lose all of us because of matters of importance to only those few. We do believe, however, that the deleted charges will not come before the Court."

P. Comingal was not pleased with the less than one page of important charges, each of which took up less than one line. The five pages of charges the team decided were unimportant peccadilloes gave him another heartburn. The entire list just seemed too much. He asked, "Why are 'Failure to abide by your oath of office' and 'Fraud' first and second on the team's list?"

Judge Bolton didn't know the real reason the charges were first and second, but he explained as best he could. "Because they were first and second on every one of the charge files. The charges are not listed chronologically; the most frequently encountered charges are at the top of our list. The less frequently encountered charges appear at the bottom. The charges we deleted, because we considered them to be peccadilloes, were nearer to the bottom of the individual lists in the majority of cases."

Comingal and those on his team of experts ignored the importance of the much larger file they had been offered but had refused to look at. The ignored file documented the chronology of the charges in each individual's personal life and explained why the charges were listed in a specific order for the person charged. The large volume of personal information was meant to be used with the small personal charge file to establish the motivations and historical accuracy of the charges listed in the small file. None of the remaining accused had, as yet, asked for, received, or considered the importance of the larger personal volumes to their defense.

P. Comingal moved away from the group for a respectable distance and sat alone, looking at the pages of charges as though he was in deep thought. When no one was looking, he quickly fished his own file from his jacket pocket and compared it with the charges the team had compiled. He noticed the team had not subtracted any of his own major charges from the main list. Some of the charges Comingal thought were his peccadilloes were on the main list. Only a very few of the rest off his self-proclaimed peccadilloes were not included in the five page compilation of the groups peccadilloes. His own peccadilloes that were not on the compiled list were peccadilloes he thought he could most easily explain.

Comingal's attempt to get the Court to agree to a list of reduced charges, even if the list was acceptable to the Court, seemed to leave himself, President Clint Comingal, swinging in the wind. He didn't think his personal record was good enough win in the Court, and the record compiled by the team was just as bad as his personal record.

Feeling betrayed and desperate because the team hadn't reduced his personal danger, he had to calm the storm raging inside himself to handle the situation. First, he blasted his emotions to the back of his mind. Then he raised himself from his chair, stood tall, and faced the team who, by any measure, had not fulfilled his dream of an easy defense. Yet, he still had confidence in his own ability to pull it off.

He spoke with a sincerity that was a credit to his past ability to face a problem and triumph over it. "You gentlemen and the ladies among you have done a magnificent job. You are all a credit to the effort. However, I need to caucus with a few of the experts I am most familiar with to determine if we can further, reasonably, reduce the number of charges against us. Your wonderful work will of course be the basis for our consideration of this matter."

He looked around with what he hoped was meaningful sincerity before he called for his familiar experts. He asked, "Will the following people step to the other side of the room please: James Cornball, Supreme Court Justice Alan Coffin, Mr. Flim Flamm, and the members of my cabinet?"

James Cornball was a longtime friend of his. Judge Coffin, Comingal felt, could be counted on because of the difficulty Comingal had faced in getting him confirmed for the Supreme Court. His Cabinet members were all in the same boat he was in. Comingal felt he could rely on those few, chosen for a more intensive effort to reduce the charges, to do the right thing him and themselves, and keep their mouths shut about it.

VP Patsy was stunned, and beginning to feel left out. His name hadn't been called, but P. Comingal grabbed his arm and pulled him along as they crossed the large room. One of the cabinet members wheeled one of the large carts loaded with the files of accusations to the far corner of the room where the meeting was to be held.

As Comingal and his small crew sauntered across the room, Comingal noticed the progressives were in deep discussion that silenced as they passed it by. Comingal caught the eye of their leader and was shocked to realize he was being looked at as though he, Comingal, was a dead man. Comingal realized that he really was a dead man, but he didn't like that look anyway. He knew the look signified they had a plan that didn't include him.

The other members of the larger compiling team weren't happy with not being a part of the new effort. Many of them began having left-out and left-behind feelings. They had no other choice but to wait for the results of either skullduggery or a better plan coming from fewer people. Most of them were lawyers and trained to use time efficiently, even under stress. They used most of that time to discuss the possibilities of various strategies when the actual defense began. Some arguments ensued between those who thought they best understood the situation and those who didn't believe them. The thousands of people who hadn't been selected for either team were also in discussions, some heated, some calm.

P. Comingal and his gallery of seventeen appointed experts walked confidently to the empty end of the room as though the solution to the problem was already at hand. Only the Bailiff in his corner near the door had a suspicion of how shaky their confidence was. They paid no attention to the Bailiff standing silently at his station, and he did nothing to call attention to himself.

The newly appointed experts wanted to be out of earshot of the other accused in the room as they managed the progress of the problem. They knew they would need to speak very softly in view of the good acoustics of the place. The loud arguments going on at the other end of the room would serve to help cover the sounds of their own machinations.

As they took seats at the table nearest the corner, P. Comingal quietly addressed the small group. "If there have been any reductions in the original charges, the reductions have been so insignificant that I can't find them. The charges have been compiled but not changed. Our own lawyers apparently found nothing wrong in the charges as they were written. We must in some manner reduce the number and severity of the charges we face or lose, and losing is not an option.

"It looks to me as if we must mount a technical defense against the charges. The only chance we have of winning is to reduce the charges to something we believe the court will accept instead of the original charges. All right! I want everyone to take a copy of the six pages of charges and come up with every angle we can use to reduce any of it or get rid of all of the charges with a legal maneuver. One thing we haven't considered is calling in outside help. Do any of you know a lawyer who is available in Heaven and might be able to add some expertise to the problem?"

None of them had given anything but an Election Day nod toward Heaven, and they were unable to produce the name of a lawyer who could help. Brice Blivit, a Cabinet member, admitted, "I don't believe a lawyer who has the wisdom of Solomon can help us do what we are trying to do. We can't hope to win with a strictly legal defense."

James Cornball, misunderstanding Brice's statement, complained, "Sulaman was the dirtiest lawyer I have ever met. He wouldn't be in Heaven in the first place. He could make a victim look so guilty juries thought the victims committed the crime. If we could get him on our side, I would be all for it, but he's still alive."

Brice knew the Sulaman Cornball was referring to, and whether he held the same opinion of him or not, he replied, "Cornball, I'm not talking about Sulaman DePresski. I'm talking about Solomon, as in Solomon and Delilah. You know, in the Bible.

Cornball returned, "We don't need any more long-haired lawyers on this case—no matter how strong they are. We've already got too many."

The upshot of that general misunderstanding was that the experts among them had the only expertise available. To use it, they had to get down to the hard work of improving the larger team's work on what was supposed to have been a meaningful list of reduced charges. The new charge reduction plan had the further burden of convincing the Court that all of the accused were wrongly charged in the first place and must be returned to their pre-bubble living status. Big order!

The smaller but more expert team of blame dodgers made a military style attack against the pile of accusations that would have done credit to any desperate action against life and death odds. The logic of certain charges being on one list instead of the other list necessitated conferences between members of the larger and smaller defense teams. No reductions were made in that manner, although those discussions caused a great deal of traffic between the two groups.

Brice Blivit reasonably wondered aloud, "How did rape get among the peccadilloes instead of the major charges?"

No one was interested in getting rape added to the major charge list, but it did seem to be a question an adequate defense would probably need a logical answer for in the near future.

Supreme Court Judge Calvin Bolton arrived from the main team to explain the old team logic to the newly formed team of super experts. "Some of the seemingly serious charges were put on the list of peccadilloes because only a few in the group were accused of them. The team felt those few charges would only compound the problems of defending the group as a whole. We had to consider the preponderance of the charges most of us have been accused of. Strangely," he said, "misappropriations of government funds was a minor charge because of the small number of people accused, while outright theft was a major charge because there were many accused of theft."

James Cornball asked, "What's the difference between misappropriation and theft?"

Judge Bolton thought for a minute, then stated, "We aren't in our own court, and we may need to clarify the meanings of some of the charges to defend ourselves. That hasn't been done because you are still attempting to reduce the charges, and that process, as of now, is incomplete. When a court makes the distinction, it's up to the court to clarify the difference."

The super team wrangled about the solution. One side considered it best to surprise the Court at the trial and insist on a standard definition that included both charges as equals and thereby reduce the charge of theft to a more manageable level. The other side didn't want to take that chance because the Court may have already decided that theft and misappropriation weren't equal. P. Comingal, who settled all arguments, feared that not knowing might sink the defense into even deeper trouble than they were in so far. He decided to act immediately to clarify the Court's difference between misappropriation and theft. He dispatched Judge Bolton to ask the Bailiff for a clarification.

Judge Bolton proceeded to the Bailiff and explained the need for a clarification of the two accusations. The Bailiff left briefly and returned with the Court's written answer, which he handed to Judge Bolton.

Judge Bolton read the short explanation as he returned to P. Comingal's super expert defense team. He handed the explanation to P. Comingal, who read it aloud. "Heavenly Court Number 666. Explanation written by Judge Carl Bullman! The misappropriation of funds occurs when government funds are collected by the government for one purpose and then redirected by an individual or group to serve another purpose without proper authority or legislative action. The seriousness of this charge varies greatly depending on the level of competence of the offender and his intent in using the misappropriated funds."

P. Comingal continued, "The charge of theft is incurred when one or more persons are engaged in taking money from another or others who are not willing to give it freely. The charge of theft occurs even when one or more of the victims are unaware of the theft. The seriousness of the theft is not mitigated by the expertise of the individual thief or thieves. The theft is just as serious if the unwilling victim or victims are unaware of its occurrence. The theft is just as serious when the stolen money is taken from tax revenues, taxpayers, or individual citizens. Theft also occurs when persons in government or associated positions raise tax revenues with the knowledge that the tax money will not be used expressly for the originally requested purpose or for the benefit of the taxpaying citizens. Tax money used for the purpose of increasing partisan political power is theft—even if all of the stolen money benefits ordinary citizens in some manner."

James Cornball vented his spleen at Judge Bullman's unexpected attack on his Party's taxing policy. "That judge don't know anything about politics. He's a danger to the whole business of politics. Our democracy can't run without political power. Don't he know we'll make everything better when we get enough power? Everything in politics is political, and everything that is successful in politics increases partisan power. If we don't take power, our enemies will take it, and then where would we all be? You all know I'm right in this. Every dime of every tax dollar expands somebody's political power. I'll go and give that judge a quick lesson on how we do things. He'll see we did the best we could. Tax money makes our democracy stronger only when it makes our Party stronger? What kind of a judge is he, anyway?"

In a fit of wild abandon, VP Patsy spilled the beans. "He isn't a real judge; he's a plumber."

James Cornball's spleen ruptured when V. P. Patsy forced him to face what he thought was not only a life threatening, but a ridiculous, assault on judicial appointments. He shouted, "What! What the hell do you mean, he's a plumber?"

P. Comingal realized his vague hope of using the ersatz judge's shaky judicial background at a more advantages moment had been thwarted by VP Patsy's early announcement. Cornball's loud reaction required an immediate and serious explanation. He quieted Cornball and explained, "Jobs in this neck of the woods are assigned on the basis of the talents and abilities that were not necessarily evident in someone's past life. Those who have the right qualifications and want the job can get the job.

"I think it is possible for us to use this situation to our advantage. We may even find someone who was a plumber in his former life to be easier to deal with than someone who was a judge. An experienced judge might be more inclined to reject our plan for a collective defense."

Cornball was thoughtful after listening to Comingal's logic. He considered the type of people on whom he had used his ability to spin bad news into good news. Those who believed the spin weren't lawyers, judges, politicians, or people familiar with Beltway politics. The people he aimed his talents at were ordinary people who were usually less familiar with political tactics, like plumbers and such. He thought, *Comingal is the smartest politician I've ever known; he's probably right.*

Cornball was mollified, but his shout had reached the other end of the room. It was buzzing with questions about who the plumber was. Some wondered if the room had been bugged. Some of them worried that someone might have been listening to all of their conversations. A few of them looked at the Republicans in the group but couldn't think of any way they could have brought listening devices with them. The Republicans were only more of the accused.

Big Sam Pilfry was resting quietly in his chair with his shoes off and his feet on a table when Cornball's shout raised him from his thoughts. He didn't know what it was all about, but he didn't think it was anything likely to benefit himself. He made the decision to privately check out the management of the court. Sam's close, long-term association with the members of the collective defense team had made the Comingal-hand-picked team become, for Sam, a source of personal worry. Sam hoped he could find some way out for himself without having to defend Comingal's entire administration. He reasoned, "A team reduced to Comingal's Cabinet and a few of his favorite lawyers isn't likely to be of much help to Big Sam Pilfry. They might even try to make me one of their scapegoats."

Big Sam Checks the Progress of His Problem

Big Sam picked his large self out of his chair, put his shoes on and slowly ambled across the big room to the Bailiff. He, in an unnaturally quiet voice, asked, "Might I ask a few questions of Judge Bullman?" The Gray Angel smiled and answered affirmatively as he showed Sam into the judge's chamber. The judge seemed friendly as he asked Big Sam "Is there something I can do for you?"

Sam asked, "What do you think of the defense they are preparing out there?"

"I can't comment on that," Bullman replied, "until the defense is ready and presented to me or makes a request for my help. If a request is made, I will give the most help I can give. Do you have a request you would like to make?"

Sam was thoughtful for a moment before he said, "I have a lot of misgivings about the defense they're planning, but I need more information before I can decide what to do."

"Have you read the personal file concerning your own actions?" Bullman asked. "It was meant to accompany the accusation file, and you were supposed to read both."

Sam admitted, "I actually haven't read either. All of the accusation files were bunched together by the old defense team and are now in the hands of Comingal's new cabinet defense team. None of us have received or even asked for the larger file."

Bullman shook his head up and down and then said, "I'll give you a copy of each. You can read them in the room behind me. Take all of the time you need. Time is not important here. You may find the information you need to make up your mind. If you wish to discuss any of it with me, I will be glad to help."

Sam hadn't bothered to read his own file or any of the others while he was on the first defense team because he'd considered it more important to remain in a self-protective watch-and-listen mode. Sam opened his small file and was surprised that it had such a short list of accusations. He expected to see a long list of things beginning with "The sin of," but nothing on the list began that way. The first thing on the list was, "Failure to honor your oath of office." After that, the list included fraud, murder, theft, bribery, wrongful influence, and lying. He slapped the file closed without reading the remaining items on the list.

Sam believed he was innocent of some of the charges and some of the others just didn't seem realistic to him. Sam thought, *I have never stolen anything in my life, and I for sure haven't killed anyone. So I've done a few favors here and there for one reason or another, and I have taken some money from a few people, but not enough to go to Hell for.* Sam decided to talk with Judge Bullman about the charges he knew of, so far, and get this stuff straightened out. He thought he could read his personal file later.

He returned to the Judge's Chamber, where Judge Bullman was waiting for him. Judge Bullman inquired, "Have you already finished?"

Worry was clearly in Sam's voice. He said, "Not yet. There are some things here I think are wrong. There others I think are not accurate. I would like to discuss those with you."

Judge Bullman gave Sam a long look and then said, "Begin."

Sam, unprepared by the information in his large personal file, walked headfirst into the muddy waters of his personal culpability. He stated,, "First, this stuff about not honoring my oath of office. Everyone knows the oath of office is just a formality. It is just something we have to repeat after someone else to take our office. New congressman may take it seriously for a while, but they quickly forget it in the hubbub of their legislative duties. All of the deals they have to make to do anything the Party leadership wants done pushes the oath out sight and out of mind. The real issue is doing what is right while we're in Congress. Every congressman faces up to that problem, and I am no different than those who are still there."

Bullman said, "You took an oath to uphold, and do your work, within the constitutional laws of the Republic of the United States. You promised to faithfully perform the duties of your office. That is, to faithfully perform the duties of your office within the boundaries the Constitution requires you to give your oath to obey. Your oath is given to God and the citizens of your Republic. God expects the oath to be the guiding light of all of your actions in Congress. It is first on the list of charges against you because most of your other failures in office stem from the failure to abide by the oath of office. You gave no respect to your own oath, which was also your word to those who elected you. Your oath represented your promise to do what they elected you to do. You not only ignored your oath, you pretended it didn't exist."

Sam replied, "If I had kept it, I wouldn't have been able to do any good at all. I would have been out of there at the next election because I wouldn't have received the support of the Party, or the support of the special interests who gave the money and advertising I needed to pay for my reelection."

Bullman rubbed his chin, took another long look at Sam, and then told him, "Your oath was between you, the American people, and God. It wasn't between you and your Party. It wasn't between you and the special interests you served. It wasn't between you and your campaign contributors, or the people you served with. The oath you freely gave was a public affirmation of your personal honor to do the best you could possibly do for your constituency within constitutional boundaries, whether your political Party, or your associates liked it or not. If you had accepted your duty to the constitutionally required oath, you appeared to voluntarily accept as your most important public obligation, your personal honor would be intact. Even though you might have lost the next election, you might not be here."

Sam felt injured but not defeated. If he could prove one point wrong, he might be able to use that proof as a game changer. Any small change might allow him to return to the other points and, perhaps, fight his way out of Hell. Sam pressed on, "All right, let's go on. What about this charge of murder? I have never killed anyone. Who is this person I murdered?"

Judge Bullman replied, "It isn't one person, it is all of those people you helped to murder. You have voted yes on every bill promoting abortion while you have been in office."

Sam felt relieved. "Abortion isn't murder. After all, murder is a legal term meaning to illegally take the life of another person. Our Party protected the legality of abortion. There isn't a court in the land that would try a case for murder against a legal abortion, and most abortions are legal."

Bullman informed him, "This Court isn't in the land you are talking about. In your present situation, the laws of this Court supersede the laws of that Court. This Court makes an important distinction in the charge of murder. Crimes are more serious when committed by a government than when they are committed by an individual. Murder is more serious because the victim of government murder has no legal pathway to pursue justice on his own behalf when the government is the criminal. The Government's use of its legislative powers to pass laws to protect a Supreme Court decision that made murder legal increases the seriousness of a charge of murder in this Court. The entire population of the world began life as unborn babies. Not one may be murdered by his government at anytime in his life. That's the law of this court."

Sam replied, "People in government haven't aborted one fetus. The Supreme Court made abortion a constitutional right, and neither I nor any other congressman had anything to do with that. We in the legislature only protected that existing right. We want abortion to be legal and rare. That's the Party line."

Bullman stated, "Your Democrat Party has caused many laws to be passed to increase abortion's legality, and it has allocated tax revenues to make it easier for some of those desiring an abortion to have one. The Democrats in Congress have not only condoned, they have encouraged abortion. Your Party has insisting that newly appointed judges must support abortion to be confirmed in the Senate. More than fifty million babies have been killed in the United States since that new, and immoral, constitutional right was established. Your party is also doing the best it can to make money and support available for the same thing in other countries."

Sam felt Bullman was applying to much pressured at this point. He decided to move on Sam said, "What of this charge of theft? I feel the charge is unfair."

Bullman responded, "Sam, if you really want to fight that charge, here is the fight. On the record, you have in every one of your campaigns used campaign funds donated for your reelection by your supporters, to pay off your personal debts. That is theft. More serious thefts were committed during your activities as a legislator. You initiated legislation for many pork barrel projects that benefited your powerful friends. Those friends, in return for the pork, increased the amount of money they gave to your election campaigns.

That still isn't the big theft. The big theft is in the tax revenues you helped to raise for programs to benefit the general public. The programs did help the general public to some extent, but the purpose of those programs wasn't to give that help. The programs' purposes were to build a Democrat Party bureaucracy and constituency that could not lose an election. Your use of tax revenues for partisan political purposes is the big theft.

"You then used your constituent's fears of the loss of those services to assure yourselves they would continue to vote for you and your party. Arousing fear where there should be no fear constitutes wrongful influence in this Court."

"One of the charges is fraud," Sam complained. "I've never been associated with a con game in my life. How have I committed fraud?"

"Fraud is an intentional deception to cause a person to give up property or a lawful right," explained the judge. "The United States is a republic—and you know it's a republic. You called your Republic 'our democracy' many times in your reelection campaigns and in your congressional speeches. You asked American citizens to give you money, which is property, to finance your reelection to a non-existent democracy. That is fraud.

"Your were one of the designers of the healthcare system that was supposed to make healthcare less expensive for every family. The Democrat's healthcare system wasn't a healthcare system. It was a political party fraud using healthcare as the excuse to legislate it. It was a system designed to allow Democrats permanent control of the political system of the United States. Even the healthcare claim to redistribute wealth was a fraud. The fraudulent redistribution of wealth would have broken down the financial base of the working people in the middle class. It would have destroyed the middle class businesses. It would not have improved the national health. Those financing, or friendly to, your Party, were exempted from its financial collapse in the body of the healthcare legislation.

"Those you deceived gave up, money, property, and lawful Rights. The revolution you were engaged in was the process used for taking away the people's lawful right to their Republic and its Constitution, forever! You failed in your attempt to take their laws and Republic away from them. You were put on the bubble express to this place because of that revolution. You are guilty of fraud in the most criminal sense of the word 'fraud' in all cases."

Sam, angered by the accusation, spit out, " Our Healthcare plan might have worked in the distant future. History would have exonerated us of our present criminal wrongdoing as we established our benevolent power over the American people.

"As for our Democracy, we Democrats have been calling the Republic our democracy for several decades. I had no intention to defraud anyone. I only used the term as an accepted means to raise campaign money."

The Judge countered, "Democracy as a form of government isn't a fraud. If there has ever been an actual democracy somewhere, and I don't know of one, it wouldn't have been a fraud, but the United States doesn't have that form of government. The United States is a Republic, an entirely different form of government. When you called the United States 'our democracy,' you committed fraud by intentionally calling it a different type of government. The purpose of the fraud was to raise more money for your reelection. Just because you used a long-standing lie that has become accepted as truth by your constituents, doesn't relieve you of the consequences for committing fraud. You knew you lied when you told them the Republic of the United States is a democracy. You used the 'accepted means for raising campaign money' even though you knew the 'accepted means' was a lie. It didn't matter to you that it was a lie as long as it raised the money. Deceiving others for money or votes is still fraud, no matter how old, or successful, the fraud has become."

Sam dared not get into the bribery part. He asked, "Is there anything I can do to help myself?"

Judge Bullman replied, "First, you really should read the personal history volume I gave you. If you want to do that, I will have an operator to go over it with you. The operator is very good and will give you all of the help possible."

Sam agreed, and was shown into the seclusion of a room where he could plunge into everything he had ever done wrong and never wanted to hear about.

The Team's Decision

P. Comingal's team of experts examined every legal trick, and every other avenue they could think of, to reduce the number of charges against the group. They failed! They weren't even sure the major charges could be successfully separated from the list they hoped the Court would consider unimportant peccadilloes. They despairingly accepted that a plea bargain would be out of the question. They had already been convicted of their many crimes and had nothing to bargain with that would interest a court. They had little faith in their ability to show any of the charges to be false. The consensus was that an entirely new type of defense was needed. They needed a defense so unusual it could float the already convicted to a judgment of innocent in a court that was unwavering in its insistence on truth. They were in desperate need of a presently unknown, but spectacular ploy that would save them from a fate worse than drowning.

Xavier Xanker, from the Department of the Interior, suggested, "There doesn't seem to be any witnesses against us; perhaps we can bluff. If we all tell the same story, who can deny the story is true?"

V.P. Patsy made a riveting speech about personal honesty. He ended his master piece with, "Forty thousand people can't tell the same lies at the same time, and get away with it. Some of them will screw it up so bad no one will believe it. I like the President's idea of a technical defense, but what kind of a technical defense will work?"

P. Comingal looked down at his hands for a few seconds, and then rubbed his forehead before he said, "That's what we're trying to figure out, Patsy."

Jane Rantthru, the Attorney General, gave her opinion. "I have exhaustively examined every type of legal defense I am familiar with. I can't think of any as a good choice." Jane didn't realize that the large volumes they had been offered, and had rejected, contained the evidence against them that was being used as the Court's testimony against them. Jane enlarged her errors with, "We have no idea of how conclusive the evidence against us will appear in court. Without that information, it is difficult to form a defense."

P. Comingal addressed Jane and the group. "We are not in our courts, and we are not looking for one of the typical legal defenses we use. We are looking for a type of defense this Court will agree to as an alternative to all of the legal stuff we use in our courts."

Brice Blivit suggested, "We haven't explored the legality of the accusations themselves. We should look for a way to challenge them. If we can show the accusations were unfairly laid at our door, we can win the case with that one legal maneuver."

V.P, Patsy agreed, "With no witnesses, the accusations should be easy to nullify."

P. Comingal didn't think Patsy's idea was good, but he considered, "Any port in a storm is better than no port at all." He advised, "Patsy, you take charge of that element of our defense. Find some high-powered legal advice and give it your best try when we get to court."

Elmer Gron, of the Department of Education, asked, "How about a biblical defense?"

"What do you have in mind?" P. Comingal asked.

"I don't have anything in mind," Elmer Replied, "but our options have dwindled to no options. The Bible is something we haven't considered."

P. Comingal stated, "The only mass extinction in the Bible where anyone survived was Sodom and Gomorrah. Only Lot's family survived; everyone else died."

Jane Rantthru said, "But they all died because ten good men couldn't be found in those cities. Maybe we have ten people in our group who are good enough. If we have the ten, those ten might be good enough to get all of us off. After all, we all died at the same time in the same disaster. It's something we should consider."

"Any other ideas?" asked P. Comingal.

Herald Crochen, head of the Department of Defense, offered, "What about Nineveh? In Nineveh, the entire population escaped when they were about to be killed."

VP Patsy answered, "Yes, but they lived and we didn't. We are where they would have been if Nineveh had been destroyed."

Bert Croney, head of the Department of Commerce, went to the heart of the matter. "But how did they avoid the sentence on themselves?"

VP Patsy explained, "They did it by putting on sack cloth and ashes, repenting, and changing their lives. God allowed them to live after they repented. In our case, we are past the point where we can repent and be allowed to live."

James Cornball tried his spin on the situation. "Neither of those defenses sounds any good to me. I think we should go for a defense showing the judge to be unqualified because he was just a plumber and get the whole case thrown out of court. Maybe we can get him to recuse himself by appealing to his honesty. When we get a new judge, we can say we weren't treated fairly in the first case. Now that's a technical defense."

Judge Calvin Bolton disputed Cornball's logic; "Bullman was assigned to his bench by a higher authority. The higher authority thinks he's qualified to do what he does. We are not in a position to challenge the integrity of that higher authority by saying it doesn't know how to assign judges properly."

Cornball retorted, "We're back to Sodom and Gomorrah, then. How can anyone build a defense on that?"

The team sank into silence, mulling the possibilities in a mental circle of despair. They couldn't find a way to plead innocent. The Court had already confirmed their guilt. It was utterly necessary for them to successfully dispute their guilty conviction. They couldn't move to another jurisdiction. There was no other jurisdiction. There was no public involvement. They couldn't change public opinion in their favor, and none of them could answer James Cornball's question. Their hope lay in the facile mind of P. Comingal and his monumental ability in the past to pull his irons out of a fire. If he couldn't find a way to save them, they would all go to Hell.

P. Comingal thought deeply before making a statement. He was aware that the silence of the team was a demand for something special from him alone. At last he spoke, "We're between a rock and a hard place, here. The Vice President is right in saying it's too late for a defense based on changes in the lives we have already lost. The Nineveh defense is out because it says our lives were all wrong. If our lives were all wrong, how could we possibly defend them? That admission would leave us at the mercy of the court. I don't think this court will have any mercy on people who were all wrong.

"The Sodom and Gomorrah defense is desperate. We all died in the same flood, and all of us have the accusations against us as proof of the reason we all died. We can't escape blame by using the assumption that there are ten good people among us. If that were true, there would be ten people here with no accusations against them. There are about forty thousand of us here, and all of us have been accused. Yet, in this large group, we have done a lot of good. I think we may be able to mount a defense based on the fact, that among us are the collective accomplishments of ten good men. I believe, many more than that. As I see it, we have a chance of winning this tough battle using a Sodom and Gomorrah defense."

Comingal looked at the team sitting before him—looking back at him in a stunned silence. James Cornball was the first to recover and give it his approval. "Now that's what I call a clever defense. I think we can slip through on it. I'll go along with it."

The others began talking among themselves, most with more hope than they had enjoyed since they'd arrived.

Xavier Xanker exclaimed, "That's a defense for the history books!"

Jane Rantthru added, "We could win with a defense like that in the Supreme Court, maybe even in this Supreme Court."

Out of sheer desperation, they all agreed it was worth a try and they had nothing to lose by trying.

Bolton's Bolt

Judge Calvin Bolton took the super team's profoundly innovative defense rhetoric in as he sat quietly pondering the problems he saw coming his way if they tried a defense like the Sodom and Gomorrah defense. He raised himself from his chair and quietly proceeded to the Bailiff's station. After speaking quietly with him, the Bailiff left the room for a moment and returned with a large book that contained the information about Judge Bolton's life experiences. Judge Bolton sat at a table near the bailiff station and began to read.

After immersing himself for a long time in the faulty choices he had made in his life, he once again rose from his chair and proceeded to the other end of the room. He spoke quietly and at length with some of those he knew best, those who were not directly involved in defense planning. They in turn began speaking with others in the same group.

Judge Bolton returned to the bailiff's station as the room began to buzz with quiet conversations behind him. He approached the Bailiff's station again and asked the Bailiff if he might have a discussion with Judge Bullman. The Bailiff preceded him to Judge Bullman's chamber.

Judge Bolton's actions didn't go unnoticed by P. Comingal's super team on the other side of the room. They wanted to know what was said and what Judge Bolton was doing, but they kept their curiosity to themselves. They wanted to ask the Bailiff where he was taking the judge, but they didn't want to appear uninformed about the activities of one of their own. P. Comingal's team of experts decided to continue with the work they were doing while hoping Judge Bolton was in the process of discovering some new defense angle they hadn't previously considered.

The Bailiff introduced Judge Bolton to Judge Bullman. Immediately after the introduction, the Bailiff returned to his station, leaving the two judges to discuss whatever was on Judge Bolton's mind. Judge Bolton retained a contemplative silence for a time as if trying to put his thoughts into words.

Judge Bullman inquired, "What is the subject you wish to discuss? Are you here representing your group, or is this a personal matter?"

Judge Bolton answered, "I don't believe the plan they have to answer the charges will be successful. I have read my own personal file, and I realize how my personal actions caused the accusations against me. I don't believe any of the actions I might take in their defense would minimize or maximize their own defense efforts. I don't believe their actions would contribute to my defense. The only reasonable course of action for me, for their sake as well as mine, is to separate from them and pursue whatever help I may be able to receive alone. Can this be done at this late date?"

Judge Bullman replied, "Yes, it can, and that's what you were meant to do in the first place. That's why all of you were told about the two separate files in the beginning."

Judge Bolton asked, "This is a very strange court by our world's standards; why does it operate the way it does? You are judge, prosecutor, and defender in a court where the punishment has been set prior to the action of the court. Also, the punishment was set by the highest authority, from which one would assume there is no appeal."

Judge Bullman informed him. "If I explain this court to you, you may not return to the others, but you will receive the help this court can give."

Judge Bolton replied, "I accept that. I had no intention of returning to them."

Judge Bullman explained, "The bubble of water in Washington was put there because God wanted to prevent the future activities of those he arranged to be in it. You and the others were close to beginning a revolution to change the form of government of the Republic of the United States into what you and your fellow revolutionaries were going to call a democracy. The new form of government would not have been a democracy. The new form of government would have been a socialist state and would have very quickly become a tyrannical oligarchy. The oligarchy would have lasted only until one of you anointed ones became strong enough to overcome the others. You and the citizens of the Republic would have been forced to serve a dictator.

"This is not a court of law as you see a court of law on Earth. This special kind of court was established to do everything in its power to soften the sentences against you individually because of the method used to bring about your premature deaths. However, the Court was ordered not to interfere with whatever methods the individuals themselves, or different groups, or the group as a whole chose to use in its own behalf."

Judge Bolton thanked him for the information and then stated, "All right, so we were leaning heavily toward an undefined but socialistic democracy. Many of us felt the Constitution was outdated. It prevented government from forming an enlightened rule of the people. The Bill of Rights was too negative for strong government control. We had to find a way to set the entire Constitution aside, but we couldn't just throw it out; that would have caused a counterrevolution. Without a revolution, the only way we could change the Republic to the positive centrally controlled government form we wanted, was to change each of the ten amendments piece by piece. We wanted to quickly establish our regulation of everything in the Constitution and the very important things the Constitution prevented us from doing. We could not establish a permanent and different type of state using the present Constitution as a base. Our revolution would have given us the power too make fast changes.

"We felt we could force the United States into socialism forever if we could put our socialist type of democracy in place during one, or possible two, four-year terms of office. We felt our government regulation was necessary to rebuild all facets of human life. We believe a government must impose the regulation for the welfare of every large population like the United States. However, the people must have a feeling of being free, even though they are not free."

"Did your Democrat Party or anyone in your Democrat Party seek to be reelected on a platform of total replacement of the Republican Form of Government, or of government regulation of every facet of every life?" asked Bullman.

"Of course not," replied Bolton, "nobody could be elected on a platform like that, especially since most Americans have some knowledge of their constitutional rights. A large percentage of Americans believe they already live in a democracy. They think their Rights came from, and are a part of, that democracy. Very few know the difference between a republican government and a democratic government. We constantly tell Americans the United States is a democracy, and we publicly refer to it as our democracy."

Judge Bullman asked, "So, you Democrats didn't trust your political fate to the judgment of intelligent citizens who know they live in a republic. Worse, you didn't trust your fate to your own dupes, the people who actually believed the lie that their Republic is 'our democracy?'"

"We couldn't trust the future of the nation to either, but our revolution would have been good of all of them," Bolton responded.

Bullman asked, "If it is to their good to have their lives regulated by political means, then who is it good for them to be regulated by?"

"By our new democratic form of government," Bolton answered, "and by the regulatory processes approved by that government. More precisely, the people would be regulated by the intelligent socialist chosen to be regulators, and by those hired into our revolutionary system that was formed and approved by our government's leaders. Supervision designed to insure the regulators fidelity to the process would control all regulators. The same regulatory process would, at the same time, insure the greatest benefit to the people."

Bullman stated, "A democracy is a very simple form of government. It requires a political structure with only one purpose, to guarantee that the majority will of its citizens is the law of the land. Socialist bureaucratic processes cannot be substituted for the will of the majority in a democracy. By definition, a democracy requires its majority to be free to decide its true will. Every law and every government process in a democracy is subject to change or repeal by the free will of the majority of the citizens. Democracy is a type of government with no standard rule of law and no supreme bureaucratic process. A democracy has only one compelling reason for its existence, to guarantee that the majority of its free people rule the government—rule by the ruled.

Bolton reasoned, "Ah, but you see, it's the will of the majority to be regulated by caring experts who understand their problems, and we were those caring experts."

Bullman probed, "How can it be the will of the majority to be regulated when, as you have said, no party or politician has ever been or can be elected on a platform founded by a socialist oligarchy whose agenda is total government regulation of all of the people?"

Bolton reasoned, "When we offer regulation in small amounts and make the regulations appear necessary, or beneficial, to a particularly needy or important segment of society, we can make those regulations the law of the land. We never refer to regulatory laws as regulation of the people. Our regulations are referred to as 'needed changes in government.' Most of the people don't connect 'needed changes in government' with themselves being regulated; the people think of those 'needed changes in government' as politicians regulating other politicians.

"We haven't been able to offer a broad field of regulations all at one time, but we have kept a constant stream of regulatory items in the public's mind and presented them as necessary and good for some purpose. As long as the regulations appear good for somebody, the people will support the regulations."

Bullman accused, "It is a lie to say you believe in democracy or even your socialist corruption of democracy while at the same time admitting you can't put your entire program before the people. You certainly know that the majority your socialist democracy is supposed to benefit will reject it as soon as they know what it is. How can your democracy be called any kind of a democracy when it is unable to survive the will of the majority it is supposed to establish as its supreme authority?"

"We don't see democracy in the same way you see it," Bolton replied. "We view democracy as having the distant goal of being accepted by the majority. We don't see the necessity of having a majority that accepts our democracy before it comes to power. We revolutionaries believed that once we gained control of the government, and the broad spectrum of our democratic programs were established, the majority of the people would eventually understand our message and be happy we forced the basic changes in their way of life to occur."

Bullman jabbed back with, "The laws of the Republic require voters to make the decisions concerning who governs. The Democrat Party and the Republican Party both use the laws of the Republic for voting purposes, and neither of you receive a majority of the voting population. You don't usually receive a majority vote from the voting population that is registered to vote. All unregistered voters and many, sometimes most, of the registered voters do not vote. The Republican Party rightly governs from whatever percentage of votes it receives within the law. That is sometimes a little more and other times a little less than the percentage of votes your party gets. Each of you might get one or two percentage points more when your party is elected.

"If all of the registered voters of both parties, who vote, voted for your party, you Democrats would still not receive a majority vote from the voting population of the Republic. How do you square that fact with majority rule? After all, you call yourselves the Democrat Party. The supreme governing principle of a democratic government is majority rule. Without majority rule, you can't have a democracy."

Bolton felt he could reconcile the democratic discrepancy of majority rule. After all, he was speaking with a world-wise, intelligent man. Bolton began, "As a general rule, governments aren't changed by a majority; they are changed by a dedicated minority who are able to successfully overthrow an existing government, and manage the new government using their own revolutionary plan. The democratic majority would rule the new government; but, the democratic majority would need be informed of the proper times and conditions when the majority could rule after the change in government.

` "We didn't have the necessary support from a majority of the citizens of the United States for an open, public change in government. We couldn't legally insure the success of the change in government from the Republic to our democracy at this time. However, we felt the time for the change was quickly approaching, and we were ready for it. We had managed to install a very strong Democrat Party majority into the federal bureaucracy, and something less of majority in the bureaucracies of the fifty states. The government we needed to manage the change from a republic to our democracy was in place. We felt we were close enough to begin the final move from a constitutional republican form of government to our socialist democracy."

Bullman said, "There is still one more thing I would like to know about your revolution. What was your plan if the American people got the upper hand and successfully rejected your socialist democracy? What would you have done next?"

Judge Bolton didn't like the question, or any of the others, but he couldn't avoid it. "There is a trick that can be used when people are paying too much unwelcome attention to something going on in one of our offices. If we don't want to stop doing whatever we were doing, we change the name of the office and move it somewhere else. The office personnel and purposes does not change.

"The new name for the failed revolutionaries would change from Democrats to 'Progressives.' The new office would take the form of a new type of politician no one had experienced before. He would be a politician who could campaign on new claims instead of past deeds. Our new man's new approach, right on the heels of the failed attempt, would be too unbelievable for the people to accept as just one more try. The old message in the new package would sound so different and so couched in new code words that the people wouldn't comprehend that the man and the message were just more of the same old revolutionary business as usual."

Bullman inquired, "In case they did understand, was your constant chopping away at the Second Amendment Rights of the American people a part of your plan to gain acceptance for the total Democrat Party program by force, if needed? Perhaps you feared that a small minority of dedicated individuals would mount a counterrevolution that would overthrow your revolution. Or were you more fearful of a majority with guns of their own? Revolutions always end up bloody. How did you intend to support your revolution with enough guns to make sure the spilled blood wasn't yours?"

Judge Bolton was startled by the blunt question. The one topic he feared most in the conversation was counterrevolution. He had personally hoped for a bloodless revolution, but he had known it might end up very bloody. He answered, "Armed citizens are the worst enemy of any revolution, or any armed attack on a nation by outside forces. Of course we wished to prevent the bloodshed of any of our citizens, but we knew that some blood would probably be spilled. We hoped to remove all guns from the hands of the ordinary citizens through incremental regulation. That would leave the Second Amendment within the legal spectrum of the law but impossible to use. We were only marginally successful, but we felt we were close enough.

"We realized that our programs would cause some kind of a counterrevolution. We had to minimize the abilities of our enemies to respond with lethal force. A revolution need not be bloody if the revolution is well planed. The people we thought might become immediately active as a counterrevolutionary force were not well organized, and they were out of position to respond quickly. We expected our revolution to be so powerful and quickly accomplished that we would have an overwhelming force capable of putting them down by the time they became fully organized. There could be no respectable counterrevolution under those conditions. Our democracy would have been safe for us to bring forth all the good things we wanted to do."

Bullman insisted, "Your change in government wasn't from a constitutional republic to a democracy. The change you describe was from a constitutional republic to a socialist oligarchy. A few politicians that consider themselves powerful enough to control a nation would control the oligarchy.

"No matter what flavor of tyranny it became, it would be controlled by people you kept in total control of the weapons of the ruined republic. You would have ruled with a bureaucracy of henchmen you managed to clandestinely and illegally install in the Republic of the United States. The only democratic element of your democracy would have been its name."

"It may seem that way," Bolton argued, "but we always had the interest of the people at heart. We would have selected the people's representatives and the bureaucracies to share the same love of the people we had ourselves."

Judge Pullman leaned closer to Judge Bolton and asked, "How would you have done that? One of the major arguments against politicians and bureaucrats is that they are out of touch with mainstream America. Do you have a love meter you can use—on yourselves—to insure that you and your bureaucrats love the people you are out of touch with more than you love yourselves?"

"Of course not," insisted Bolton. "Party oversight would have insured that the actions of those involved in our regulation of the people would remain within the norms of our Democrat Party's government principles."

Judge Bolton's answer caused Judge Bullman a moment of stunned silence. Bullman's criticism returned at a much higher intensity, "You mean all of this talk of bringing about a national democracy was to be done so you could force an entire self-governing population to be put under the thumb of your political Party? Your Party, in its entire history, hasn't shown a shred of democracy at any point."

Bolton felt Bullman's criticism put him down, but he thought he was still a long way from out. To give credit to what he thought was obvious, Bolton stated, "Our Party was the key element in the revolution. The Party was to become the government, and the government was to become the Party. We, over a long period of time, organized our Party to take much better care of the people than the people could do for themselves. We had sympathetic experts in every field to guide the people every step of the way through the dark labyrinth of life."

Bullman countered, "Give me the names of ten of your party's politicians who in the past have always had the benefit of the people at heart and have had enough support from your Party to guide anyone through the dark labyrinth of life. There could be ten or even more, but your Party has always put its plans for power above the needs of the people. You don't solve problems or let a crisis go to waste; you manage both for maximum Party advantage. I can think of no time when the Democrat Party sacrificed its power-seeking agenda to anyone's desire for doing good for the people."

"I can't name them," Bolton replied, "not from the standpoint of what must necessarily be done to secure power. From the standpoint of the eventual good many of us hoped to do, the names of all with that hope would suffice."

"I believe you, and many like you, seriously believe the end justifies the means," Bullman answered. "However, daily honesty can't be replaced by daily dishonesty because the hope of a general good might arise from the dishonesty at a later time.

"You were about to destroy constitutional liberty under a rule of law that has protected both the majority and the minorities over the course of the life of a nation. Your replacement for the freedom insuring constitution would have been a fraudulent democratic system. The fraud's changes in laws would be driven by changes in contemporary political agendas. Such weak laws can easily be mismanaged by the many politicians who prefer to have no standard of protection for anyone but themselves at any time."

Judge Bolton replied, "We believe the majority will always protect the minority because the majority will always be well intentioned."

Bullman pressed, "But your democracy would not have sought the will of the majority for the protection of the minorities. Your majority would have to be told when and under what conditions it may exercise its majority rule. Your democracy wasn't seeking the majority will that was necessary for you to put your democracy in power. You haven't sought the will of the majority on any issue at any time. The will of the majority wouldn't have been sought when minorities needed protection from the government. Your democracy would have announced that the actions it took against the minorities had the backing of the majority, and neither the minorities nor the majority would have any way of knowing you were lying.

"The majority of American citizens will not rise up in popular support and give you a democracy. Your kind may continue to deceive the people into believing their Republic is your democracy, but deception is the basis for revolution, not for majority will, and not for democracy.

"If your strange brand of democracy overcomes the Republic, its leaders will owe nothing to the majority it deceives to take power. Your majority is non-existent. The real majority will be nothing but silent pawns in the game of revolution. The American people are not the deceivers, they are the deceived, and the deceived cannot govern the deception.

"Your kind will use the fraud of majority will to destroy individual liberty! Individual liberty is where majority will comes from. Without individual liberty, the individuals who make up a majority are lacking in the liberty necessary to form a majority will. You weren't offering liberty or the safety of protective laws, only unending regulation of the people by politicians like yourself. The purpose of the phony democracy's regulation is to insure its power to control the people can never be challenged by the people.

"Your party was ready to throw away a good rule of law providing specific protection for all of the people, minorities and the majority, equally. The Constitution restricts government control of the people while it maximizes individual freedoms. You were preparing to throw the protective rule of law away in the name of a fraudulent democracy. You felt the rule of constitutional law, specifically written to protect your nation from people like yourself, whether they are well intentioned or not, was restricting your ability to establish your Party's agenda.

"That's why the founders of the Republic required public servants to take the oath. The founders believed the oath would be so personally powerful it would cause honorable men to restrict themselves from taking the freedoms you were in the process of taking from the people. How much personal honor is left for a person who knowingly violates his personal oath? What province of truth and honor does his ability to govern come from? Any man who gives his oath as a mere formality has no honor, no truth, no fairness, and no ability to govern a liberty-loving nation.

"You Democrats routinely violate the constitutional protections of the people, and I must mention those personal protections because of their importance. Article four, section four of the Constitution states, 'The United States shall guarantee to every State in this Union a Republican Form of Government...' You violated the American's Right to their Republican Form of Government with your decades-long reeducation program to convince the people that they live in a democracy you know is nonexistent. You were right about the many people who believe that lie. How do you defend yourself against that accusation?"

Bolton sat back in his chair and thought for a while before he answered. "The First Amendment guarantees us freedom of speech. How we use the First Amendment is up to us. There are also laws that protect us while we are performing our duties as judges, congressmen, and in many other positions in government service. Our constitutional freedoms are very broad in that respect."

"You were using the constitutional freedoms, given to the people in the Constitution of the Republic, to destroy the Republic," Bullman asserted.

"The Constitution is a very weak document," Bolton countered. "If it is so weak it can't defend itself from revolutionaries, it should fail. I can guarantee that our democracy would not have had those same weaknesses."

"What about the Ninth Amendment in the Bill of Rights?" probed Bullman; "Did you ever violate that part of the Constitution?"

Bolton was uncomfortable as he attempted to remember. "The Ninth Amendment is never quoted—even by those in the Republican Party. I don't believe I can quote it from memory. Most Americans are familiar with their First Amendment rights, and many know the Second Amendment. A few know their Fourth Amendment rights, and the Fifth Amendment is very well known. Very few know the others. Most people don't understand the very important Tenth Amendment right. You could probably ask any thousand people anywhere in the United States and not find one who knows what the Ninth Amendment says or what it was written to do. It just isn't important in the conduct of government."

Bullman looked at Bolton in disbelief for a moment before he said, "You were a presiding justice at the time of your death. I can't believe a presiding justice would make the Ninth Amendment protection of the rights of the people appear insignificant. I will quote the Ninth amendment for you and explain it so you will be able to understand one of your most grievous errors as a judge. The Ninth Amendment, as it is written in the Constitution, states, 'The enumeration in the Constitution of certain rights shall not be construed to deny or disparage others retained by the people.'

"The much-ignored Ninth Amendment was put into the Constitution to keep people like you from violating the rights not written by the founders in the Constitution. The Ninth Amendment's specific protection of rights not mentioned in the Constitution also insures equal protection to those rights, which are mentioned. Your revolution would have denied the American people every unwritten right, and every right written in the Constitution. All the American people would have left is regulation by politicians. Some of them may have believed, for a while, that democracy was bringing them greater freedom and more control of their government, but they would quickly come to an understanding of the emptiness of those promises."

Bolton saw things beginning to slip away from him. He thought he had one more ace up his sleeve. "Whether the United States is a republic or a democracy, the laws were administered fairly by me and in most other courts. No one suffered because we used our benches to promote our democracy. We administered the Constitution of the Republic and the Bill of Rights fairly."

"First," Bullman advised, "there is no Constitution and Bill of Rights. There is one Constitution, including all of its amendments, and the first ten of the amendments are referred to as the Bill of Rights. I realize you wished to separate and do away with that part of the Constitution you are calling the Constitution, but retain, for a time, that part of the Constitution you are referring to separately as the Bill of Rights. The first part of the Constitution has that ugly R word, Republic, in it, and you can't legally solidify your democracy as long as the American people have the proof of their Republic in their Constitution. Retaining the Bill of Rights would help to maintain the false perception that those Rights still guarantee freedom for the people.

"Secondly, you and Democrat politicians, with your help, were violating the Bill of Rights with impunity. You believe you can regulate the Rights listed in the Constitution. In your democracy, a Constitutional Right would no longer be something recognized as beyond the government's ability to change it. A regulated right is nothing more than something people are permitted to do within the limits allowed by politicians until politicians change the limits.

"Mr. Bolton, your case fails in every respect. If you had been in charge of the effort to change the Republic of the United States into 'your democracy,' you would have made just as big a mess of the United States as Mr. Comingal would have, but I must confess, you would have done a slower job of it.

"Do you have anything else to discuss, Mr. Bolton?" Bullman asked. "Or shall I call an attendant to help you improve you future?" Bolton knew he and Bullman had nothing more to discuss. He asked for an attendant.

The Sodom and Gomorrah Defense

P. Comingal addressed his team, "The technical aspects of our Sodom and Gomorrah defense are paramount. We must show that our activities as politicians were beneficial. We must show those activities were carried out by all of us. We must prove that our collective actions constituted enough good to deserve a pardon for whatever mistakes we may have, incidentally, committed along the way. We're going to stand on our collective record rather than on our individual records. Technical advantages we have yet to discover from other sources will certainly be used.

"What we need most is a list of successful programs this administration and this group at large were involved in supporting. Secondly, we need arguments pro and con that are likely to be used in the presentation of those programs in court. Third, we need to solidify our defense against the counter arguments and criticisms we may receive during the court process.

"Our problem is to force the judge to understand, and accept, our good work as a warming coat of many colors. We must present the Social Security, Poverty, and the Medicare programs to our best advantage in court.

"I expect the Court to attack us on Constitutional Rights issues. We will probably need to defend programs the administration supported because we found it absolutely necessary to regulate some of the constitutional rights of American citizens. We must show why it was necessary to regulate rights if we, ourselves, find it necessary to bring rights activities into our defense. The most important charge against us is that we violated our Oath of Office. This charge is one we all share. It must be shown as insignificant.

"Also, we must include the many instances where this administration returned money to the states and the people from federal tax revenues. I'm sure there are many programs we will want to consider, but these will get us started in the direction we want to go. If the judge understands our message, I'm sure we will be exonerated in his court."

James Cornball added, "We can show all the work we've done to increase population control. We've supported abortion from day one, and there is euthanasia on the horizon."

Constitutional lawyer Flim Flamm jumped on Cornball's suggestion. "We don't want to disturb the Court with a program the administration has supported, but supported entirely on the basis of a new right for our democracy. The choice of using that right was, specifically and unmistakably, the responsibility of the people. The administration had no responsibility at all in this matter. The Court may see some activities performed by the people as government supported even though this administration has made it clear it personally disapproves of those activities."

Cornball refused to buy it. "That's one of our big successes in every administration after 1973, including this one. We can't just ignore the advances this administration has made in the area of population reduction. We have too many people in the world. President Comingal and company did as much to reduce the numbers as anybody. Our people were sent to the UN and all over the world supporting these programs."

Xavier Xanker threw some logic into the discussion. "We have thirty-three million illegal aliens in the country, and there have been about fifty million abortions. What if the judge asks if we supported abortion so we could bring more illegal aliens into the country? At some point, all of the illegal aliens could be made citizens by an act of Congress. That would make them legal citizens with the ability to vote. How do we come up with population control when it appears we have a population replacement program that kills American babies and replaces them with foreigners who vote for Democrats?"

Cornball gave his angry reply, "Who cares? Poor people don't vote."

Xavier retorted, "Don't they? What about the drive to get one million aliens naturalized so they could vote in the last election? That wasn't a project to elect Republicans. We can't go into court with our own defense ready to sink us. The stuff you mentioned might help sink us."

P. Comingal stopped the discussion with, "We aren't trying to justify any particular program. Our goal is to do what any average politician can do under ordinary circumstances, escape blame. Lets concentrate on that. Abortion, population control, and illegal aliens are out."

Herald Crochen thought a Department of Defense angle might work. He offered, "The wars we were in have been against some really bad people. We can show that our own casualties have been very low. Our administration has been really good to foreign combatants who were captured. Our past actions have been as clean as new snow. We're in good shape on that subject."

John Gruff, from the Department Of Labor, replied, "There is that thing with illegally giving the Chinese our missile guidance technology, and everyone knows the President signed a waiver on the delivery of the technology after the technology was delivered. Then there was the part about our letting the Chinese government take over that naval base in California. The Chinese didn't get the base because the Republicans stopped us from giving it to them, but some people still said the base was a payoff for illegal Chinese contributions to our election campaigns. The Chinese took over both ends of the Panama Canal, and our administration said nothing about that takeover. Virtual safety might not be good enough if we are asked how a Communist base in California and their takeover of the Panama Canal increased our security.

"Our Party voted to begin the war with Iraq and then called it an unjust war. Do you think the judge might suspect we had bad motives in one case but not the other? Or would he believe both were entirely political? We were the ones who said those really well-treated prisoners in Guantanamo Bay were being tortured."

P. Comingal became very irritated with the questioning of the time-based political positions he considered nothing more than standard political maneuvers. He said, "We're not here to defend the nation or hash over old political strategies. We are here to uncover new defense strategies for ourselves. If there is something we can use from the defense angle, we'll get back to it later."

Hank Beef, from the Department of Treasury, offered, "What about the economy? Well! I know the economy tanked on us, but we inherited that situation. We were about to see the light at the end of the tunnel before our quick trip to wherever here is kicked us off the job. We were spending our way out of that mess by printing trillions of dollars of new money. The taxpayers are taking it in the shorts for that; but they will eventually, in two or three generations, be able to pay that debt off.

"If we had been able to keep the American people confused about what we were doing for another few months, we would have put the entire country into our socialist programs. We had the average American dripping with sympathy for the people with no medical insurance. Our socialized medical program would have succeeded if the right wing television, and the radio talk shows had kept their mouths shut for a while longer. We might have made our socialist revolution a political fact even before we were bubbled out of existence—if they had just kept their mouths shut."

P. Comingal replied sarcastically, "Thank you for sharing that with us, Hank. We all needed to know whose fault it is we arrived here soaking wet and choking for breath."

Hank Beef replied testily, "You said you wanted all of the pros and cons; I just gave you the pros."

P. Comingal gave Hank a sour look and said, "Next time you give us some of your Beef, make sure it isn't while we're in court. If the judge listens to you and believes what you say, he'll believe we are all guilty, and that will be the end of the road for our defense."

James Cornball upchucked his opinion on the matter. "What the hell is the use of giving a suggestion and then demolishing it in the same breath? Don't you have any damn sense? We're trying to get out of bad situation here. We need information we can use, not something even you can beat us over the head with. What about Education? We're really good on that."

P. Comingal jumped on Cornball's lead. "Where's Elmer Gron? Oh, there you are. Can you give us some good news on our Education program?"

Elmer Gron kind of groaned as he looked at the ceiling and rubbed his chin. "The last time I checked, American students were very low in the scholastic achievement area in the industrial world. A rather large number of parents are choosing to send their children to private schools instead of public schools to get them educated. Our own scholastic achievement tests show children going to private schools are better educated than the public school students. Even home-schooled students are doing better on scholastic achievement tests than public school students. Teachers with degrees are not instructing the home-schooled students in most cases. Even students instructed by parents with no degree are doing better than public school students.

"Our critics say most of this downward trend occurred after the Department of Education began federalizing the public school system. I don't believe that for a minute. After all, we introduced some of the tests that confirmed the downtrend. Look at it this way: however poorly the public school system is doing, we have at least shown some interest in changing it."

P. Comingal retorted, "Elmer, is it your opinion that we can build a defense on being interested enough to recognize the public school system is in the toilet, and all we did was make tests to prove it?"

Elmer replied, "It certainly is. We inherited this situation, and we are, or were, doing the best we could under difficult circumstances. We have that on our side."

Hank Beef added more of his beefy analysis. "How long had the downtrend been going on before we recognized it? Can we get a pass for not paying attention to the education system until then? Will some hard case want to know why we assumed federalizing the education system would make it better and didn't bother checking to see if it actually did until it was a national disgrace? Is that hard case a plumber who became a judge?"

P. Comingal felt a little stressed. Without answering, he sat down at the table with the others on the team. After a short time, he said, "What about the Welfare system? The Welfare rolls have decreased somewhat; maybe we can make something out of that."

Aaron Shum, one of Comingal's political advisors, was approaching the team to see for himself if they were selling him and the others down the river. He overheard the question and decided to give them his opinion. He said, "It's not true that the Welfare rolls have declined somewhat. If it were true, that might be a plus. The real problem with Welfare is the system itself. The Welfare system keeps more than seventy percent of the tax money collected for Welfare in the bureaucracy. The flimflam factor on that is over seventy, and that means the government keeps over seventy percent while the Welfare recipients get less than thirty percent. That's not a very equitable mix.

"Another problem is the economic situation we hoped to rectify with our socialist programs. Many within the vast reaches of the newly unemployed are older people who would have difficulty finding new jobs even in better times. Some of them are opting out of the work force and going on welfare. That changes the flimflam factor a little, but not enough to make the entire system look good."

P. Comingal answered sharply, "I can do simple arithmetic, and I don't need new buzz words for old bad news, so lose the flimflam factor stuff. Do you have any usable good news about the Welfare system?"

Aaron Shum replied, "The Republicans have been all over us on that one. Every time they try to change it, we have our spinmeisters and Mediacrats all over the country accuse them of trying to take Welfare away from children. Judge Bolton told me Judge Bullman is no fool, and spinmeister rhetoric won't work in his court. The first thing he'll recognize is how many of our own bureaucrats are ours because we keep the system going with most of the Welfare money going into bureaucratic pockets. The second thing he will recognize is that ninety-five percent of Washington's bureaucrats vote as democrats. We could even be accused of building a bureaucracy for voting purposes if someone considers the country at large doesn't vote as a democratic majority. We could have a problem explaining any political department in Washington, DC. No matter how much of the country the Republicans win, we always control the national bureaucracy, and the bureaucratic vote is always ours."

P. Comingal wasn't shattered, but his plan was beginning to look dented. He said, "I want all of you to relax, put your minds on our specific problem, and tell me how many of the nation's problems we have actually solved as a Party, specifically in my administration."

The team sat back and began their ruminations, cogitations, and thought-provoking memory exercises. As they did all of the above, they stared at each other. They stared at the ceiling. They stared at the floor. They rubbed their heads or their chins. They scuffled their feet. They cleared their throats. They scratched their butts. They put their hands in their pockets and then took them out. Jane Rantthru, not realizing dead people don't need to go to the bathroom, asked, "Where is the bathroom?" They popped their hands together. Two of them whistled a few notes. They scooted their chairs around as they sat in them.

Finally, James Cornball blew some of his hot wind into their sails to float them out of the doldrums of invincible non-performance. "We done a lot of good things. We put more policemen on the streets to make the people safer. We passed more gun legislation than anyone ever has. We tried to put more teachers in schools and promoted smaller classrooms. We provided money for new artists to show their work. We sent a lot of money back to the states. We could be in pretty good shape if we stop listening to naysayers and start pumping up our successes."

Jane Rantthru gave her reluctant objections. "If we were in one of our own courts, or even an impeachment proceeding in the House of Representatives, we could beat this hands down. Unfortunately, we're in a strange court where rhetoric will be measured by truth, and our logic must be based on facts. If we found it necessary to put more policemen on the street, it's because there is a bigger crime problem, not because we solved a crime problem. We have indeed passed new anti-gun legislation, but that hasn't translated into any less use of guns by the criminal population, and may have made the general population more susceptible to becoming victims. Washington, D.C., had the most stringent gun laws in the nation, but it wasn't safe to be on Washington streets in some areas at night. Then, there are those thousands of federal gun law violations in the D.C. area with very few prosecutions. Our successes in the past have been measured by political standards that are based on trying to do something and getting it done, not because what we did solved a problem. Implementing an agenda may be a political success, but it does not prove the agenda is a national success."

Elmer Gron answered the comment about teachers. "There's lot of talk and suppositions from various interested parties about smaller classrooms, but there isn't any credible study showing smaller classrooms mean better grades. There is a study showing students in large classrooms do as well or even better than those in smaller ones. We might be able to go with that on our intention to do well; if we are wrong, we can say we made an honest mistake. For myself, the mistake would be true, but there is one other element I can't answer for. The teachers unions are big contributors to the Party. My question is this: was the legislation we were trying to promote for smaller classrooms a pay back so the teachers' unions could add more teachers to their union or a real attempt to solve an education problem? If it was a pay back to the teachers unions, it won't wash, even if we were right, and I'm not sure we were right."

Aaron Shum stepped in for the artists. "If we try to promote what the federal government has done for the American people through the art angle, I'm out of here. I'm not going into this court defending a crucifix in a jar of piss and homosexual nudity."

Comingal observed, "He's right; the art angle is out."

Hank Beef drudged up enough common sense to handle the returning money to the states angle. "Sure, we return a lot of money to the states. We also get all of the money we returned to the states from the states. Taking money from the states and then requiring them to accept our regulation to get part of the money back is one of the ways we enforce our federal control of the states. The federal bureaucracy takes its cut in the form of salaries and upkeep. The bureaucracies also use some of the money for things the various states don't approve of, but the states almost always knuckle under just to get a part of their money back. That is a violation of the Tenth Amendment of the Constitution. Need I mention what every one of us shares as the first accusation against us? We are accused of violating our oath to uphold the Constitution."

P. Comingal needed a diversion from all of the bad news. He looked toward the Bailiff's station and noted a few hundred people at nearby tables reading books. He said to James Cornball, "Find Judge Bolton and see if he can make any sense out of what those people are doing over there."

The Thinning of the Ranks

Cornball left the team to search the crowd for Judge Bolton. After a fruitless search, he returned with his report. "No one knows where Bolton is. He seems to have vanished. Large groups of people near the stage are talking about being treated unfairly. They think they should have been included in our planning session. Some of them are disappearing like Bolton did. They go to the Bailiff, get one of those thick books, read the book, and then go somewhere else. If this keeps up, we may not have the actions of ten good people left in the group."

P. Comingal retorted, "There were never ten good people in this group in the first place. We don't need ten good people. What we need right now is for someone to ask those who haven't left what their problem is. We need to know how many are going to stay. We need the largest number possible when the court convenes. Somebody take a poll and find out how many we can count on."

Gladys Shalot, from the Department of Health and Human Services, who had been fruitlessly trying to contact her Master of the World spirit guide for help, decided to give it up and take the poll. Gladys spied an old acquaintance, Sandy Glock, as she crossed the room. They recognized each other at about the same time and began walking to meet. As they came within talking distance, Gladys said, "Are you leaving, Sandy? I thought you would surely want to stay with us."

"I'm not sure, Gladys," Sandy replied. "There's a lot of talk about a better way to do this. It seems help is available to anyone who wants it. All we need do is get our personal history from the Bailiff, read it, and then decide. A few of the people who were at your end of the room before you took it over read their personal histories, and they are gone. None of us know where they went. Judge Bolton told some of his friends that you guys couldn't build a defense if they let you put a moat around it. He also said the best chance we have is with Judge Bullman and his team's help. Judge Bolton disappeared with his personal history book under his arm. He went somewhere with the Bailiff."

Sandy continued, "We don't know what you're planning or how you intend to make your plan work. We hear Cornball shout occasionally, but we haven't a clue about who he is accusing of what. Some of us are afraid the defense might be all of you saying you can't be personally responsible for the actions of your subordinates. Maybe Comingal's team will try to get themselves off that way. Others think Judge Bolton was right, and you just can't come up with a reasonable defense. You're in the center of the planning, Gladys; you tell me."

Gladys attempted to reassure her. "Don't run off, at least until I've had a chance to get the President to explain what we've been doing. He'll tell everyone what our defense is really all about. I need to talk to a few more people. I must get back to the President when I've finished. I'm sure he'll want to tell you all about it. Our defense strategy looks very hopeful to me."

Gladys talked to many of the accused and confirmed her assessment of the situation. She tried to spread reassurances throughout the crowd in the hope of stopping the flow of people from the room. After she had done as much as she could, she returned to the defense team to speak with P. Comingal. Gladys immediately remarked to the President, "There isn't any way to take a poll of people who are still making up their minds about whether to stay or go. We have a problem. They don't trust us because the only input they hear from us is the sound of James Cornball accusing someone. They're suspicious because they don't know who he's accusing or what the accusation is about."

Cornball jumped in energetically, "Who says I'm accusing them? I ain't accusing anyone. What are they talking about? I love them like my own cousins. If I want to accuse someone, they'll really hear it."

Gladys replied, "They hear you all right, and you always sound like you're accusing someone. We're not concerned with your accusations or how you sound. We're concerned with their wrong perception of what we're doing, and if we don't change that perception, we'll lose them all."

P. Comingal thought for a moment and then said, "I'll speak to them from the podium on the stage. I'm sure I can get them to believe our message."

He walked briskly through the large room, shaking a hand here, saying a hello there, appearing affable and in control as he approached the podium. He looked up thoughtfully from the podium for a moment and then spoke reassuringly. "I'm glad to see most of you still with us. You with your core beliefs in our democratic process will not be disappointed. Our defense isn't quit finished, but we are approaching the end of the difficult task. I thought we would be able to finish before the plan was presented for your approval.

"When we are finished, all of you will have an opportunity to include any input you feel would enhance your personal defense. It seems we need to offer some reassurances to you on the sweeping nature—and the probable success—of our plan. Those dissidents who left before we could inform them must have thought our plan would be a failure. We will not fail.

"The plan is simplicity itself," he continued. "We have decided not to try to stand on our personal records, some of which are not, really, impressive in this venue. Our collective record is, however, very impressive. We have done great things for our democracy, and we expect those great things to more than balance out the few blameworthy difficulties we may have encountered along the way. Still, all of us have major allegations we must address. I feel those allegations can best be disposed of as a block, balanced against the major contributions we have collectively, and I must emphasize the word *collectively*, made as a team of hard-working government employees of the American people.

"I hope all of you will stay with us to maintain the team effort we have all benefited from thus far. I must soon return to the floor and finish the difficult work we are about to conclude on all of our behalves. If any of you have questions, now is the time to ask them."

A voice from the crowd asked, "Where are you getting the material you need for this defense?"

P. Comingal replied, "We have everything we need from the accomplishments of the two terms we nearly completed. All of those accomplishments are available, and we intend to use whatever of it seems useful."

There were some worried stirrings at that point. A few of the accused began moving toward the Bailiff's station to ask for their personal histories, but most of the accused were still in tune with the team.

Another asked, "Why are there only you and your friends on the team making the plan? Why have those few separated from the rest of us instead of remaining in contact with all of us?"

"You must realize the intense nature of this process," Comingal answered. "We need uninterrupted privacy in order for we, who are the experts, to be able to apply our minds to the problem at hand. We separated in order to do the very best we can for all of you. We feel your pain and your anxiety, and we know your pain and anxiety are justified. All of my team has been working very hard on your behalf. We expect no thanks for our hard work, but we do hope for your cooperation and forbearance. Our privacy is nothing more than a simple tool to help us do the very best job we can possibly do—for all of you."

Someone else from the crowd asked, "How is one defense going to cover us all? I didn't read the accusations, but I know they came in individual files as though they were accusations against individual people instead of the group as a whole."

P. Comingal tried a soothing voice. "Yes, they certainly did come in individual files. After an intensive study of all of those individual files, we decided the most defensible approach would be to combine the files into one large file and defend the group as a whole instead of the impossible task of dealing with thousands of separate defenses."

Sandy Glock put in her gripe. "Judge Bolton said you don't know how to build a defense. He said Judge Bullman's offer of the best defense he could offer was the best defense we could get for ourselves. What have you to say about that?"

P. Comingal un-soothed for his reply. "Judge Bolton is gone, and no one knows what happened to him. How good of a defense is that? As far as Judge Bullman goes, he is the accuser, and he wants himself, our accuser, to be our defender? If you think that's a good idea, try it yourself!"

Sandy and a few others headed for the Bailiff's station, talking about a windbag defense being no better than the wind in the windbag.

Another face in the crowd said, "There are those of us who think you are engineering a defense for yourself. They say you are using our personal records to overcome the personal accusations against yourself. What do you have to say about that?"

P. Comingal shook his finger at the questioner as he replied. "My personal record isn't any worse than anyone else's. It's just more public than any one else's. That's what I have to say about that."

James Cornball shouted defensively from the floor, "We all got bad records; nobody's perfect. None of us are saints. Everybody's got things they don't tell their mothers. Those people who left, calling our defense a windbag defense, are a bunch of ignorant nobodies. They can go to Hell all alone if they want. I don't want to go there at all. Even if I do go there, I don't want to go alone. I want a lot of friends with me. We don't call our defense the windbag defense. We got a better name than that for it."

Another voice from the crowd directed his question to P. Comingal. "What is the better name for it, Mr. President?"

Cornball interrupted before P. Comingal could smooth things over. "Tell them about our Sodom and Gomorrah defense, Chief."

The room exploded with the noise of many questions being asked at the same time. No one question was coherently heard, but their collective drift was really clear. The drift being, if that's the best you can come up with, maybe we had better just chuck the whole thing. But first—we demand an explanation!"

P. Comingal winced; he would prefer to explain anything rather than a defense plan with a name like Sodom and Gomorrah. Thousands of voices in the room loudly buzzed with the words, and the voices were becoming ever more insistent. Comingal thought he could deal with the concept easily enough, but with those names added to the concept, an explanation was tough.

He faked enthusiasm bravely and spread his hands for silence. As the crowd quieted, he said, "Listen, I can explain this. As us guys were back there just kicking things around, one of the guys said we should consider our position from the perspective of a biblical defense. Well, someone thought our position was like Sodom and Gomorrah, only wetter. While we were talking about that, someone else said Sodom and Gomorrah were destroyed not so much for what they had done as for the fact that they didn't have ten good men in the place. If Sodom and Gomorrah had ten good men, they would have been spared. We couldn't say we had ten good men either, because we had read the accusation files, but there was something different in our case.

"Obviously, our whole town wasn't destroyed, and just as obviously, the group of us who drowned wasn't all bad. We have done a lot of good in our lives, and we weren't getting credit for it in this case." He smiled again, and in a lower voice, confided, "Now I'm the one who thought of this; we have done more good than harm in our lives, but we were still treated like Sodom and Gomorrah. I thought our best chance to reverse the judgment against us is to enter a common plea of not guilty for all of us. We will use the collective good we have all done together as the evidence for our common innocence.

"There's a whole lot of good on our side, more than any ten good men could do. We have the collective good of my entire administration to work with, and all of you had nearly as much to do with the good as I did myself. We have all stood for collectivism in our Democracy for a long time. Whatta ya say? Let's make a collective defense work for us in this case."

There was no spontaneous outburst in the crowd. There were many quizzical looks, some guttural muttering, and a noise beginning with a few that slowly climbed to a crescendo, a disenchanted roar aimed at P. Comingal and his team of experts. Erupting from the center of the noisy crescendo came a loud yell. "Sodom and Gomorrah defense! What's that, something Cornball thought up to blame the Republicans for after we're all in Hell?"

Someone else shouted, "Anyone who would think up a defense named Sodom and Gomorrah deserves fire and brimstone."

Another yelled at Comingal's whole team, "If you guys can't scare the judge with your Sodom and Gomorrah defense, tell him you'll take his social security away from him. That should do the job."

VP Patsy was shocked by the vitriolic reaction from those few. He looked deeply into himself for an inspired response. Finding none, he shouted over their noisy objections, "Why can't we all just look at it as an exercise in the logic of charge reduction?"

A bellow from the crowd, maybe from one of the Republicans, burst out, "Patsy, why don't you just tell the judge there is no compelling authority to bring a charge against you because you're the first politician caught committing that crime?"

The few hundred in the crowd, spewing expletives behind but hope in front, slowly spread itself toward the Bailiff's station and away from the Sodom and Gomorrah defense. They were soon reading their personal files and being shown out of the room by the Bailiff.

The Sodom and Gomorrah Final Plan

P. Comingal, his Cabinet, Cornball, and the remaining members of the original team, along with the accused who still believed a collective defense was possible no matter what its name happened to be, were still in the room.

Elmer Gron remarked, "Not one of those who decided to leave has changed his mind. You'd think at least one of them would come back saying he made a mistake. None of them have done that."

Jane Rantthru said, "We haven't changed our minds either, and we have finally gotten down to those who are committed to a defense for our collective, and they are the one's who will stay with us to support it. I think we can take heart from the small number of those who left."

P. Comingal agreed wholeheartedly. "We've only lost the losers, and they weren't very important to us anyway. What we need now is...what we need to do is, well, we need to decide on the parts of our record we're going to use for a defense."

Gladys Shalot asked, "Can we use the Sodom and Gomorrah defense with some of us gone? We can't make a claim on their good records unless they're here to share in the benefits from their own records."

"Yes we can," P. Comingal disagreed. "We aren't defending ourselves with their personal records. We're defending ourselves with *all* of our collective accomplishments under my administration, and they were under the supervision of most of us who are left here. We don't need them for that, and we don't want them milling around here. There's always a possibility that one of them will mess up our defense. Besides, the better the Court treats them, the better we will be treated. If they are treated poorly by the Court, we still have a chance of being treated better than they were because of our collective—just as well say it—our Sodom and Gomorrah defense."

Gladys bubbled with enthusiasm, "Brilliant, just brilliant. If they have done good, we can benefit from their best work, even if they can't. That's just too precious."

"They're all a bunch of traitors," James Cornball added. "Who needs them? We got everyone we need right here. They'll get just what they deserve, and we'll be walking free."

Hank Beef seemed irritated as he said, "Let's just wish them the best they can get from the Court, while we continue to develop our defense plan. So far, our only definitive input is our own expectation of success. We don't even know how to present what we will present if we ever get around to deciding what we should present."

Aaron Shum caught the edge in Hank's voice. Aaron quietly suggested, "We have to get it started to get it done. What's the format? That will give us a starting point."

P. Comingal said, "I thought I would start off with a speech about our accomplishments and then answer any questions Bullman may ask. The speech should be in generalities; generalities are easier to defend and harder to attack. We want to avoid specific programs if we can because, politics being politics, they are usually filled with political compromises and can easily become controversial. Remember, we are not answering specific charges; we are putting forth a common-good type of defense with ourselves as the ones who acted in the common good."

P. Comingal's plan was now in the open, and everyone in the room could hear and agree or disagree as he saw fit. There was no loud disagreement in the room about the logic of the defense, nor about the way their defense would be presented.

One Gentle Lady in the crowd stated, "I insist that we have a chance to answer questions in our own defense. Surely, you don't expect to do everything yourself?"

"I think each of us will be able to say whatever we choose to say," P. Comingal replied. "Some answers to the Court's questions may require an expert response, while others will require an individual response. We can't plan positively on which because we don't know what the attitude of the court will be. Since we are defending our collective. rather than individual records, I expect most questions asked by the court will require some expertise to answer."

Another asked, "Is this presentation of yours going to take the form of a speech with a question-and-answer session like you do with the press?"

P. Comingal answered, "Pretty much the same, but of course, this is going to be much more serious, and the judge will be asking the questions. I'll need a more thorough expert backing than I needed for the press. That won't be a problem. I have all of the necessary experts right here on the team. You, yourself, could be called on as an expert witness in some case."

A leading bureaucrat stopped and whispered a few quiet words in P. Comingal's ear. He finished his few words and left, quietly walking toward the Bailiff's station. James Cornball called after him, "Hey, where are you going?"

The man stopped, turned to Cornball, and said, "Where I'm going is into court. I'm sure as hell not going into court with a bunch of crazy people trying to defend themselves with a press conference. You're all as crazy as Hell itself. Good-bye and good luck."

Cornball yelled after him, "You're a traitor. We don't need the likes of you, white trash. You're a traitor to the American people, that's what you are. We're all lucky you're gone."

John Gruff brought the proceeding back to the business at hand. "I think we had better get some speech writers here. Our only choice is to put whatever we have on paper so we can all get a look at it."

John Caughess and Bill Presser were chosen to write the most important speech any of those present had ever been involved in. Its success would be life itself. A failure would plunge the personal future of thousands into the darkness of Hell. Everything for all of them would be made or lost on the strength of what was written. The philosophy for the speech was simple. It had to prove to the satisfaction of the court that the public work of the group as a whole was equal to, and worthy of, the efforts of ten good men and thus worthy of freedom from Hell for the entire group.

Hank Beef voiced a disagreement with the format. "I think we should look into those personal files to see if there is any possibility of forming at least part of the defense on what they contain."

James Cornball disagreed with Hank's disagreement. "We don't need a lot of personal stuff messing up this defense. If that personal stuff could help us, we wouldn't be here. All of those who read their personal files are gone. We are still here, and we will be the winners."

P. Comingal added, "We have all had an opportunity to make a decision about the type of defense we think is best. All of us have entered into a collective agreement, and we proved that by staying with the group. We think the choice we have made to defend our collective is our best hope. I agree with James."

The Court

The speechwriters did their best work. They followed the instructions they were given and entered the most appropriate politically correct icons into the defense. P. Comingal read it and thought he had made better speeches. He felt that, under these circumstances, the speech he had for the defense of his fellow Democrats was the best speech he could make to defend himself.

VP Patsy was chosen to inform the Bailiff that the defense was ready to begin. The Bailiff signaled for the large crowd to enter the Court. The first to arrive was P. Comingal and his entourage of core defenders, closely followed by the lawyers, who had compiled the short list of charges the defenders wanted to force the Court to accept. Following the lawyers were the various groups making up the body of the whole body of the recently deceased that still believed in P. Comingal's ability to defend them.

Judge Bullman waited patiently for the large crowd of the accused to enter the court. Behind him sat a stranger, whose purpose was unknown to the accused. Judge Bullman waited for the crowd to complete their entrance and then introduced the stranger. "This is Mr. Clause; he is my assistant and a student of law." Judge Bullman banged his gavel on the bench and stated, "These proceedings are now in session. Each of you may enter the plea of your choice."

P. Comingal addressed Judge Bullman with confidence. "Your Honor, we are not entering individual pleas. We have chosen a defense for our collective as a body of defenders. I have been chosen to present that defense."

Judge Bullman looked with some disappointment over the crowd and then advised them, "The failure of a common defense will demand a common judgment. Equal and severe punishment may be meted out to all of those entering the common plea. I advise each of you to accept the responsibility for your individual actions and present individual pleas. A common plea will not mitigate your actions to less than they were or allow you an average punishment based on the best and the worst actions you are collectively guilty of. A common plea may cause you to suffer the most severe punishment meted out to the worst of you.

"I will give you a few minutes to reconsider your position based on the information I have just given you. Those who choose the wisdom of an individual defense may leave this chamber through the door on the right. Those who insist on a collective defense may remain in the chamber."

Soul searching is a thin description for the shock Judge Bullman's words let loose in the crowd. Most of them expected, at the very least, to find the Court would have a technical appreciation of the defense for their collective as a collective effort. Most of them thought that at least a word of praise would be forthcoming for their willingness to sacrifice a small part of their own futures to the collective good of their fellow Democrats. They received no praise for that effort under these most dangerous circumstances. None of in the Court were willing to admit to their own intense fear of facing their own guilt alone.

The noise from the crowd grew with each moment. The pro common defense, and con common defense antagonists found it increasingly difficult to be heard over the voices of loyalty and dissent for the collective's plea. The loud, angry arguments dragged far past the few minutes Judge Bullman promised for the resolution of individual decisions.

Each of the convicted wanted all the other convicted to accept his individual decision to leave or stay, and not break what most of them felt was the established protective common bond. After all, right or wrong was a matter of consensus in their minds.

The self-serving consensus had been broken by Judge Bullman's rude remarks about extent of individual punishment. The interpersonal creaming, invective, and accusation were meant to reestablish the common bond shared during the preparation of the defense of the collective. Each had stayed with the Comingal defense because of how much they felt they needed that common bond, and it was very difficult to walk away.

Judge Bullman realized the divisive discussions could never be resolved to the satisfaction of all factions. He pushed his Banshee button and the loud, unpleasant noise emitted throughout the court. The noise of the many voices ceased as the noise of the Banshee wail forced the accused to cover their ears.

Judge Bullman, having caused the silence, addressed the accused, "You have ten minutes to make your decisions and leave the Court or stay."

Faced with the necessity of making an immediate choice, the crowd began to break up. As it turned out, about half of the accused chose to make individual pleas and began leaving the room. P. Comingal and his team remained, joined by the survivors of the political breakup who were still pro collective defenders. James Cornball, somewhat stunned by the large exodus, announced in an unprecedented quiet voice, "We'll be the ones who get out of Hell. I know Comingal will pull this off."

P. Comingal asked to no one in particular, "Where is the thousand or so Chicago clique? I've lost track of them, and that's a bad group to lose track of."

Cornball informed him, "I saw them traitors leave with the others. I thought they would be with us all the way. I know they were plotting some way to take over our action, but they never said anything."

P. Comingal didn't say anything to Cornball, but he breathed a big sigh of relief as he thought of Judge Bullman's threat, that everybody could get the worst punishment given to the worst of the offenders. Comingal knew that bunch pretty well, and he felt a lot closer to winning his case with them gone.

Judge Bullman waited until the last of the accused exited to the right, waited for an additional amount of time to assure himself that none of the others would follow the course of his suggested wisdom, and then addressed the accused. "You who have chosen to the defense of your collective may enter your plea."

Lawyer Flim Flamm advance to present the plea. He introduced himself as the chief counselor for the accused and addressed the Court. "We plead not guilty to all charges. Our plea of not guilty is predicated on our actions as a whole and the actions of those who were in President Comingal's Cabinet, his Administration, and his associates who were closely related to the actions of his Administration. All are present for this proceeding.

"We recognize that we have all made errors in our lives, but we believe a careful analysis of our public record will show the balance of our actions proved to be good for the citizens we served in our Democracy."

Judge Bullman's new assistant, Mr. Clause, listened closely to Flim Flamm's statement. When it was finished, he stepped forth and said, "Let us examine one of the important points in your plea statement. You mentioned serving the people in your democracy. Isn't it a fact that the nation you are calling your democracy is a republic? I have it listed as the Republic of the United States of America. This proceeding requires absolute accuracy. Please clarify your remark."

Mr. Clause's criticism allowed the accused a closer look at the one who would remain their most important critic. He was an unusually tall man, about seven feet. He was dressed in a dark gray three-piece suit and had an intimidating dignity about him. His smile was friendly, but his smile didn't reach up and gather his dark, penetrating eyes into its warmth. His voice was quietly powerful, and he spoke his words with an easy authority none of them had heard coming from a law student in the schools they had attended.

Flim Flamm took Mr. Clause's criticism very seriously, "Our nation is commonly referred to as a democracy. Democrats almost always refer to it as a democracy, most of the news media people refer to our nation as a democracy, and even some Republicans occasionally refer to it as a democracy. Most of our constituents believe it is a democracy."

Mr. Clause wasn't satisfied with Mr. Flamm's response. He pushed further, "You, as a constitutional lawyer, must be familiar with Article Four Section Four of your Constitution, which states, 'The United States shall guarantee to every State in this Union a Republican form of government...' Are you suggesting that every state and the entire land mass of the United States is a Republic, but the nation is a Democracy?"

Mr. Flim Flamm paused for several moments while he tried to form a coherent, legal sounding response. P. Comingal noticed his problem and feared Flim Flamm might blow it. Comingal stepped in to repair the damage. "I believe it is my duty as Chief Executive to make a response. Over a period of many decades, we have managed to create a shift in the common language used to describe our nation. That shift was brought about by the ascendancy of our Democrat Party to national power for most of that time. During those years, our Party solidified the facts of freedom for our people. We began new programs for their benefit. The federalization of the Welfare system, the Medicare program, Social Security, and many public works programs, to mention a few, were Democrat programs. We zealously guarded the people's constitutional rights. Our favorable shift in language was effective and found favor with the people. During those many years, not only a very large number of people in the United States, but the people in most other countries came to think of the United States as a democracy. Mr. Flim Flamm, within the broad region of descending political effluence, was linguistically correct, though he was legally inaccurate. Our democracy is, legally, a republic.

"We fed the poor. We healed the sick. We clothed the naked. We established new levels of freedom for our people, and we did it in the name of our democracy. Our record of service may be blemished, as all political records are, but we worked very hard for the American people, and the balance of our hard work produced a tremendous record of good works for our democracy."

Judge Bullman sat back in his chair and looked with envy at P. Comingal. He kept his admiring eyes on Comingal for a long moment and then stated, "I can see how you became the President of a great and populous nation. That was a beautiful speech, full of everything a deluded constituency would see as far-reaching evidence of your dedication to duty. Unfortunately, this court demands facts, not pumped-up political rhetoric. Your speech had no facts whatever, just claims of doing what you are accused of not doing. My assistant, Mr. Clause, will have some questions for you, Mr. Comingal."

James Cornball, the master accuser, became irritated with Judge Bullman for calling President Comingal "Mister Comingal." Cornball vituperated, "Comingal isn't a 'mister,' he's a President. You should call him President Comingal or Mister President. He deserves some respect from this Court. He's the reason we're all gettin' out of here with a whole skin. Comingal deserves some respect."

Judge Bullman explained the procedure to James Cornball and to all of the accused, "Your former titles are of no concern during this proceeding. All of you are mister, misses, or miss. No other title will be recognized. If you wish to maintain your former titles among yourselves, you are welcome to do so, but don't expect the Court to accept that burden."

During Judge Bullman's answer to Mr. Cornball's critique of the Court, Mr. Clause came to the bench from his place behind Judge Bullman. He said, "I will direct my questions to Mr. Comingal, but I would like to make it clear to all of you, anyone who believes he may help the collective case with his own answer may also respond to the questions. If you have something to say, just blurt it out;

you need no one's permission to make your response."

Mr. Clause stood for a moment after Judge Bullman's announcement, as though he was having trouble forming a question. He finally stated, "I intended to ask Mr. Comingal to explain how he uses the broad region of descending political effluence to call the Republic a democracy and be linguistically correct but legally incorrect. To prevent further confusion, I will not ask and this Court will use the legally correct word. The Court will call your Republic a republic."

Clause continued, "Mr. Comingal, please be as precise as possible with your answers. You spoke of feeding the poor; how did the Democrats do that?"

"The beginning of the national Welfare program was before my time," Comingal replied, "but I may be able to explain the process. In a former time, each state had its own Welfare program. Their different programs depended on each state's ability and determination to care for the poor. The poor in the richer states were well fed, but others in the poorer states were poorly fed. We Democrats federalized the system to even out the care each of the poor received without regard to the state he lived in. The welfare system was increased over the years, usually at our insistence, until it became what the United States now has."

Mr. Clause asked, "The poor were being cared for but not cared for well enough to suit the Democrats? Are you giving Democrats the bulk of the credit for the present Welfare system?"

Comingal responded cautiously, "We have had some bipartisan support most of the time, but we Democrats created and maintain the present welfare system."

Clause paused before he continued, "More than seventy percent of the tax money collected for poverty programs remains in the bureaucracy as salaries and costs. With that much money remaining in the bureaucracy, the Welfare system appears to be a bureaucratic support system more than a Welfare system. The poor it was created to serve, and is being maintained for, receive less than one third of the money the American people are being taxed to support those poor people. The Democrats turned the national Welfare system, whatever intentions they held originally, into a system to support Democrat bureaucrats who are the body of your power system. The majority of the American people are unaware of how little of their tax money is actually used for its original purpose. Do you wish to challenge my statement, Mr. Comingal?"

Mr. Comingal offered no challenge. Mr. Clause began again. "I would like to continue with a question about how you healed the sick. What means did you use to accomplish the healing?"

"I want to be clear on this point," Mr. Comingal cautiously stated. "I wasn't a member of the federal government when the Medicare program began. "My administration did everything we could to control costs and assure each of our elderly citizens of the very best medical care. There has always been very heavy bipartisan support for Medicare, and we Democrats who are here, and who became associated with the program after it was already in place, have no particular responsibility for it. The earlier Democrats are responsible for it, not us."

Clause stated, "I realize you aren't personally responsible for initiating the Medicare program. It was originally designed and brought into the lives of the American people as a program for retired citizens who were too poor to afford their own medical treatment. The nation's entire aged population was then put into the program almost immediately.

"Your Administration has, however, attempted to forced the entire American medical system into your party's brand of socialism. Included in that socialist plan is medical rationing. Bureaucrats will decide who, when, and how much medical care shall be given to each individual. The additional tax revenues needed for long-term support of that system is in the trillions of dollars. You knew then, and now, the nation can't possibly afford that system.

"The increase in the number of bureaucrats needed to support such a system could raise the number of votes you receive from state and national government employees to a high enough level to assure your party will be reelected in every election.

"A large number of people will die or suffer permanent impairment while waiting for a bureaucrat's permission to continue medical treatment. Others will suffer the same fate from being refused medical treatment by the bureaucracy responsible for their care.

"Medical costs will skyrocket far faster than they did after the over 65 group was forced into Medicare. The cost to the young and the middle class entrepreneurs will impoverish many who would otherwise prosper. The cost of medical care will climb to the point that more people will lose medical care than will be provided with medical care.

"One of the charges against you, and many of those with you, is Using Undue Influence. As you have stated, the Democrats have had heavy bipartisan support for the Medicare program, but that support ended when socialism, with its changes in the national character, arose. In the past, Democrats consistently used a threat of Medicare changes that would occur if their opponents were voted into office. That tactic tended to keep the older citizens voting for Democrats. That threat constitutes undue influence. Creating a false fear to gain party power or votes for specific candidates is using undue influence. Undue influence is so common in politics that I will not labor the point unless there is someone brave enough to challenge it.

"We will skip your claim of clothing the naked. There is no specific federal program to cloth the naked, and I assume you are referring, again, to nationalized Welfare. You may address your claim for clothing the naked if you feel you can establish an actual case for it that will aid in your defense."

None of the accused came forward to defend a national program to cloth the naked, and Mr. Clause continued, "I want to pursue your claim of bringing new freedoms to the American people. Government actions are highly restricted in the Constitution of the Republic. All rights not expressly given to the federal government in it are reserved to the states or to the people. All of the freedom they have had in the past, and that is a great deal of freedom, was codified for them in the Constitution either directly or by recognition of their unwritten rights in the Ninth Amendment or by the constitutional restrictions on the powers of government.

"I'm not sure how you mean new freedoms. Constitutional rights are sometimes referred to as freedoms, but a constitutional right is more accurately defined as something *beyond the government's ability to change it*. Freedom means liberation from the control of another or from some arbitrary power. I know of no case where your Administration gave either a new constitutional right or a new freedom to the American people. You must testify to specific instances of providing new freedoms or rights to use them in your defense."

Comingal stood pierced by his own rhetorical petard. One of the congressmen in the group had publicly announced that Congress had the right to regulate the rights of the American people. All of the accused had voted for or helped promote the regulation of constitutional rights. Even with the regulation of some rights, the United States was still the world's bastion of liberty. *New freedoms aren't easy to come up with by someone more concerned with running a government his way than running it the constitutional way.* To make the problem even worse, Mr. Clause had accurately defined both a constitutional right and freedom.

To the best of Comingal's knowledge, the Democrat Party had never defined either rights or freedom. He had no standard democratic definition to fall back on. Further, the weasel language usually used in press releases and interviews just wouldn't work in this Court. Comingal knew there weren't any new freedoms the Democrats had provided at any time in the past.

Unfortunately, Ray Blather, the Mediacrat representative of the people, was still with the collective plea group, and he believed Comingal was on to something with the new freedoms angle. Ray broke the silence in the Court. "We have consistently supported choice for women, and we are the pioneers of gender equality. Millions of people are enjoying more freedom because of our efforts."

"What choice for women did you support?" Mr. Clause asked.

"The women's choice for reproductive freedom," Ray stated.

"You're speaking in riddles, Mr. Blather," remarked Clause. "Are you telling me the women in the United States were not free to reproduce until your party gave that freedom to them? Will you please be specific about your statement and include the actual choice or choices women have been granted in their use of the new freedom?"

"Women have always been free to reproduce, but the new freedom allows them to choose to become pregnant or not," Blather reported, "or whether to abort the fetus or to carry it to term if they do become pregnant."

"If a woman chooses to become pregnant," asked Clause, "why wouldn't she choose to carry the baby until it's born? If she can choose not to become pregnant, why does she become pregnant?"

"Most women who choose to become pregnant also choose carry the fetus to term," responded Blather, "but life styles differ, and many women suffer unwanted pregnancies within their choice of those life styles. Those women, who through sexual misfortune become pregnant, often choose to abort."

"Mr. Blather," Clause asked, "are you telling me that the accused in this Court consistently supported killing unborn babies because women who did not choose to become pregnant became pregnant anyway?"

"Certainly not," replied Blather. "We only supported the woman's right to abort her fetus. We did not advise anyone to do that, and most of us in this Court wouldn't abort our own children."

Mr. Clause didn't insist on Blather's explanation of his intricate logic for supporting something the supporters wouldn't advise anyone to do and wouldn't do to themselves. He seemed to have something else on his mind. "Mr. Blather, would you mind explaining what type of people seek abortion?"

Ray Blather thought he had a good answer for that. "People from all races, all social and financial levels, all religions, and every political persuasion seek abortions."

"All of the major religions are against the killing of children by abortion," stated Mr. Clause. "Are you telling me that abortions are performed by good Catholics, Jews, Protestants, and Muslims?"

"I'm not sure what you mean by *good*, unless you are referring to those fundamentalist who are very strict in their religious practices. The good ones, in that case, do not abort their fetuses," replied Blather, "but many others who belong to those religions have had abortions performed."

"Are the people who call themselves pro life, the ones who are against abortion, are they democratic voters?" asked Clause.

"Not as a general rule," responded Blather. "I think we receive very few votes from pro life people, ultra right wing Christians, conservative Catholics, or from what we sometimes call the fundamentalist Christians in the Protestant religions. They don't seek abortions, and they don't vote for Democrats. They have never understood our message."

Mr. Clause paused for a moment to consider what Ray Blather had just said. He continued with, "Is it fair to say that the voters who seek abortions are the most likely people to vote for Democrats and support your platform?"

Ray showed only a small amount of hesitation before he answered, "Yes, it's accurate to say that."

Clause looked toward Judge Bullman before he proceeded. Bullman nodded his approval, and Clause continued, "Judging from what you have told me, and I know what you have said is correct, the Democrat Party will eventually go down in history as the only political party to kill its own fetal constituents. Your consistent support of abortion is primarily reducing your own Democrat Party's ability to increase its membership from the birth of newborn babies. Your opponents, as you have admitted, don't abort their babies. The people who do abort their babies are those who vote for democratic politicians and support the democratic platform.

"With fifty million abortions already performed in the United States, your party must be feeling the pain of those lost votes. I find it difficult to believe Democrat party leaders are not aware of the loss of those voters to the party. Your opponents aren't losing a source of new voters because of abortion. Do you have any information about your Party's plan to replace its lost votes with new Democratic voters?"

Ray Blather was drained from what Clause had said. He didn't want to talk anymore, and he felt the hot breath of Hell blowing down his back. Ray admitted, "I'm not one of the planners of Democratic strategies. I don't have an answer to that question. I think you should seek whatever information is available from someone who is more involved in making decisions for the Party."

Clause looked around the silent room and asked, "Is there someone in the Court who is aware of a Democratic strategy for replacing Democratic votes lost from abortions, or someone who knows where the new source of voters will come from?" The silence was so total that not even breathing was heard. No one wanted to answer Clause's question.

Clause's dark, penetrating eyes searched the crowd. Finally he turned to Mr. Comingal and asked, "Are you aware of such a strategy? I hope you will answer truthfully. Please keep in mind, your future and the future of the group is in the answers you and the group give. There is no room for verbal machinations to make a bad answer appear good or to hide the truth."

Mr. Comingal considered his answer carefully. "I have not met with any group of Democrats to discuss the situation. I'm sure some Democrats are aware of the loss of voters, but I know of no Party-wide plan to cure the loss."

"In your last election," Mr. Clause stated, "you instructed the Immigration and Naturalization Service to speed up the process of naturalization for one million new citizens. Was that an effort to help insure a Democrat victory in the election?"

"Well," Comingal replied, "It occurred to me that most of those votes would come to the Democrat Party, but I didn't consider that as a move to counter the loss of voters from abortions."

Clause continued, "Your Party platform for the last election suggested democracy training for school children. Do you think democracy training for school children, and all American children are growing up as citizens of the Republic, would be used to strengthen the Democrat voting position in the Republic of the United States? Would teaching those children to accept your version of democratic government cure some of the problems caused by the loss of democratic voters from abortion?"

"I'm sure it would," Mr. Comingal admitted, "but I, personally, don't know that curing the loss of voters caused by abortion was the *specific* purpose of democracy training for school children."

Clause didn't dispute Comingal's answer, but he pressed further. "Do you believe the Democrat votes lost from abortion would be, in large part, replaced if the Democrats managed to naturalize the thirty million illegal aliens in the United States?"

Comingal was becoming very worried with Clause's line of questions. He didn't know where clause would end up with the questions, and there was no way for him to give an answer that was good for the defense. Comingal gave what he hoped would be the final answer. "I have no definitive information on the number of votes the naturalization of illegal aliens would replace, but most of the newly naturalized people would believe they owe their newly acquired social welfare and citizen status to Democrats. Most new immigrants vote for our democracy, and I have no doubt the new citizens from that source would do the same. I think we have exhausted this line of questioning. I have no answer for the voting loss problem."

Clause stated, "The voting loss problem was used to show how much damage this group and its Party is willing to sustain to support one of the icons of your democracy, abortion at any cost. It was also used to show the probable method your political party would have to use to bring your voting levels back to normal because of the loss of voters due to its abortion policy.

"I would like to continue with the first accusation on each of your lists. You gave your personal oath, witnessed by God and your fellow citizens, to perform your duties within the laws of the Constitution of the Republic of the United States. The accused usually refer to the United States as "our democracy." A democracy, if your politicians could have made one possible, is a very simple system of government with only one goal: to do the will of the majority of the people in the democracy. Supreme power in a democracy is vested in the majority of its people. The oath you took was not to a democracy; it was to your Republic.

"The Republic of the United States has a system of government with a president as its highest officer and representatives elected by a majority of those who vote in its states. It has a constitution that is its rule of law, and its president, officers, and elected representatives must govern according to constitutional law. Supreme power in the American Republic is vested in the body of citizens who are eligible to vote. Those who are registered to vote and do vote in the nation's elections use that supreme power.

"None of you can say you didn't know you lived in a republic. If I am incorrect in that statement, those who did not know they lived in a Republic, please raise your hands, and I will apologize for my error." Mr. Clause checked around and saw that there were no hands raised.

"There are many lawyers among you, and some are constitutional lawyers. Lawyers, public servants, and all who take the oath of office know they are taking an oath to uphold the laws of the Republic they live in. All of you violated your Oath of Office. You gave your oath no honor and no meaning except that it was constitutionally required of you to take the oath in order to take your positions in government. Once in office, you did not bring your personal honor to your oath—you ignored it completely. That alone should have gotten you a quick trip to Hell."

The Flowering of Democracy in Court #666

Mr. Clause complained, "So far, you have done nothing but try to impress this Court with the same tactics you used during the press conferences you presented in your political lives. Those deceptions have proven to be unacceptable. You have not attempted to address even one of the charges included in the accusations against you. I wish you no ill fortune, and I realize you did not prepare your defense within the boundaries this Court originally set for this proceeding.

I have spoken privately with Judge Bullman about your request for a manageable list of charges, and he has given my request his consideration. Judge Bullman and I have made a deal on your behalf. This is your challenge before this Court, if you accept the challenge. You must convince the Court that your effort to change the Republic of the United States into the type of government you would have called your Democracy of the United States, if that effort had been successful, would have benefited the American people more than the Republic they now have. Prove your revolution would have been better for the people, and you will win your case. All of your useless attempts to manipulate the Court in your favor will be forgotten. All of the accusations in your individual lists will be ignored, and you will win your freedom from this Court."

There was an audible sigh of relief from the accused. Each felt certain a collective effort by all of them could do that one thing. James Cornball shouted, "Sticking with Comingal was the best thing we ever did. He'll pull us out of this without a scratch." The entire collective of lost souls buzzed with new life.

Comingal was both relieved and apprehensive. He had finally succeeded in having his own personal charges reduced, but he was worried about the freedom issues in his version of democracy. He raised the question, "How may we proceed to provide the proof for our democracy? Will you be asking questions, or are we expected to provide a body of proof showing our heart-felt confidence in our democracy?"

Clause remained cautious; he knew Comingal's offer to provide heart-felt confidence was designed to trap the Court into allowing the accused a broad array of warm and fuzzy claims no one could prove would fail in a democracy. Still, he wanted to give the accused all of the room they needed to maneuver while keeping himself in control. He stated, "As you are all equal in this Court, any of you may contribute as you see fit. You may ask questions, challenge the Court's opinions, or remain silent as you choose. The Court shall retain control of the proceedings and demand truth. I or Judge Bullman may ask questions, and Judge Bullman is the final authority on the truth of what is said."

Addressing the heart-felt confidence ploy, Comingal had suggested to avoid factual truth, Clause stated, "Your heart-felt confidence about the final outcomes of activities generated by a future democratic government is not admissible. However, if you can show how your heart-felt confidence was generated by a procedure or process that was actually tried and worked to the benefit of the people, then it is admissible. You may not say democracy is or would have been better unless you can show how democracy has been better. If you require time to organize, the time will be given you."

Comingal immediately asked for more time. Judge Bullman banged his gavel and ordered, "This Court is in recess for the amount of time the accused may consume to organize their defense. The accused may retire for consultation to the room they formerly used."

The Comingal crowd liberally consumed the time they were given to organize their defense. Judge Bullman and Mr. Clause began to worry about a permanent retirement for consultation; still, the defense was finally ready. The Bailiff informed the Court that the accused had completed the preparations for their defense and were ready to enter the Court.

Mr. Flim Flamm made the opening statement, "With due respect to the Court, we must challenge the Court's definition of *democracy* and submit our own as a more practical definition than the Court's. We maintain that all governments must establish laws, and democracies are no exception. While the law is in place, the law is the supreme authority in the democracy. The ruling majority must make its objections to those laws, policies, procedures, etcetera, etcetera, within those established laws of the legal framework regulated by the democratic government for the convenience of the majority. The majority of people may take their rightful place as the supreme authority only when the majority recognizes the necessity of influencing the members of government. The government must in return recognize the majority of people and manage the majority's authority to the benefit of the democracy.

"We recognize that the government must make changes demanded by the majority when the government becomes aware of the majority's will to change. We maintain that it is the majority's duty to make its will known to the government as a necessary part of the process for change. We believe, due to the enormous challenges of both determining and administering the will of the majority, the Court must use a more liberal definition of *democracy*. We believe the definition we are giving to the Court is more reflective of the actual political conditions as they presently exist in the United States."

Mr. Clause responded, "You are informing the Court that the democracy you prefer will be governed by those who may ignore the will of the majority unless they are informed by the majority of the majority's demand for change! Further, the laws made by the governing politicians are supreme until the majority becomes aware of the necessity for a change in the law. The majority must then come together without any organization that can bring them together. Then, acting as a dutiful majority, take specific, positive action using an undetermined format of future design to make their demands. If the majority does not—or cannot make its majority demands known to the governing political establishment, the democratic government has no duty to the majority. Mr. Flim Flamm, have I correctly stated your revisions in the processes of a democratic government and the methods you would use to govern it?"

"The terms you used are more graphic than mine," replied Flim Flamm, "but they are reasonably accurate."

Clause eyed Flim Flamm closely for presenting such a sweeping reversal of the definition for a democratic government and then said, "There have been few up-swellings of majority demands at any time in history. Governments usually identify, or cause, a problem and then present it to the people. The people are generally dependent on a government, as the primary source of knowledge in the development of the majority will. There are big problems with important government information going to the people; it is almost always twisted by a political agenda. Have the accused, as members of the hierarchy of the Democrat Party, diligently presented the truth to the people of the United States and then made an honest effort which discovered the truth of the majority's will and used that truth as the majority directed?"

Flamm thought it was a reasonable question asked by someone who was unfamiliar with the American political scene. He felt uneasy with the discovery of majority will part of the question, and using it to their advantage was too difficult for a real answer, but he had answered tough questions all of his life, and he felt he could wing it. Flamm answered, "We have an adversarial relationship with the other major political party. We inform the public of our political position, and the other party presents its position concerning the same effort. We know they will try to show our position to be deeply flawed and their program to appear better for the public. We cannot give the public the deficiencies we see in our position, because the other party will pounce on them and then add their own perceived deficiencies of our program to destroy our position. If they succeed, they will win the electorate's legislative support for themselves. They inform the public at the same level we do in the same circumstances. Neither of us dares to tell the whole truth."

"Since neither Party is telling the whole truth," asked Clause, "how can the electorate determine the truth from two political parties who only tell them enough to entice them to support their party's political agenda?"

"Well," replied Flamm, "most of the people are usually too busy or too uninformed to understand the legislative political maneuvering of either political party. Only hot-button legislation or personal issues force them into political action to support either Party's position. Both Parties have a base that will support them no matter what each proposes. That base support is, usually, not enough to insure legislative success. If we can influence the opinions of the political activists in the independent center to our side, we can assume a majority consensus for our agenda, and win the case for Democrat Party legislation. There is no possibility of and actual majority in the majority of cases."

"But," insisted Clause, "you aren't just one more political party. As a party dedicated to specifically democratic actions by government, you can't assume you have a majority that you know you don't have. Your political strength is usually, and by your own admission, based on a politically active minority. You cannot truthfully claim that minority support to be the majority will. You are democratic politicians. By the proclaimed purpose resulting from the democratic qualifier in your title for your Party, you have cemented your public purpose. You say you are dedicated to the majority will of the people.

"I find you are not really interested in, and you do not have a standard method of determining what majority will is. Your main political support comes from political activists, and people only occasionally aroused from their political disinterest for a compelling personal reason. Those people might, or might not, support your legislative agenda effort. The information given to the hoped for supporters by your Party is politically motivated half-truths, and outright lies, provided by aggressive politicians who are most interested in the supremacy of the Party agenda, not the will of the majority. Politicians lying, or even giving less than the truth to American citizens are perpetrating an obvious government fraud.

"You began this discussion with your criticism of the Court's definition of *democracy*. You have not succeeded in changing the definition, but the Court did not provide you with a standard definition. The Court provided you with the same definition, but it was not in precisely these same words. I will now provide you with a definition this Court is judging to be the true definition of *democracy: Government in which the majority of free citizens hold the ruling power either directly or through elected representatives; rule by the ruled. Majority rule* is the most commonly understood definition that is used by most of the people. Less than majority rule by free people does not fit a definition of democracy.

"Your task of showing that a democracy would be or has been better than the government of the Republic of the United States still stands. Your group may caucus for a brief period to reconsider the original task."

The caucus was filled with anger. Most of the accused had never bothered to define the word *democracy,* within democracy's political actualities. To them, being a Democrat didn't mean they had to actually be democratic. They lived in the comfort of collective political ignorance. They had depended on their leaders and the actions of the Democrat Party to be following a politically acceptable democratic paradigm. Few had ever questioned the democratic nature of their leadership. Very few had ever bothered to consider if their own actions would be permissible by an actual democratic government.

The only one left among them with a deeply held confidence in Comingal's ability to pull it off was James Cornball. The others, though lacking in confidence, knew they had only two choices: win or go to Hell. They had chosen the collective defense, each of them had bought it and was stuck with it, and each feared his individual defense was even more dangerous than following Comingal's poor plan.

Most in the caucus no longer recognized a team of saviors. Each was intensely and vociferously interested in the outcome for reasons of personal safety. Their desperation was reflected in their questions and comments.

"What do you mean our democracy is supposed to be ruled by the majority of the people in the United States? I thought it was ruled by the majority of us Democrats," one commented.

Another blurted loudly, "That judge said our democracy is our Republic. When did it become a republic? My grandfather was a Democrat, my father was a Democrat, and I'm a Democrat. All of us called it our democracy. When did our democracy become a republic? Nobody told *me* it's a republic."

James Cornball was not to be silenced under such trying circumstances. He complained, "There is a bunch of us here who have never taken the Oath of Office, but they still have violating the Oath of Office as our first crime. Few of the lawyers or Mediacrats took the Oath of Office. Ray Blather and I checked with the judge on that one. He said we helped the politicians violate their Oath of Office, and that's why we're charged. That's unfair, and someone has to do something about it!"

Comingal was fed up with complaints shouted to no useful purpose. He stood up, his presidential countenance set in grim determination, surveyed the crowd of overheated bubble-nauts, and said, "We are not here to prove what the United States was, is, or shall be. We are here for only one purpose, to prove our democracy would have been better for the United States than the Republic. That is a difficult task because the United States has never been a democracy. It has always been a Republic, no matter what anyone's father or grandfather told them or called it. All of us *must* put everything else out of our minds and deal with that one issue. If we put our minds to it, I think we can offer enough proof to get that one thing done."

There were no clocks and no change from day to night. Time was nothing at all. The only weight on their heads was their fear of the looming failure, and no certain way to defeat it. The various debates continued for an undetermined amount of time. The groups were not disturbed in the lengthy discussions. The discussions were finally completed with some hope of remaining as a group, and the accused returned to Court to renew their defensive assault on the only issue left to prove.

Judge Bullman called the Court to order and asked if the defense had completed its preparations. Mr. Comingal stated, "We have, and the defense is prepared to continue." Comingal's opening statement was short. "The United States has always been a Republic. We cannot show specific instances where a non-existent democracy might exceed the good function of the existing Republic, but we have always maintained the Republic to be flawed. We can show those flaws and suggest how it would have been better if a democracy had been selected by the founding fathers instead of the Republic. If that is an acceptable premise on which to proceed, we will proceed."

Judge Bullman looked at Mr. Comingal closely and stated, "You were to show specific instances where democracy had succeeded. Your unproved conclusions were not to be submitted to the Court. Unless Mr. Clause has an objection, I must pass the Court's judgment based on your lack of performance on what you were assigned to prove. Mr. Clause approached Judge Bullman and whispered quietly into his ear. Judge Bullman sat back in his chair, folded his hands, and contemplated what Mr. Clause had whispered. He then moved forward once again and stated, "Mr. Clause has asked the Court's permission to allow the trial to proceed. I have agreed to Mr. Clause's request. Mr. Comingal, you and your group may continue your collective defense, but the original Court demands are still the rule of the Court."

Mr. Comingal stepped forward and addressed the Court. "A democratic government is established on the basis of doing the will of the majority of the people in the democracy. We maintain that the majority of the citizens in a democracy are more frequently right than people who may chose to vote or not vote, such as in the Republic of the United States. The majority of people who vote do not represent a majority of people in the United States. Presidents are usually elected by a minority of the registered voters and are sometimes elected by less than a majority of registered voters who actually vote. The majority of the voting population in the United States is usually not registered to vote and is therefore not eligible to vote. The nonvoters are always the actual majority of the adult population.

"If all elections are considered, less than fifty percent of the eligible voters exercise their right to vote on a consistent basis. The present voting patterns in the United States show a weakness of representation in that pattern of both the eligible voters who do not vote and the citizens who do not register to vote. A seventy percent turnout of the eligible voters in national elections is considered unusually high, and the highest turnout in the twentieth century was sixty-five percent. The upshot of these boring statistics is that the nonvoters in all elections, national and local, would come under the purview of a democratic government."

Mr. Clause responded, "Are you telling the Court that your democracy would be better because it would represent the present majority of citizens who are refusing to take part in choosing the people who represent them?

"Using current voting practices for all elections as a model," Mr. Comingal replied, "the nonvoters, who could vote if they would, could certainly form a majority voting block for every election. The non-voters in the voting population do not represent themselves by voting and are not directly represented in the election process. American children must also be added to those numbers, and they are not directly represented in the voting process of the present Republic."

"What method for determining the will of a politically inactive majority would be used in the democracy you are describing? I have failed to discover a method of determining the majority will of people who don't care enough about governing themselves to vote in their government's elections. I don't see how lazy or childish citizens can improve any type of government over any other type. Will you please enlighten me, Mr. Comingal?" begged Clause.

"The determining method would be chosen by a majority of the citizens," Mr. Comingal acknowledged. "In a democracy, there is no requirement for the citizens to vote. The will of the majority may be determined by any method that guarantees the government will perform its legislative duties according to the will of the majority. Voting may be used and probably would be one of the many methods. Other methods such as polls, electronic opinion responses, and electronic canvassing of neighborhoods might be used. Any number of methods might additionally be used by a diligent democratic government to determine the will of the majority."

"*Probably*, *might be*, and *could be* do not make a case for democracy," accused Mr. Clause. "You are trying to prove that a democracy would be better for the United States. You have only ' suggested' that democracy might be better. The methods you want the Court to accept as proof have never been used by your Party to establish a majority will of American citizens. No political party, present or past, has attempted to determine the will of the majority of American citizens. All political parties have relied on the laws of the Republic in their attempts to climb up the political ladder of success.

"You have mentioned how the will of the majority might possibly be found if there were a democracy and politicians used those or some other means to discover the will of the majority. Your supposed democracy assumes to represent the children and use them as a part of your national majority, but your administration was very diligent in its support of abortion that kills children; many of those children would have been your Party's voters, but they can't grow up to vote because they were aborted.

"You stated that a diligent democratic government would determine the will of the people. I ask you, among the Democrats still living, or present in this Court, were those democratic politicians actually seeking the will of the majority, and presenting the majority will to the Democrat political establishment?"

Ray Blather, bristling with indignation through Clause's entire dissertation, bristled a question. "Would you define what you mean by the Democrat political establishment? Does that mean the entire Democrat Party?"

"Well! I apologize for being less than pure in my speech," stated Clause with his own unapologetic boldness. "I do not mean the Democrat Party with respect to all of its voting members. I mean those Democrats in the Congress, in leading positions in the party, news commentators, lawyers, and large contributors—those decision makers who form the Democrat Party agenda. Those who only vote democratic or send money without particular influence on the party's agenda are exempt.

"Most democratic voters believe they already live in a democracy. They believe their national voting process is a product of democracy. They don't know a democracy is a different form of government than the Republic they live in, and they don't know that its voting practices are governed by the laws of their Republic."

James Cornball had been listening to Clause with growing anger. He'd had more than enough, and he wasn't going to take any more of Clause's attack on Democrat Party processes. He blurted, "You mean to tell me that you think Democrat voters have no voice in forming the Party agenda. We send questionnaires before every election to get their opinions. We have Town Hall meetings, we read our mail, our people tell our voters where we are going politically all of the time, not just at election time. They know every move we make."

Mr. Clause considered Cornball's outburst a legitimate concern that he had to answer. "The questionnaires are sent to voters to form Party unity and to guide the voters in the direction the Party wants to take them. Questionnaires are used by the Party to help form a consensus opinion among the voters, not to seek the will of the majority. Questionnaires are sent to Democrats you hope to receive money and votes from, not to the vast number of Americans who would form a democracy. There is no search for a national majority will in politically motivated questionnaires.

"Your Town Hall meetings are attended by a very few highly active Democrat Party supporters you expect to be your cheer leaders. Town Hall meetings do not represent an effort to discover the opinions of a majority of the people of the United States.

"Your mail is generally from constituents appealing to high-level Democrats to perform some legislative function as the sender desires. I'm sure they are important as a tool for the Democrat Party politicians and may, on rare occasions, reflect a majority passion of Democratic voters, but receiving and reading the mail from a Democratic constituency does not represent a search for the will of an American majority, nor is it an American majority's confirmation for democracy.

"You do, indeed, keep Democrat voters informed of where you are going, but you don't ask them where they want you to go. You just spin them, in the most agreeable terms you can think of, to let them know what you have already decided to do. That is one more attempt at consensus building. Your information to them and theirs to you is not a function of democracy; it is a function of the freedom of speech guaranteed by the First Amendment. The Democrat Party deserves no credit for the freedom of speech given to it by the laws of the Republic. In fact, in a democracy, if the majority was convinced to abolish freedom of speech, a democratic government would abolish freedom of speech, and with that loss, all of the other freedoms would vanish.

"The most compelling work of a democratic government is to truthfully determine the will of the majority of free people. Democratic politicians must then accept that majority will as their only choice for action. If the democratic politicians ignore or cannot determine the will of the majority, the government is a failure and cannot be a democracy."

Mr. Clause maintained a long pause to allow the fullness of the information about democracy to sink in. He then stated, "That brings us back to Mr. Comingal's problems. First: how to truthfully inform the citizens of the democracy of problems that must be solved by the will of the majority. Second: how to determine the will of the truthfully informed majority. Third: how to find politicians who will faithfully administer the majority will."

James Cornball wasn't one to be quelled by simple facts. He was an attacker, and his usual method of attack was to make accusations that forced his opponents to appear guilt ridden while defending themselves. His very nature demanded he attack Clause, and what Cornball believed was Clause's simple-minded stupidity for insisting on the purity of political purpose. Cornball sucked in a deep draught of air and blew it out hot. "You ain't nothin' but a political ignoramus! No government is as pure as you want us to prove our democracy is. Republicans can't prove the Republic is that pure. Everybody in government does things wrong. If we can get ourselves elected, we won the day! You and no other do-gooders can stop us from doing what we think is right. Running a government is wheelin', dealin', spielin', an' reelin'; it's half con or all gone! It's power plays and everything from laying low when it's too hot to shouting from the roof tops when its not. The winners make the rules! Rules made up from some simple-minded format for government won't work. The politicians have to run the people because the people can't run the politicians; we all know that! The people trusted us enough to elect us, and they expect us to take care of things from there on. It's your job to be realistic and allow us to be what we were when we were and accept what we wanted to do when we did what we did. You got to forget those things we did wrong along the way. We're the good guys, and you can't even figure that out!"

Mr. Clause appeared unmoved by Cornball's tirade, but he knew he had no other choice but to answer it. "I will overlook your insults and handle your last suggestion first. I cannot forget the things you did wrong when you were what you were, although you may have wished for a different result after you did what you did. Some of your intentions may have been good but your actions and the results of those actions spread from the unwise to the criminal. Some say the path to Hell is paved with good intentions, but I don't believe your intentions were good enough for paving bricks.

"Actions done for the benefit of politicians have consequences for the people they govern, and those consequences may stifle the freedom and opportunities of the people. Politicians of every type of government are charged with serving the people—not a political party. Citizens of nations are neither required to be, nor do they wish to become, useful objects politicians manipulate to build powerful political parties.

"Governments have no money except the tax money paid by the citizens. The citizens are the ones who pay your salaries. Politicians are required to serve those salary-paying citizens to earn their pay. The things politicians do to benefit themselves are frequently illegal, and none of you were hired to become powerful enough to break and remain above the laws you were required to sometimes legislate and *always* maintain to protect the citizens of the United States.

"As to the form of government, the form wouldn't matter if all politicians were capable, compassionate, honest, and intelligent. There are some who are all four, but most fail in at least one area, many fail in two, and some fail in all four. Every politician will claim to be all four, even though most know they are not. Their personal political deficiencies make it essential to have a form of government that forces politicians to follow a governing rule of law designed to control politicians, judges, and public servants. Without a rule of law that controls the government, the people have no power and, indeed, are at the mercy of whatever group is in power. Power of that kind begets more power of that kind, and tyranny is the result.

"The power of a nation cannot at the same time be in the hands of government and the hands of the people. One is supreme, and the supreme power makes the rules. When supreme power is in the hands of government, the people are only as free as the government will allow them to be. Politicians and political parties aren't known for their willingness to decrease their own power over government to provide more liberty for the people. Politicians and political parties are known for taking liberty from the people to make themselves more powerful. That is why the form of the government is so critical to freedom, and only critical then if it controls a nation's politicians, political parties, and the political structures that secure the liberty of the people.

"I dislike being repetitive, but Mr. Cornball's spin took us from the search for a democratic method of informing a democratic government of the will of the people, and prevented us from discovering those faithful politicians who will administer that will. We will now return to that democratically necessary search."

Mr. Comingal angrily retorted, "You have made it impossible for us to find a way. All we have done and all we propose might be done is immediately torn to shreds by you."

Mr. Clause replied, "I have not made it impossible. If a democracy is impossible, finding politicians who will honorably and faithfully govern it using political and administrative methods based on its one democratic principle, majority rule, has made it impossible. It may not be impossible to establish a true democracy, but it is extremely unlikely for a true democracy to be established, given the nature of the politicians and the political methods they use to govern.

"Thus far, you, yourselves, have failed to present a democratic plan you could have used as democrats. As you so belatedly admit, your democracy was a Republic, and a democratic plan to govern a republic is not possible. Your Democrat Party could have used a democratic plan for its own political conduct, and that would have proven your point—but you didn't. You left that most valuable point untried.

"You have also failed to offer this Court a plan for *any* democracy, if you could find one and govern it. That failure may be because there isn't one among you who actually worked to support democracy's only principle, majority rule. There isn't one competent democrat among you, but nearly all of you belonged to the Democrat Party. You frequently spoke of the superiority of democracy, but none of you trusted democracy enough to use it. Instead, you used the peoples' confused understanding of democracy as a tool to increase your party's power.

"Your Democrat Party has no standard definition of a democratic government to give to the people who vote for it. You have not defined democracy for yourselves. Your Democrat Party hasn't informed its voters that democracy is a different form of government than the Republic.

"You were attempting to force their Republic to become your strange brand of a democracy. You did that without ever defining a democracy and how it should work. You refused Americans, who by necessity would have to rule your democratic form of government, your definition of your democracy. Your Party hasn't given a standard definition of *democracy* to their constituents—or even to themselves. From your neglect of defining a basic form for a Democrat Party, or government, and from your lack of democratic principles in your political actions, one must assume democracy has no substance in the Democrat Party.

"I have denied you nothing except misinformation, disinformation, misconceptions, and lies. You were given an opportunity to prove something you have claimed to be true during the entire span of your political lives, that your democracy is better for the American people than their Republic.

"You're between a rock and a hard place. I don't think you have a prayer of proving your case, but if you can, the proof doesn't rest on the shoulders of Mr. Comingal and Mr. Cornball. Proving this case rests on the shoulders of the silent accused who have stood quietly, and hopefully, by throughout this proceeding. They have hoped your strength would succeed where their weakness could not. If their weakness is not stronger than your strength, the rock and the hard place are both yours, and theirs.

"In order to strengthen the resolve of the silent accused to win and spur them to speak out, I'm going to show you the door the losers go through. You may turn and look directly behind you."

The blank wall behind the accused had disappeared. The wide room they were in stopped abruptly at the beginning of a walkway made of hot, bubbling lava. The super-heated walkway ended at the largest, most terrifying door any of them had ever seen. The terrifying metallic Portal of Hell appeared ancient; two red-hot iron sections of the Portal joined their burning edges at the center. Two burning metal snakes undulated in eternal anger from the top to the bottom at the center of each section. Shards of fire spit into the hot lava as the metallic serpents squirmed against the Portal of Hell. Each fiery serpent struck endlessly at infinity in an eternal trap that formed the handle for each section of the burning Portal.

Nothing could be seen beyond the glow of the burning Portal. The darkness was blacker than space. No glow of star or errant speck of light could penetrate the darkness around the Portal of Hell. Only a thick, black coating of soot, barely illuminated by the burning metal of the Portal, hinted at some unknown horror connected to the hissing terror of the burning Portal.

Suddenly! The wall reappeared, and Judge Bullman banged his gavel to get the crowd to face the Court. He announced, "The court realizes you need time to overcome the terrible experience of seeing the Portal of Hell. The Court will recess for a brief period while you gather your thoughts. You will be given the time needed to consider your participation in the proceedings. The Bailiff will call you when we are ready to begin once more."

For the first time since their arrival, the assembled political wheelers and dealers realized that going to Hell was not just a possibility; it loomed in their future as a fearful likelihood. Each of them had felt the proof in the blast of heat from the Portal. They were on the horns of a deadly dilemma. They had willingly agreed to base their plea of innocence on a collective defense that failed. But, the failed collective defense had to be won to escape Hell. The defendants could not recognize their failure, apologize, and enter a new plea of innocence. They knew a winning defense for the collective group must appear from among themselves, not P. Comingal and his personally picked experts. Comingal's team of experts had failed at every turn.

They, at long last, had a definition for *democracy*. They had all applauded the dismissal of all other charges to prove the one point they thought would be easiest to prove. They had to prove that the United States would have actually been better off as a democracy than as the Republic.

The Court expected the true definition of *democracy* to be used. There was the real problem. Their lives as self anointed democrats had never prepared them to defend the actualities of a truly democratic government. To them, democracy had been nothing more than an excuse they used to avoid their responsibility and ignore their duty to the Constitution, while imposing their fraudulent brand of democracy in its place. For many of them, democracy was nothing more than the battle call used against their most active political enemy, the Republic Party.

If they as Democrats had been able to force the United States to become a democracy, all of them would have been satisfied with what the democracy would be under party leadership. They had no sense of personal responsibility for whatever the government actually was, as long as their leaders called it a democracy. But, they were now faced with deep desires to escape blame for the charges brought against them. They had to understand a real democracy, and consider what the United States would become, if it became "our democracy."

The defenders of the differing democracies broke up and began as large groups in discussions. Those discussions ranged from logical consideration of the problem to vitriolic denunciation of everything about the problem. The large groups broke apart under the failure to find credible champions to successfully address a defense. Many of the smaller groups became even smaller, and some among the accused decided to defend themselves using their own individual capabilities.

The loners had lost all hope in the collective defense, but perhaps a few had some small hope in their own ability to defend the collective group using their own defense. The larger and smaller groups retained some hope for success in a collective defense approach, if that approach represented their personal plan for a defense, and some found likeminded support among the others.

For those who had repudiated the Comingal team's leadership, the heated rhetoric soon cooled to become an objective rationale concerned with the available possibilities for their defense. Comingal and his chosen experts never considered following the lead of the body of the whole body of the accused to prepare a more diversified defense. Comingal's team, and its followers still believed that, somehow, they could win by sticking together to pursue a successful search for a technical loophole in the charges against them. That loophole would free them from the odious court and return them to life itself. They were still the largest group to face the Court. That was the status of the accused when the Bailiff informed them the Court was ready to begin.

Judge Bullman called the Court to order, but Mr. Clause made the opening statement. "When you wish to make a statement about your defense, simply raise your hand to do so. It will not matter if someone else is addressing the Court at that time. I have an excellent memory, and I will call you in the order you raise your hands."

One of the loners was the first to raise his hand, and he offered the following testimony. "There are some of us here who were not actually engaged in transforming the United States into 'our democracy.' We worked our way up in the bureaucracies we served and recognized the Constitution as the basic law of the land. We should not be punished for following the leadership of those who were actively engaged in the transformation. I ask for the release of myself and those in that group because we lacked both revolutionary intent and performance."

Mr. Clause replied, "Your leaders also recognized the Constitution as the basic law of the land, and the worker strengthens the hand of the leader. Your leaders ignored the Constitution whenever they thought they could get away with it, and you helped them get away with it. You would have remained a follower no matter what your leaders did, if they let you keep your jobs. You also supported your leaders by helping other Democrats, who would not have been considered for government jobs except they were Democrats, to be employed in your bureaucracies, even though it is illegal to consider political affiliations in the hiring of new employees.

"Your paycheck did not come from your political party; it came from American taxpayers who expected an honest day's work for the pay they provided. Political parties do not own bureaucracies. Government workers owe nothing to their political party, nor can they legally use their government positions to serve the interests of their political party. You served your political party first and the American people last. You, and those like you, may not have had the zeal of your leaders, but your less than zealous actions on their behalf served the same purpose as their zeal. Your request for dismissal is denied."

The next to be recognized was the spokeswoman for a small group. She made a political social worker's approach to the defense. "We, the average Democrats, were less interested in politics than we were in social issues. We didn't consider the Democrat Party to be attempting to bring forth a different form of government. We believed we were already citizens of a democracy. We thought of our nation as a democracy because our Party presented its programs as social programs for the majority of Americans. We wanted everyone to be brought into the mainstream of American life regardless of race, creed, ethnic origin, gender, or sexual orientation.

"If the Democrat Party had managed to change the Republic of the United States into a democracy, the minorities would have made up our majority along with the forward-looking people in the actual majority of the nation. All of the people in the United States would have benefited equally under a democratically controlled government. I propose we be released because of our commitment to the least of our constituents and the American people as a whole."

"I think you have made a valiant effort," remarked Mr. Clause, "but there are some serious errors in your assumptions. Minorities aren't necessarily the beneficiaries in a democracy. The majority rules a democracy, and minorities can only be beneficiaries while the majority allows them to benefit. In the American Republic, the Constitution makes all citizens equal under its rule of law. When the Constitution is allowed to work in the fruition of its liberty, it provides equal protection and opportunity to minorities and the majority of citizens of the United States.

"The actual majority in the United States has nothing to do with which minority or a supposed majority one addresses. The actual majority of citizens in the United States are the taxpayers. Small children who spend only a little bit of money still pay taxes on that money. All citizens pay taxes in some form from the time they are born to the time they die. Every child is born into a tax system he already owes money to, and must pay for throughout his life.

"In a democracy, if the taxpaying majority wants a government program to benefit themselves, while excluding one or many minorities, a democratic government would have no other choice but to comply with the majority demand. The minorities, you hope will make up your majority, can easily be excluded by the taxpaying majority if the minority is an identifiable part of the majority. Those minorities might be ethnic, racial, economic, old aged, youthful, geographic, or any minority the majority may target at different times. The laws of the Republic prevent that kind of skullduggery. Equality for all under the rule of law of the Republic's Constitution is one of the Republic's major strengths.

"Social programs should be an attempt by government to address deficiencies in a nation's society. The recipients of the help from those programs do not and should not share equally. They must deal with many different levels of the problems they are having, and each should receive the support he needs to overcome his problem. The taxpaying majority who pay for the social programs can only benefit when the social problems are solved and they no longer need to pay the taxes to support the problem individuals. I recognize that some problems are life long and require life-long support, but that is not in most of the cases. Under the American Constitution, all of whatever minority or the majority must be included in all social programs if their problem is within the boundaries of a particular program. The majority does not rule, and it cannot include those the majority likes or exclude those the majority does not like from government programs. Constitutional law rules, and it includes all equally. Those who were included in the social programs you supported were included under the laws of the Republic; Democracy had nothing to do with it. Your misplaced commitment to a non-existent democracy does not qualify you as innocent of the many charges brought against you personally or exonerate the group as a whole."

One of the loners, Judge Pussyfoote, who was bubbled off of a federal bench, was recognized next. He gave his testimony in his own behalf. "I am a Democrat, and I have always been proud of my political position as a Democrat. I have done my best to make my court a reflection of justice within the laws of the American legal system. The political preferences of defendants, witnesses, juries, lawyers, or anyone else subject to my court had no bearing on the outcome of my cases. I believe I have been wrongly accused and should not have been sentenced for a crime I did not commit. I petition the Court to reverse the judgment against me."

Mr. Clause commented, "All of those selected for jury duty in your district were forced to watch a video tape giving them your instructions. In that tape, you instructed the jurors to faithfully apply the laws of "our democracy" to their deliberations. You do not live in a democracy. Your judicial district and all judicial districts of the United States are in the Republic of the United States. Since your Court procedures were based on your stated conviction that the United States is a democracy, you denied the jurors in your court of their right to the Republic and its Constitution.

"You were in violation of the constitutional rights of all who entered your court. Article Four, Section Four of the Constitution states, 'The United States shall guarantee to every State in this Union a Republican Form of government...' That Article is the legal forty-four magnum that protects the Republican form of government for each citizen of the Republic of the United States. Your personal decision to force the courts in your district outside of the guaranteed Republican form of government to serve a non-existent democracy, denied the right under Article Four, Section Four to every person who stepped into your court— defendants, witnesses, juries, lawyers, or anyone else subject to your court.

"If your court represented a democracy, then the nation was a democracy for those who were in your Court while they were subject to the decisions and conditions in your Court. There is no way for a judge to faithfully fulfill his oath to the laws of the Republic and perform his court duties for that Republic while the judge presides over his court as if it is the judicial arm of a democracy or a political party. A democracy is an entirely different form of government.

"If you knew your Court was established by the laws of the Republic, and you were knowingly denying that knowledge to those subject to your Court, you were also guilty of fraud—and you did know. Your petition has no credence and is rejected."

Mr. Clause turned to recognize someone else, but he hadn't heard the last of Judge Pussyfoote. Outraged by Clause's charge of fraud, he angrily shouted, "I resent your high-handed, scurrilous, and unproved charge of fraud. Your mean-spirited accusation does this Court no credit. I demand proof of fraud. Proof must exceed the demented mumbling of a mere student of law and rise to the level of factual truth."

Being accusing of demented mumbling really pissed Clause off, but he managed to hold his peace. After a slow ten count, Clause retorted, "Proof you want, proof you'll get. Let us examine the proof in small steps to make it clear for you.

"Fraud is an intentional deception to cause a person to give up property or a lawful right.
Democracy is a government in which ruling authority is vested in the majority of its free people, rule by the ruled.

"The Republic of the United States is defined by its Constitution, and you know that Constitution very well. I will only mention, in that respect, that the Constitution defines the United States as a Republic. Since 1789, that fact has remained a legal truth.

"You know the United States is a Republic, not a democracy. That factual truth makes your deception intentional. Jurors and defendants in your Court were too timid, ignorant, or too frightened to challenge your lie that your court represented a democracy. Lawyers know which side the bread is buttered on and do not politically challenge a judge in whose court they expect to work more than once. You defrauded everyone who was subject to the rules of your court. Your deception forced them to give up their right to their Republic while they were in your court. You violated their Ninth Amendment right to truth from judicial officers in judicial proceedings. You defied your own Oath of Office. The truth is that your court was a part of the judicial branch of the Republic of the United States.

"Your intentional deception to cause a person to give up a lawful right is fraud, and you caused many people to give up their lawful rights. You are a fraud. Your case is rejected on its first appeal."

A congressman, Mr. Fringe, was recognized next. "We Democrats have been wrongly accused. We were forced into this desperate situation by a method, and for reasons most of us do not understand. We never, at any time, would have endangered our fellow citizens by attempting to change our Republic to a democracy—and I will present the proof for my last statement.

"Our party platform clearly states that we Democrats are dedicated to the Constitution and a rule of law. As politicians dedicated to the Constitution and a rule of law, we could not have overthrown the Republic of the United States. The only Constitution and the only rule of law in existence in the United States are the Constitution and laws of that Republic. I insist that all of us be released from the accusations against us because of our Party's platform expressed a commitment to the Republic."

Clause eyed the congressman with astonishment for a moment and then stated, "Let us examine your fidelity to the Constitution and its laws. When you were told by a witness in a congressional hearing that you couldn't do away with constitutional rights, your answer was, 'No, but we can regulate them.' If American liberty fails, that statement will be written on its tombstone. No one in your Party has objected to your statement. The definition of a *constitutional right* is this: 'A Right is something recognized as beyond the government's ability to change it.'

"No government gives people their rights. Rights are a part of the natural order of humanity to be freely used by all people. Good government recognizes the natural order of those rights and is prohibited from infringing on them, Mr. Fringe.

"The lack of government recognition of rights or a government's regulation of rights is a sign of the oppression of the people by their government. The rights of the citizens of the United States are abundantly recognized in their Constitution, and no one has a right to regulate them. Your regulation would have caused *constitutional rights* to have a new definition as follows: something people may lawfully do within the limits permitted by politicians until politicians change the limits. Your regulation of constitutional rights would have destroyed the people's protection of the Constitution, including its Bill of Rights, and left them at the mercy of government regulators who are willing to destroy every right—regulators like yourself, Mr. Fringe."

Mr. Fringe assumed his most impressive posture of one whose dignity has been offended as Mr. Clause finished his accusation of destroying every right. "Your opinions are absurd, Mr. Clause. I would have regulated the people's rights fairly with their best interest always in mind. I had no plan for the future destruction of rights. However, periodic changes of constitutional rights are required, and intelligent men must make changes, as they are required. My efforts were based on the necessity for contemporary constraints, as I, and my congressional associates, viewed contemporary conditions. No one has been more sincere in those legislative efforts than myself."

"Mr. Fringe," returned Clause, "you were not hired by your constituents to revise their rights based on your opinions of contemporary conditions. You were hired to protect rights, not to make your opinions about them the law. Your personal oath was given to uphold the laws and rights included in 'the people's' Constitution. You were, indeed, sincere in all of your efforts. You sincerely wanted the best for the people, but not if it interfered with what you sincerely wanted as the best political position for yourself. When you were challenged, by one lone American citizen, for regulating constitutional rights, you sincerely didn't give a damn because you had the protection of your entire political party for regulating those rights.

"I hope you won't mind answering these questions, Mr. Fringe. If your revolution had been successful, would your sincere commitment to the Constitution have faded when you realized a democracy has no demand for a rule of law? Would you have discovered the rights of the people are even easier to regulate in a political system that has no way and no intention of determining majority rule? Would you have at any time in your regulatory zeal sought the will of the majority before you regulated their rights? Would your Party platform have protected the rights of the American people from your regulation when your personal oath to protect their rights did not?"

Mr. Fringe knew that truthful answers would be self-incriminating, and he wanted a means of refusing to answer. Fringe supplicated, "The Constitution's Fifth Amendment allows a defendant the right to refuse to answer self incriminating questions. Does this Court have a similar provision I may use at this time?"

"It does not, Mr. Fringe," responded Clause, "but I will not force you to answer the questions. The answers to the questions are obvious, and the truth is inescapable.

"Your violations of the Constitution, including its Bill of Rights, were more thorough than most in this room. You were willing to reduce the Constitution of the Republic to ignored words written long ago. You had no commitment to the Constitution, the Republic, or your party platform.

"Your political Party did not violate your Oath of Office, Mr. Fringe—you did. You are one of the worst offenders in this Court. Neither you nor anyone else in this Court can bail himself out by using a Party platform statement none of you cared enough about to use. I congratulate you for one thing: grasping at the only straw you had. That showed an enterprising mind. If you had been that enterprising while performing your congressional duties, within the laws you took an oath to uphold, you wouldn't be here. Your request for all of you to be released on the basis of your Party's platform statement, which usually refers to your Republic as 'our democracy,' is absurd and denied."

The next to be recognized was the spokesman for the remaining members of the Republic Party. He began his plea very logically. "We are Republicans and the very name of our Party ties us closely to the republican form of government. We have never tried to change our government to any other kind. We have faithfully represented our constituencies and performed our congressional duties to the best of our abilities. I don't understand why we were brought here under these circumstances. I assume there was a bureaucratic error made that included us. It is our plea that we are here due to that error, and we petition the Court for our immediate release."

"There was no error," Mr. Clause responded. "You did not represent your constituencies or perform your congressional duties as you should have. You are the Vicars of Bray of politics. You are Republicans in name, but you represented the Republic and its Constitution only when it was personally beneficial for you to do so. You changed sides on the issues as you determined a change in the political wind, not because of constitutional restrictions. Neither the Constitution nor the Republic was a consideration in your Vicar of Bray changes in your decisions. You were ready to sell out and join this group or any other group the instant you felt they would succeed.

"Most Democrats in public life refer to their Republic as 'our democracy'; and you, with other Republicans who are not yet here, frequently refer to the Republic in the same words. Not one of you—ever—rose to correct the lie that the United States is a democracy. If there weren't so many other reasons for you being here, I think your Republican silence in the face of that one Democrat lie, repeated endlessly, might do the trick. The very name of your party should have demanded you speak out."

A lady from the Government Printing Office, who represented a small group of feminists, was the next to approach the Court. She was just as interesting and made a more passionate plea than the Republicans. "Everyone knows the Constitution is an outdated document written by a group with only men in it more than two hundred years ago. Time and circumstances have taken their toll on the once-grand Constitution, and we find it is no longer entirely relevant to the American citizens of today. Much of it should be replaced with a more modern document that supports these times and the more advanced thinking of today's wiser politicians. Many in the Democrat Party, and a few Republicans, have noted the deterioration in the Constitution's ability to service a larger, more technically complicated and diverse population.

"The search for cures to the Constitution's inability to promote modern values is very difficult. Those cures must come from outside the Constitution because of the difficulty of bringing them forth from within it.

"Our party is the oldest of the present-day political parties; our founder was Thomas Jefferson. We Democrats have worked from that beginning to keep the laws of the United States within the social boundaries of the majority of our contemporaries. We have been faithful to that trust throughout the years of the existence of our party. We Democrats, who are here, have done well in that field of endeavor. If we had been able to bring about a change of government from the Republic to a democracy, it would have been because a majority of people understood and responded to our message. It would have been a bloodless change of government. The democracy revolution would have benefited every American citizen."

"I must commend you on being the only group so far who have clearly addressed the challenge the Court gave to you," replied Mr. Clause. "However, you have brought up some very important issues in your presentation. You mentioned the difficulty of changing the Constitution, and I agree with you that it is very difficult. The founders made it intentionally difficult, and that difficulty does not force those who disagree with it to use outside means to make constitutional changes. There are, at present, twenty-seven amendments to the Constitution. Each Amendment was made within the constitutional system for changes. The Constitution requires a two-thirds majority of both Houses of Congress, and a three-fourths majority of the states to ratify the amendments. That system is still in force and actively protecting the American people from unwanted changes in constitutional law and the republican form of government. All other methods used to change or supersede constitutional laws are illegal. To date, none of the methods used outside of the Constitution to make changes have sought the approval of a majority of the citizens of the United States, Congress, or the states before they were used. Those methods were neither constitutional nor democratic.

"You claim the Democrats are doing well in protecting the contemporary values of the majority. They are more adept at responding to a selected minority value and promoting that value as a constitutional right of the minority than they are at defending the majority values of the American society as a whole. For instance, Democrats use Separation of Church and State instead of the constitutional rights written in the First Amendment as follows: 'Congress shall make no law respecting an establishment of religion, or prohibit the free exercise thereof'; many people have been prohibited the free exercise of their religion on public property because of the use of Separation of Church and State. Eighty percent of the citizens of the United States profess a belief in God. If the Democrats were protecting the majority rights for these times, that eighty percent would be freely exercising their constitutional right to practice their religion wherever they are, including public property.

"Now, to finish off the old lie about Thomas Jefferson being the founder of the Democrat Party. Thomas Jefferson was a republican, a leading founder of the Republic of the United States, and was a strict constitutional republican in the sense of being a citizen of the Republic. He didn't like political parties, and there was no Republican Party, or any other political party, as we think of political parties during his lifetime. Jefferson died several years before Democrats became a political party. When Jefferson was alive, he was not just active but intensely single minded in his promotion of republican principles. Republicanism thoroughly permeated his political philosophy. Jefferson did not, and could not have been a founder of your party.

"You claimed that the change from the Republic to a democracy, if it had occurred, would have been a bloodless change of government. It would not. There are many who fear such a revolutionary change. They have the intensity and firepower to have formed a counterrevolution if the change had become obvious to them. As your democracy failed, more would have joined them. Your revolution would have been far from a bloodless change of government; it would have caused a long, bloody counterrevolution—because so many Americans dislike your message. Your reasons for a dismissal of the charges against you, while showing your heartfelt confidence in democracy, were specious, and I must reject your plea."

A representative, Mr. Hert, from one of the more populous states was recognized, He nervously stated, "Without objection, I reserve the right to extend and revise my remarks."

Objection!" cried Clause. "No one is allowed to revise and extend his remarks. This is not your Congress!"

The congressman apologized. "I'm sorry about that! Old habits die hard!" Having failed in his first effort, he pumped himself up and demanded, "We Democrats have never attempted to overthrow the government. All we have tried to do is change the American voting practices to insure that nationally elected candidates are elected by a majority of voters. I demand we be set free on the basis that we were not attempting to change the government from a republic to a democracy."

Mr. Clause eyed the congressman with some suspicion because of his trick of going directly from his apology to his demand. Clause asked, "Are you suggesting that senators and representatives from each state be elected by a national majority? Senators are already elected by the majority of voters in their home states, and representatives by a majority of votes in their state's Congressional Districts."

Representative Hert barked, "Certainly not!" Then he paused and thought it over for a second before he said, "I don't believe we could actually do that. I'm speaking of the Offices of President and Vice President."

"In recent memory, the Democrats have won presidential elections with less than a majority of registered voters who voted," stated Mr. Clause. "Why do you want to change to a system that requires a majority of registered voters to win? Are you a Democrat who wants to refuse the Office of President of the United States unless you receive a majority of those votes in national elections?"

Representative Hert retorted, "I refuse to answer that question. It has nothing to do with my demand. My demand concerned your accusation of being revolutionaries trying to overthrow the government, nothing else. We were not trying to overthrow the government."

"Your objection to answering the question must be sustained or overruled from the bench," Clause stated as he turned to Judge Bullman and asked, "Your honor, how do you rule?"

"The court overrules the objection," judged Bullman. "The question is pertinent to the case and must be answered."

"The majority vote for the presidency has nothing to do with democracy," was Mr. Hert's unwilling answer. "It has to do with allowing each voter's vote to count equally. Our Party would not refuse the Office of President when it receives less than a majority of votes."

"Then does it have anything to do with abolishing the Electoral College?" shot back Mr. Clause." Doing away with the Electoral College would take the Office of the President out of the hands of all of the states and put it in the hands of a few heavily populated states. Does the Democrat Party have enough political control of those heavily populated states to insure a victory in presidential elections if they can count on the minority of votes they would receive in the less populated states?"

"I resent your question, Mr. Clause," blurted Hert. "Are you impugning the integrity of my defense?"

"Yes," admitted Clause, "I am, and I insist you answer the question."

The angry Mr. Hert looked back at Mr. Clause for some seconds before he replied, "We think we have enough votes in the more heavily populated states to win with whatever minority of votes we receive in the less populated states. Still, the Electoral College is an antiquated system that denies the American people voting equality, and it should be done away with."

"Mr. Hert," suggested Mr. Clause, "I believe you are familiar with Article Two of the Constitution. It establishes the method of election for the President and Vice President. You are also familiar with the reasons it is done that way. Using the Electoral College system, all of the states retain power in an election that is equal to their populations, and the voters in their states do have voting equality. The Electoral system was designed to prevent the political power struggles that would deny the weaker states the national representation they need to maintain at least some kind of equality among all of the states. I also know you are aware of the power struggles that would occur in the United States if the Electoral College was abolished, and it would be abolished if you, Mr. Hert, could abolish it.

"Your defense is predicated on your not being a revolutionary attempting to overthrow the Republic to establish your democracy. How much closer to your democracy would the United States be if the Electoral College was abolished in the manner you have suggested?"

"The President and the Vice President could then be elected by a democratic majority of eligible voters who bother to vote," Mr. Hert replied, "and that would bring the United States closer to being our democracy, but the change would not make it a true democracy by the Court's definition."

"What of Article Two of the constitution?" asked Clause. "Would the Democrat Party insist on its removal by amending the Constitution, or would the Party depend on a court action for the removal, or would they try to use congressional legislation to remove it from the Constitution?"

Mr. Hert was a little weary of the truth of the matter, and he showed his angst. "We could never get the vote of three-fourths of the states for a constitutional amendment. A constitutional amendment would cause most of the states to lose some of their power in the national government. A change by Court action, even by the Supreme Court, would be illegal, and so would congressional legislation without a constitutional amendment ratified by the states. We have suggested a Constitutional Convention, and we would have tried to make many changes including the change to a democratic vote for president and vice president. However, two-thirds of the states must ask for a convention, and two-thirds of the states aren't willing to ask. I don't know what method we would have used to change the voting practices in Presidential elections. I still say the method of electing presidents needs to be changed by some method."

"You are a revolutionary, Mr. Hert," remarked Clause. "You don't care how the changes in constitutional laws are made, as long as they are made as you want them done. You have worked for and gained political position and salary from the people of the Republic you have been revolting against all of your political life. You took a personal oath to defend the Republic and uphold its laws. You have had no intention of upholding or defending either. You have done the opposite.

"You have tried to avoid the sentence against you, not by presenting your democracy as better than the Republic, but by presenting one more technical challenge to the Court's legality for demanding your presence in this Court. Unless someone among the accused can prove a democracy would be better than the Republic has been for the United States, the sentence holds."

Judge Bullman and Mr. Clause had been keeping their eyes on the largest number of accused in the Comingal group. None of them had asked to be recognized. They had been involved in quiet discussions among themselves. As their discussions intensified, they had moved ever deeper toward the back of the room. They had finally moved to the most avoided portion of the Court, the back wall near the Portal of Hell. They were formulating a last-ditch bid for freedom. They had finished. Comingal's team was now on its way to the front of the Court.

Everyone in the Court ceased their activities while the accused waited for whatever the Comingal team would produce to defend them. Mr. Comingal raised his hand to be recognized, and Mr. Clause invited him to speak. He began with a barnburner of a defense. "We realized from the beginning that trying to prove our democracy would have been better for the United States than the Republic has been was an impossible task. The United States is not now nor has it ever been a democracy. We can't prove a government that has never existed would have been better than one that does exist. By the same token, you cannot prove that the Republic is better than our non-existent democracy.

"We maintain that your position of condemnation is purely theoretical. We did not replace the Republic with a democracy and were prevented by our premature deaths from providing the proof that a democracy would have been better or worse. We further note, the fact that the Republic is now in existence does not prove it is better. The Republic can only be actually proven to be better by the hard fact of its removal and replacement by a democracy. We petition the Court to set us free for the lack of proof that our crime was committed."

Comingal had given Clause cause to pause. Clause decided Comingal's argument had a logic that made it impossible for him to ignore. Ignoring it would bring him the penalty for a Virtue Violation. Comingal's challenge to the Court's position demanded a response from him. He stated, "The people in this room were the core members of an illegal revolution the average American had no knowledge of. If you had been allowed to continue your activities, your success would have been disastrous for your nation. How can you defend yourselves from the standpoint of your personal actions?"

"We aren't trying to defend ourselves from the standpoint of our personal actions," retorted Comingal. "The charges against us were reduced to one and we are showing that one charge to be false."

Clause asserted, "You were not relieved of any of the charges you believe to have been nullified. You were given a problem, and the problem was to prove your democracy would have been better for the United States than the Republican form of government it has always had. If you can prove that one point, you will be free of this Court."

Comingal's group had done their homework on the defense. Comingal proceeded as though he knew where he was going. "We have admitted to the fact that only a theoretical democracy can be used as a guideline to prove ours would have been better. You, however, have not admitted that your premise of the Republic being better is just as theoretical. Pursuant to your own requirements for proof, but not necessarily your desire for the truth, we have a proposal that will end all theoretical assumptions on both sides and turn them into hard facts.

"We propose this Court, which has the power to do so, should dissolve the Republic of the United States and install in its place—a democracy. That action will give democracy a chance to come to fruition under the rules established by this Court and allow our defense a chance to be proved or disproved under actual conditions. Our case would be held in abeyance until enough information is received to prove the case for or against us."

Clause was stunned by the proposal and incensed with Comingal's suggestion that he didn't care about the truth. Clause knew the truth was a Virtue in this case that he could not escape. He retorted, "Where will you find the honest politicians to administer this Court-imposed democracy?"

Comingal was up to the question, and he attacked it with his trademark political vigor. "The worst offenders among the democrats were drowned and are present in this Court. I presume the ones who are still able to breathe pure mountain air are all qualified for the task."

"No they aren't!" exclaimed Clause. "They are a little shook up right now because they don't know what happened to all of you, but in the end, they are as well-qualified to screw up the Republic as you were. The reason they aren't here with you now is because they weren't as closely engaged in the revolutionary activities that would have changed the Republic of the United States into your strange brand of democracy."

Comingal pressed his case. "You will recall that my suggestion was to be carried out under the supervision of this Court. A judgment from this Court can remove rogue politicians from office and install men determined to be efficient and caring administrators into office. We know this to be true because we suffered the fate of removal at the judgment of this Court, That judgment is what we are under at this time. The judgment of the Court, in the final analysis, will determine the quality and the purity of the democracy."

"What of the people's right to vote for their representatives?" Clause asked; "Will the judgment of the Court be used to prevent them from making their own choices?"

"Let me quote the definition of *democracy*," insisted Mr. Comingal. "A government in which ruling authority is vested in the majority of its citizens and exercised by them either directly or through elected representatives; rule by the ruled.

"You will notice there is no necessity for voting in a democracy. This Court has the facilities and the power to accurately determine the majority will of the people and impose that will on the government without a vote being counted. Our conviction is that a democracy under the supervision of the Court will prove to be superior to the present Republic."

"Are you recommending," clause retorted, "that the Court must also use the same Court-ordered purity of conditions to form an American Republic so an actual determination of which is best can be made?"

"Certainly not," argued Comingal. "Our challenge was to prove our democracy would be better than the Republic, as the Republic now stands. Any Court tinkering with the present political condition of the Republic would certainly destroy the results of the proof demanded by the Court."

"Well!" wondered Clause. "Do you think it would be fair if the Court corrected all of the bungling the Democrats have forced on the Republic over the past one hundred and eighty years, just to give the Republic an even chance?"

"Again," insisted Comingal, "I must say, no! We Democrats were accepted as a legal political party within the political spectrum of the Republic and were a part of the political activities of the Republic. Removing the bungling would, once more, disturb the delicate political balance the Court has demanded to prove our democracy would have been better than the Republic—as the Republic now stands."

Clause paused again and then replied, "You quoted the definition of *a democracy*. Allow me to quote the definition of *a republic*, and this definition applies especially to the American Republic: a government in which supreme power resides in a body of citizens entitled to vote and is exercised by elected officers and representative responsible to them and governing according to law. The law in this case is the Constitution of the United States.

"Are you asking me to dissolve the Republic and its Constitution, inform the people that they now live in a court-operated democracy that will assure them of honest government subject to their will?"

"The Court has demanded proof from us," stated Comingal. "There is no other way proof can be had. When a Court demands proof and Court action is the only means of acquiring proof, it is the duty of the Court to make the means available to acquire that proof. We did not establish the conditions of the proof demanded by this Court—the Court did. We, the recently demised, are subject to conditions only this Court can produce."

Clause stared at Comingal for some moments before he spoke. "Let's get back to reality for just a while before we continue. Democracy was the biggest fraud of the twentieth century and will undoubtedly be the biggest fraud of the twenty-first century. Russian peasants didn't revolt for the sake of a Communist tyranny; they revolted for freedom and were told by the Communist leaders of the revolt that they were establishing a dictatorship of the proletariat, which means majority rule, a democracy. The peasants' try for freedom ended in a Communist tyranny. The Chinese and the Cuban citizens suffered the same results from the same class of Communist tyrants, and from the same promise of democracy in their try for freedom. They found themselves subjects of the same fraud imposed by those tyrants.

"What is wrong with majority rule isn't that a truthfully informed people are not able to govern themselves when their majority will is truly sought and accepted by their government. The problem with democracy is that there has never been a democratic government that truly sought and accepted the majority will. Democracies don't fail because of the citizens in the democracies. Politicians who govern the proposed democracies cause the failure. The Russian, the Chinese, and the Cuban people did not fail; their respective governments duped them, and then failed them without a care for what the majority wanted for themselves. Those governments cared nothing for their people, or what the majority of the people willed their governments to be. Those governments took power from the people and kept it all for themselves.

"The American people and their Republic have three things that keep them standing above all other people and governments of whatever variety. Great men, heroes who meant what they said, founded the American Republic as one nation under God. The citizens who vote exercise the Republic's supreme power. The people who care enough about their government to vote in its elections can control the government any time they decide to exercise the power of their vote. The American people share the power of law, constitutional law. Those in government must govern according to law, and constitutional law is well written to keep them from becoming tyrants. The greatest danger to the American people is from people like you who despise the people's control over their own government.

"This Court demanded nothing from you. You were challenged to prove that the democracy you were attempting to establish would have been better for the United States than its constitutional Republic. A Court-controlled democracy was not a part of that challenge. You accepted that challenge to get a reduction in the number of charges against you to one charge. You thought that one charge would be easier to beat on a theoretical basis and at the same time allow you to avoid the many charges you would have had to face on a factual basis.

"This Court will not tear down the best government on Earth. This Court will not install a pure democracy ruled by court action to keep it perfect. This Court will not allow you and your associates to benefit from an actual democracy none of you would have helped, or even allowed, to govern the United States.

"What you have asked the Court to do would not fulfill the need for proof. A Court-imposed democracy would not allow the American people to make the choices they would have to make to prove your democracy 'would have been' better for them than their Republic. It would not allow politicians to rise up from the people and be chosen by the people. It would force a court-regulated, truthful government to be installed and maintained, not in the present or the past, but in their future. The newly imposed government would have no chance for error, lies, corruption, or inefficiency; every type of government will succeed under those conditions. An imposed, Court-perfected democracy would prove nothing within the political conditions now operating in the Republic. The democracy you are suggesting this Court impose would only prove the Court is more powerful than democratic politicians. The burden of proof for your democracy is still on your heads. You are the ones who accepted that burden, not the Court.

"You didn't present the proof that your democracy would have been better than the American Republic. You have only presented one more technical assault on the validity of the Court in an attempt to avoid judgment."

The Court was totally quiet during the exchange between Mr. Clause and Mr. Comingal. The numbing silence after Clause's destruction of Comingal's plan was pierced by the furious shout of James Cornball. "This ain't no real court. The judge is a plumber, and we don't know who in the hell you are. If you're a law student, why does the judge keep looking at you like he's afraid to say anything? Why do you do all the talkin'? Don't a Judge run his own court? You're one of those dead Republicans who worked his way into court. If you were a Democrat, we wouldn't be having these problems."

Mr. Clause ignored Cornball and addressed Mr. Comingal and the body of the whole body of the accused, "I will wait a reasonable time for you or anyone else to offer whatever you think is left for a defense. After that time, your sentences will be confirmed."

The passage of time lay heavy on the accused. There were many conferences, but there was no more activity to approach the bench. After a lengthy wait and a long silence, Mr. Clause signaled for the judge to proceed.

Judge Bullman banged his gavel and rose to address the accused. "Every charge made against you while you carried out your political duties stemmed from one charge. You failed to honor your oath of office or helped someone else to dishonor his oath of office. That is why that charge was first on every list of charges." He banged his gavel once more and announced, "All accusations against you are confirmed, and the sentence prescribed for each accusation will be carried out." Bullman and Mr. Clause left the court, in a great hurry, through the door behind the judge's bench.

The emotions in the Court were many: fear, deep sorrow, intense anger, teeth-gnashing hatred against the unfeeling court; and there was a deep, quiet contemplation, by a very few, of the lost opportunities to have done better.

The doorways they had used to enter the preparation room and the doors of the court disappeared, leaving solid walls around them. Suddenly the back wall disappeared, and the blazing Portal of Hell beckoned with the super-heated malevolence of its total power over all of them. Every new inhabitant of Hell stood transfixed, cringing in mind-numbing fear and revulsion. No power on earth could have forced a one of them to walk one step toward that blazing portal of doom. Every panic-driven foot in the room moved as far as it could get from the Portal of Hell.

Hell had seen many new inhabitants with that same realization of absolute horror. Hell had its own solution to the problem. The entire courtroom slid silently and quickly toward the Portal's massive burning doors swinging open to receive them. The courtroom moved the new inmates through the blazing Portal of Hell. It streaked past the smoking heaps that were Hell's mountains. It passed the fire-seared landscapes to the shore of their own Lake of Fire. The room then disappeared. They stared at Hell from the shore of a burning cauldron of lava. They knew there was no escape.

Mr. Clause and Judge Bullman

"Well, Carl, what did you think of our orientation program for the new inmates?" asked Clause.

"It wasn't the largest, but it was certainly the strangest," replied Bullman. "Why did we go through this charade we called a trial? Everyone arrives here convicted; there is no way for us to reverse any of the sentences, and that includes our own. I do understand why you didn't tell them you are Satan, given the circumstances."

Satan's eyes narrowed, and he warned Bullman, "No one has my permission to call me Satan. I am Lucifer, the Light Giver. I was the brightest angel in Heaven, and I don't like to be called Satan. We've been friends for a long time because of your service to me, but watch your tongue."

Bullman apologized profusely for calling Lucifer "Satan." He then tried to steer the conversation onto safer ground. "You haven't explained the reason you chose to have a trial."

"The trial was my idea for those who wouldn't accept our help to reduce their sentences. You, as my representative, and I were ordered here by higher authority and given permission to do it my way. You did a magnificent job of steering those who would allow themselves to be helped, and we received no criticism from the Guardians God sent to soften their sentences. I was allowed to do as I wanted with those who would not allow the steering process of their own free will; but, we were forced by that same high authority to use the truth in our discussions with them."

Bullman interrupted, "Was it God who forced us to use the truth?"

"Not directly," replied Satan. "My replacement contacted me. He was very clear about the use of truth, and it was my own enlightened impression that he was very serious about not permitting any violations of the Virtues of Hell. I had to personally take charge of the job because I needed to assure myself there would be no violation of any of the Virtues of Hell in this orientation. One lie by you, or me, during our simulated trial would have violated that Virtue and put us both in the Lake of Fire."

"But why a trial?" asked Bullman. "Why didn't you just give them your usual one-paragraph orientation and then throw the whole bunch into Hell and let it go at that? You were given the choice of how to handle them. If you had just given them the toss, there would have been no possibility of one of us violating the Virtues of Hell."

"Actually," replied Satan, "it's pretty simple. We handle large numbers of new inmates routinely. Those headed for Heaven are the very best; ours bounce in the other direction. We can handle any number of incoming inmates with no problem. They die natural deaths, and aren't closely associated with each other.

When they are associated, there aren't enough of them to matter.

The Comingal group was special. They were more than forty thousand who came here at the same time under unusual circumstances, and they knew each other. They worked at the same type of jobs for, actually *against*, the same government, and all of them think alike. I couldn't allow a group of friends and political associates to enter Hell at the same time and allow them to remain together in one large group.

"If I had separated Comingal's team from the others without manufacturing a reason for their separation, they would have worked like hell to get back together and renew their collaboration. An uncontrolled reunion could cause problems, and I don't need more problems. The entire group may get together again at some time, but it will be on my orders for my reasons.

"I, with your help, have managed to disperse most of them over a wide area of Hell. We used their personal histories, fears, and desires to lower their sentences for the dispersal. I put them far enough away from each other to make it difficult for them to collect in friendly groups and compare notes. I even put some of them in the nicer places in Hell, far from any of the Lakes of Fire. It's almost impossible for them to become one group again without my help.

"Those who stayed with Comingal were a different problem. Damn—he was good. He tried to use the power of the Court to reverse his sentence, and it was a good plan. He had me going for just a few seconds. His Sodom and Gomorrah defense wasn't worthy of Comingal, but it was a respectable try. I'm kind of sorry I had to cut it short."

"I thought you were worried when Comingal asked for a Court-ordered democracy," Stated Bullman. "What would you have done if refusing to provide that kind of proof violated a Virtue of Hell, and we failed instead of them?"

"I wasn't worried for one second," barked Satan. "Though, if we had failed, I would have been forced to turn them over to the same process the others were smart enough to use. They thought winning their case meant they would be given back their former lives. All I told them was that they would be free of the Court, which was entirely truthful of me. I didn't say they wouldn't go to Hell if they won their case."

"Well, they lost," remarked Bullman. "Still, I thought you showed a grudging respect for them on occasion."

"*Grudging* is the right word for it," returned Satan. "Those that stayed with Comingal are hard drivers who will not quit. They must be kept together so we can keep an eye on them, and guide them in the right direction. They will soon be plotting to get out of Hell or scheming to take it over. I wouldn't be surprised if Comingal finds a way to convince some of the tyrants in Hell to join with him in forming a democracy.

I put his bunch very near one of the largest Lakes of Fire. My brilliance for doing it, my way, serves as a warning to my other little problems around that lake. They will know I'm still watching them."

"Why do you care where they are in Hell?" asked Bullman. "You're all powerful in Hell. You're the Prince of Hell."

Satan watched Bullman's face for a moment before he confided, "You and I have become close friends since your entry into this super-heated eternity, and I have learned to count on you more than some of the Gray Angels who originally came here with me. Everything I have asked you to do has been done with great diligence. I am going to need a friend like you in the future, and what I am about to tell you must be kept in strict confidence. Do you agree to that?"

Bullman assured Satan, "Of course, I would never betray the confidence of a magnificent friend and benefactor like you. I'm with you one hundred percent. All you need do is ask, and I will get it done."

Satan moved a little closer and said, "God forced me into Hell, but he didn't put me in charge. I have remained in charge because of my superior intellect and power. After the final judgment, there will be enough people coming into Hell to overcome my intellect and power. Collectively, if they get together in a large enough group, they can force me out of my position of control, and these people believe in collectives.

"That's why I have arranged Hell in subdivisions and created harsh penalties for anyone who leaves his subdivision. The subdivision system makes these early arrivals easy to control. Those who are here now will convince the later arrivals that there is no way to escape their assigned subdivision without bringing the wrath of Lucifer down on their heads.

"There are always a few exceptions. Comingal and his group will never believe in my, or anyone else's, invincibility. They must remain isolated and closely controlled. I must keep them believing I'm too powerful to mess with. I cannot have them spreading their influence to the other politicians stuck in Hell. I must protect myself from the coming influx of power-greedy politicians. I'll find a means of channeling Comingal's energy, and he'll help me control Hell."

"I know you stuck to the truth with all of that democracy and republic mumbo jumbo," Bullman remarked. "I was amazed by your command of the facts. You broke them down with the truth in every defense they tried. The information you gave me was accurate in every detail. I argued with the best of them and won easily because of the training you gave me. I know you were here long before their Republic was formed, but for myself, I didn't pay very much attention to it when I was living there. How did you gather so much information about the Republic?"

"I have some resources you are unaware of," Satan affirmed. "And I used those resources. I also knew every line in the personal history volumes they refused to read. Comingal was right about his bunch; their personal histories wouldn't have helped their case. Comingal and his collective defense champions didn't trust their own past actions enough to read why they were charged.

"Our new inmates were the biggest liars on Earth. Truth became their greatest enemy. While I was forced to use the truth in this case, I would have used it if I hadn't been forced. I've found the best way to deal with lies, misconceptions, or spin is the actual truth. Truth can be a powerful weapon in the hands of intelligent people who use it to support their agenda. It can be a very powerful tool with clever use, even when the agenda itself is based on lies. As for myself, I always know the truth, and I use it superbly when I feel like it—and I felt like it.

"I know as much about the Constitution of their Republic as any of the new inmates, and constitutional accuracy was an easy way to test their ability to deal with my superior mind. If I had lied to them, they would have known it immediately. After all, they were bubbled into Hell because of their expert knowledge and corrupt manipulation of their system of government. My more expert ability to accurately use the truth they were familiar with, and had corrupted, proved my mind is superior to theirs. My faultless use of truth made them worse off in every case. Their attempted corruption of the same truth in defense of themselves, with only me as their opponent, doomed them.

"Someday you'll tell them who I am. When you do, they'll know they won't be able to pull the same con games on me they did on the American people. They will hate me for what I did to them, but their hatred will be overpowered by their fear, and their fear will help me control them."

Bullman's curiosity was piqued to the breaking point. He had found something fascinatingly incongruous about Satan. The Father of All Lies had used the truth to work over a bunch of liars who were no match for him no matter what they did or said. Satan had gone to all of that trouble to prove to the new inmates that he was smarter than the new inmates. Mind boggling! Bullman wondered, *What kind of logic does Satan use?*

Satan had begun to show more confidence in Bullman. There was an added closeness Satan had never shown before. Bullman decided to ask something he had never before dared to ask. "I know the name Lucifer means *Light Giver,* but what did that mean in Heaven?"

"It didn't mean I was striking matches to help people see in the dark," was Satan's nasty reply. "The light I gave was the light of the knowledge of God, but things didn't work out very well for me in that job. I was fired—literally."

"What happened? Do you think God was overly judgmental?" cautiously queried Bullman.

Satan gave Bullman a long, intense look. Bullman's toes curled a little; he wasn't sure if Satan was taking a second look at one he shared many hours with, or was just thinking back on his past failure to form an explanation. Finally, Satan said, "You're a trusted friend, and I have great confidence in you. I don't think it will do any harm to explain what happened. I've shared a wealth of my personal knowledge with you, but this is special, and it is for your ears only. You're the first one who wasn't with me at the time who will hear this story.

"God created me with a truly monumental intellect, and He assigned me the work of enlightening those he wanted to teach, and what they should be told. I was told everything God wanted to be related about himself, and a tremendous amount of additional information. I was the most powerful of all. I was welcome to stand beside his Heavenly throne. I knew God hadn't told me everything, because I had no knowledge of his methods of creation. I thought I was given the essentials of everything else. I believed creation was completed and that its knowledge was unnecessary because there was nothing left for God to create.

"Everything was fine until I became dissatisfied with my work. My giant intellect was being used for the simplest of tasks. I went wherever I was sent to tell, whoever, what I had been told to tell. There was nothing personal about myself, or my great mind, I could share with anyone I was told to contact. My super mind and great power was used for answering questions and making reports. It was always the same: *God wants you to do this, and God wants you to know that.*

"God was everything, and I was nothing more than a reflection for what he wanted. For all of my power and knowledge, I was still lower than a person. I couldn't make the ordinary decisions every person makes in their lives. I was highly respected, but I could only use a shadow of the power I should have been using for my own personal purposes.

"I began to quietly discuss my discontent with my closest friends among the angels. Surprisingly, some of my own dissatisfaction with the situation began to surface in them. I was amazed at how many of them felt the way I did. We had to be very careful to stay with the truth and couch our dissatisfaction in truthful terms, but I found I could add a very fine edge of conspiracy within the truth I shared with my highly intellectual angel friends. I—very cleverly—built a revolutionary power base without once uttering a false statement.

"My revolution was ready to move just after the Garden of Eden was opened. We couldn't kill God; he is impossible to kill. If we could have, and had killed him, it would have ended the universe and all of us with it."

Bullman interrupted Satan's story. "How did you intend to control God after you won the war? You're powerful, but he created you, and you couldn't kill him."

"I thought I had found a way to use his own nature to control him," Satan answered. "We angels couldn't be killed either. God gave us eternal life, and he never takes back what he gives. I, having the knowledge of God, thought I had found a way within his own laws to defeat him. We...well, *I thought*, since we angels wouldn't be killed if we surprised him with a general uprising, we could remove him from power by ignoring him. We could, very simply, do whatever we wanted. He is the God of life, not death. I knew he had the ability to kill us, but I also knew it wasn't in his nature to do so. I thought his refusal to destroy those he had given eternal life was his eternal weak point.

"I was certain the universe had only two parts: Heaven and the physical part of the universe. There was no Hell at that time, or at least, I didn't know there was. I knew that my angel friends and I were too powerful for him to allow us uncontrolled access to the physical universe, but we wanted that access. We wanted to travel back and forth as we pleased, and do as we pleased, without any interference from God. We also wanted to keep our place in God's flawless Heaven. That was a tough problem to solve.

"I had collected a rather large backing of angels who were friendly to my plan by that time. I thought those of us who didn't like the situation in Heaven could ignore God and his laws. I didn't know any method he could use to control those of us who refused to be controlled.

"All angels have the ability to go wherever they choose whenever the want to, but they don't go without permission. God doesn't want them to go, so the don't go. They can make their own choices, but they don't choose to do things God doesn't want done.

"I thought as soon as there were enough of us to revolt, the massive number of those under my command could begin to ignore God and do as we wanted. When God did nothing to us, and I couldn't think of anything he could do, the other angels would see there was no penalty for ignoring God. They would be willing to follow me in the revolution.

"I believed, with the broad power base I already commanded, we would eventually be joined by most of the other angels in our new freedom for action. With the backing of the large number of angels I already had on my side, and those I believed would join us later, I intended to become the superior power in Heaven.

"I planned to imprison God within the boundaries of His own rule of Heavenly peace, and His rule for Heavenly life. I would force God into a quiet, eternal retirement that would leave the universe in my capable hands. I thought the Angels who hadn't already joined us would, quickly, find my leadership acceptable. After the coup, they would become happy with the new Heavenly order operating under my expert direction.

"Slowly, things began to fall apart a little at a time. After I began the final preparations for my master plan, God began giving me fewer and fewer assignments. I wasn't allowed to spend as much time with him near his throne. I began spending an increasing amount of my time pacing outside of His throne chamber. I was sure God had become suspicious of me. I knew the game was up if he began questioning any of those who were helping me plot against Him. I knew the war in Heaven was looming closer. The Heavenly coup had to be soon, or lost.

"An angered God might marshal his angelic forces before I could marshal mine. His forces, backed by his power, would defeat me. Even if he refused to harm my revolutionaries in his counterrevolution, he would still be able to remain in power. I knew he could eventually create a way to control us. I thought it was a bad idea a to hurry, but I knew the only chance I had left was to make my move before God discovered what my plan was and how many of us were in on it.

"While my plan was burning hot in my brain, God created a man and a woman to begin his new generation of mankind. He put his new generation of man above us angels; he created *them* to be higher than *me*. He gave them a magnificent garden to live in, and the only thing he refused them was a fruit he put in the garden but forbid them to eat.

"I didn't think eating the fruit was their problem, but rejecting God by eating the fruit was a problem. Who knows, he may have allowed them to eat the damned fruit at a later time when they were mature enough to handle the knowledge of good and evil.

"God frequently talked with the two by himself, and he visited with them in the garden. He didn't allow me to do the job I was created to do, and he didn't consult me about his reasons. Enlightening Adam and Eve was my job, not his. He froze me out of the most important act he had created me to do. I knew then that my job as Lucifer the Light Giver was finished. The revolution was the only way out for me.

"My vast knowledge included all of the evils mankind could do. I decided to wise up the two apples of God's eye. I quietly sneaked into the garden and talked Eve into eating the forbidden fruit, which she shared with Adam. I thought spoiling God's plan for his two favorite creations would be the best time, and the most emphatic way to begin my takeover of Heaven. I didn't know God had already confirmed his suspicions about me and was watching every move I made.

"He checked his garden after I talked his two favorite creations into eating the forbidden fruit. He must have done it the moment I left. I didn't realize he would act so quickly. I made a slow, meandering trip back to Heaven. I wanted to savor my abortion of God's plan. I had aborted his plan with the knife of my treachery on the two in the garden. I could almost taste my future conquest of Heaven. I floated peacefully, happily, along on my slow, easy way to total power.

"You talk about the shit hitting the fan; a full scale war was going on when I got back to Heaven. I couldn't get near enough to it to lead my troops to victory. I could see it all happening, but I was faced by two dozen of God's lily-white angels with drawn swords, and they kept me from doing anything but stand still.

"I watched helplessly as my angels began losing the battle. Searing-hot bolts of energy crippling came from the swords of God's angels. Nothing came from the swords of my troops. Faced with the horrible power from the swords of God's angels, mine were in retreat everywhere in the city. Leaderless angels were panicked and leaving the City as fast and as far as they could get away from it. God outnumbered us, outmaneuvered us, and out-gunned us.

"God's angels forced my angels out of his city. Twelve legions of his Angels followed and fought mine until they were forced high above his city into one group. My Angels, frantically, milled around to find an escape route.

"After my troops were under full control, the twelve angels I faced pushed me into the outer edge of my angels' position. God's angels retreated and formed a protective shield around his city to keep us out.

"I rallied my troops. I turned their rout into my tactical retreat. I knew we couldn't get back into the city immediately. I intended to return to the battle after I assessed the problems. All I needed was to form a new battle strategy. In a fair fight, we would have beaten them.

"I placed them in a tactically maneuvered group retreating into space. Suddenly, God created a Gulf between Heaven and us. It was like opening a high-speed zipper in the fabric of infinity. The zipper opened, in what I thought was empty space, and released an impenetrable fog. The ripping force of the Gulf shattered my formations and pushed my troops in all directions away from Heaven. It was a ferocious struggle to reform my troops but I finally managed to get them back together.

"I thought I could still win the war if I could lead my Angels through the Gulf to renew my attack on Heaven. The best, and toughest of my troops, tested the Gulf in many different places, but none of them found a way through it. Then the Gulf began to shrink with such power that it forced us farther and farther from Heaven. It drove us relentlessly into an area that grew smaller each second, until the Gulf forced us here—into Hell.

"I still have a few trusted lieutenants out looking for a way around the Gulf, but God is very thorough. Unless he made a mistake in construction, and I don't know of any he has ever made, the Gulf has us encircled as completely as infinity itself. I know there is a way through it, because God puts people through it all of the time. If I can find a way to breech the gulf, I can end the power of Hell over all of us. We may, even at this late date, be able to return to Heaven and rule it. If we can't, we will have the physical universe to live in, and the physical universe is a hell of a lot better than Hell.

"One of the reasons for all of my hellish control efforts is this: not all of the Angels who came here with me are as willing to accept my leadership as they were before the war in Heaven. Some of them believe that they as a group, joined with human groups, may be able to take over Hell. I can't kill them or anyone else, and I can't allow the angelic traitors to my benevolent leadership and the human results of my action in the Garden of Eden to join together in a successful effort that will destroy my control of Hell.

"I can assure you, with your help and the help of the majority of angels in Hell who are still my friends, you and I will make Hell a paradise more pleasant to live in than Heaven. It will take a lot of work, but I have it all figured out. You stick with me, and you'll have everything you ever wanted: palaces, power, money, women, and everything else. You and I will remain in the two top positions in Hell.

"I have been studying our situation from the beginning, and my calculations have produced the first glimmer of a plan to destroy the Gulf of Hell. We can still have it all. I will wreak vengeance on Heaven and turn Heaven into Hell and Hell into Heaven."

Bullman was amazed by the story. He had a lot of questions about its inconsistencies and more than a few doubts about Satan's version of the truth. Satan had offered no information on his method to turn Hell into Heaven and vice versa. Satan seemed unsure about his ability to wage a new war against Heaven. Bullman thought it was best not to push his luck by asking troublesome questions like, *How can you win a future war from a position of weakness when you lost the last one with your power at its peak?* He decided to play it safe and bring Satan back to the present problem. "Now that the Democrat revolutionaries are where you want them, what do you want done with them?"

"I'm giving you the job of monitoring them," declared Satan. "I want to know everything they do, and I want you to report directly to me, no one else. If any of the traitorous Black Angels buddy up to them, I want to know which ones and the specifics of their plan. You are to make sure the Democrats don't make contact with my other subdivisions." Satan warned, "Your methods are your own, but the results had better be mine."

A dark cloud covered Bullman as Satan said, "I'm giving you powers you have never had before. I expect you to use them for my benefit. What I give, I can take away and everything else with it. The Lake of Fire is full of my disappointing disciples."

Bullman pledged his allegiance to Satan and expressed his gratitude for being allowed to become a part of Satan's Hell of pleasantries—which might appear sometime in the distant future. The meeting ended with Satan going about his business in Hell. Bullman was left alone to think over the gift of new power and responsibilities.

Bullman couldn't think of any way Satan could change Hell. He had admitted he hadn't been given the knowledge of creation, and Satan would have to re-create Hell to make it pleasant to live in. Bullman recognized that Satan didn't have a chance in Hell of destroying God's Gulf. He decided to go along for the ride as long as there seemed a profit in it for Bullman. He had to admit that

Satan was the only one in Hell who could change Hell, if Hell could be changed.

Bullman's biggest doubt was in what Satan had left unsaid about the trial, which wasn't a trial at all. The mock trial was a rather strange orientation. Satan acted as though he was in control of everything, but he wasn't. The orientation site was outside of the normal boundaries of Hell. Neither Satan, nor his power controlled the orientation. Neither Satan nor Bullman had access to the site except when Satan was told his presence was required. Both of them were prevented from staying there any longer then they were allowed to be there.

Satan appeared to have engineered the orientation, but Bullman knew that the helpers who were available to the Democrats didn't come from Hell. Bullman thought, wrongly, that all of the Democrats who had accepted help—from whoever the helpers were—were treated better than those who did not. The "Progressive" group received that help, but had been treated worse. Comingal's collective had chosen to stick together in its own tightly bonded group. The Progressives refused to join Comingal and his collective defense. That fact had saved the Comingal bunch from being treated like the Progressives.

Satan said he had assigned places in Hell for all of the inmates, but the only ones who went where Satan wanted them to go were in Comingal's collective defense group. The others had disappeared before Satan arrived, or while he was busy with the mock trial. Satan couldn't have had anything to do with where those individuals went. Bullman knew they went to Hell, but with some improvement in their condition because of the help they'd received.

Bullman had remained in the outside-of-Hell location as long as he could. He knew the Gulf was about to close and force him through the same dreadful Portal of Hell the Democrats and Satan had passed through. While the relentless power of the Gulf was speeding him back to his place in Hell, he decided Satan was playing one of his cautious, manipulative games.

Satan was pulling every trick he could to maintain his power over those who were secretly plotting to take his power away, just as Satan had plotted to take away the power of God. Bullman wasn't sure whether the humans' or Satan's side would win the final battle, or the best way to profit for himself as he played the game. Bullman knew he was one of the human results of Satan's actions in the Garden of Eden, and he didn't like adding Satan's insult to Satan's injury by being Satan's tool.

The Subdivision

Bullman knew Satan would be waiting for his initial report on the conduct of the new inmates, and it was important for him to make a first visit. His new powers allowed him to become invisible whenever he wanted, but for this visit, he wanted them to see him. The procedure he usually followed called for good relations with everyone when good relations supported his personal purpose.

Bullman wasn't quit sure what his purpose was going to be, because it cut in two directions. On one hand, he intended to remain on Satan's good side by fulfilling his assigned obligations. On the other hand, if Bullman ever found an opportunity to make himself the proprietor of Hell, Comingal and his group would be a big asset on Bullman's side. He didn't want them on Satan's.

The Democrat subdivision was one of twelve political subdivisions surrounding this political Lake of Fire. The politicians in the twelve subdivisions knew they weren't the only politicians in Hell, and their subdivision wasn't the only political one. Satan's no-contact rule was high on each politician's list of violations of Satan's laws. Everyone wanted to violate that law, but none of them wanted to be caught.

The older political subdivisions ordinarily used a variety of methods for communications within that subdivision. All of the subdivisions were high tech, but most of the older inhabitants weren't good at using the high-tech equipment, and none of them trusted equipment controlled by Satan. Many of them used communications based on fire and smoke signals. Fire and smoke were constantly available, and they were semi-private.

The inmates in the newer subdivisions used the more modern equipment, but there were many satanic restrictions they hadn't been able to overcome. Each subdivision had fax machines; computers and telephones were available for those who had less fear of Satan.

The modern equipment could be used internally inside each subdivision or externally to other subdivisions. All of the communications devices were routed to a central communications center manned by Satan's trusted Gray Angels, one more way Satan used to keep track of what was going on. The inmates in the political subdivisions were constantly seeking ways to clandestinely make contact with the others. Walking across a boundary was dangerously anti-Satan, but those in subdivisions with contiguous boundaries could see and talk with each other across the boundary. They spent a large amount of their eternal time devising inter-subdivision, non-Satanic communications systems.

Bullman looked at the Democrat subdivision with a practiced eye. He had seen them all many times, but this one was more dangerously positioned than any of the others. It was perched on the slope of a volcano. Its major building was only a short rockslide from an edge of the cliff. There were many buildings a short walk from a cliff that plummeted to the Lake of Fire. All of the subdivision's ugly buildings were constructed of the same black, porous rock as the volcano. The volcano regurgitated its hot, seething liquid venom down its slope opposite the slope the subdivision was perched on. The Democrats were convinced the subdivision would remain safe only for as long as Satan was satisfied with his safety from it.

There were no streets, and no sidewalks in the subdivision, just spaces between the buildings. The subdivision contained no houses, no apartments, and no living quarters of any kind. The inmates had no means of transportation except their feet. No inmate possessed a personal item except the clothing each wore. They had intense desires for, but no need to eat, drink, or sleep. Rare, brief rests were taken wherever they happened to be.

Bullman's shoes crunched on the volcanic grit as he entered the main building nearest the edge of the cliff. He expected Comingal and his core defense team to be inside learning to use their new surroundings to their best advantage. As Bullman entered, he heard a familiar voice in discussion with Comingal. He jumped at the chance to use his newly acquired invisibility and remain hidden while he listened to the discussions.

Comingal stated, "At least we arrived here with a quite a few good-looking girls. Life won't be so bad with a few willing women on the staff."

The Black Angel sneered and retorted, "They won't do you any good. You can't have sex here, no matter how hard you try. Something will happen to keep you separated from whoever you think you are going to have sex with."

"They seem friendly enough," remarked Comingal, "and some of them have been sending signals saying they are willing."

"Do you remember that old canard about your worm never dying?" asked The Black Angel. "That wasn't just an old canard. It means you never lose your desires, and one of the reasons they never go away is they are never satisfied."

"I intend to test that canard under fire," advised Comingal. "I was never satisfied any other time, and my worm always crawled pretty fast; maybe I'll have better luck here. "Let's get back to this inter-communications stuff you were telling me about. How can we make contact with the other political units spread around Hell?"

"All right," replied the Black Angel, "when we came here, the place was already set up. The buildings were here, but they weren't divided into Satan's subdivisions, and the communications system was in place throughout Hell, waiting for inmates who understand the progress of technology so it could be used. The Angels, except Lucifer, were mystified by this. We didn't need to use it to communicate with each other. Lucifer knew what it was for, but he didn't share that information with us. We only began to understand all of the stuff that was installed as the Earth's technology improved.

"When people began arriving who knew how to use the telephones, Lucifer made us reroute the communications system through a central exchange. We didn't know why he wanted us to do it, and some of us were suspicious of him. He engineered the battle we fought when we were kicked out of Heaven, and he did a poor job of helping us. He stayed outside of Heaven and waited for us to lose. Since we didn't trust him, we didn't do a very good job on the communications system. We rerouted everything, but we left the means of reconnecting it in place.

"I, and some of my close friends, have been reconnecting certain parts of it. We have also disconnected some of the equipment that goes to Satan's central information system. You have two working telephones, one fax machine, and one computer that are connected to our Black Angel communications system. Our system bypasses Satan's, and connects your subdivision to the other political subdivisions that are a part of our Black Angel system.

"Everything you say on any other part of the system goes directly to Satan's monitors. I, and some of the other Black Angels, have shown the inmates from less modern times how to use the equipment. They have been shown, as you will be, which of your pieces of equipment are safe. You must remember to keep up a steady stream of useless bullshit going to Satan's monitors; otherwise, he will become suspicious and locate our new system. If he discovers our system, he will have his Gray Angels disconnect it."

Comingal was wary of the angel's intriguing revelations. He asked, "If Satan is so powerful and all knowing, how is it he doesn't know what you and we will be doing?"

"He's under the same sentence you and I are under," replied the Black Angel. "He can't avoid the Virtues of Hell any more than we can."

"Wait just a minute," remarked Comingal, "what are these Virtues of Hell you mentioned? I thought Hell was supposed to be a place without virtue."

The Black angel gave Comingal a disgusted look and then said, "The Virtues of Hell aren't virtues anyone *has*. There seems to be some kind of natural law built into Hell to keep people from doing certain things, especially things having to do with sex or personal attacks against someone else. We don't understand the Virtues, and they seem to change from person to person. The punishment for violating a Virtue seems to vary with the severity of the action. The Virtues may cause you to be unable to complete something you're doing or, in some cases, cause you to end up in the Lake of Fire without knowing how you got there.

"We call them the Virtues of Hell because they appear to have something to do with the lack of virtue in our previous lives. Every person in Hell will eventually learn the ones affecting his own problems. Learning takes a long time, and each Virtue is learned the hard way. No one knows how they will affect anyone else except for the most common virtues."

"What about Satan?" Comingal asked. "He must understand the Virtues he has to be careful not to break."

"He's never been in the Lake of Fire, and he understands his Virtues," replied the Black Angel, "but his never dying worm affects him just like it does everyone else. Lucifer's worm wants Lucifer the Light Giver to know and control everything and everyone around him. His desires, like your desires for sex, can no longer be satisfied. He doesn't know what anyone is thinking, and he can't keep anyone from doing anything except by using his power, or the fear of his power. He is still powerful and dangerous, but he no longer has the power he once had.

"A combined angelic and human effort can end his power over Hell. When that happens, we run Hell, not Lucifer, and we can do a much better job than Lucifer does. Join us, and I'll show you the safe equipment. Otherwise, I'll see that your safe equipment is rerouted to Satan's monitors. If you don't join us, you keep your mouth shut about our conversation, or I'll punch a hole in your volcano and wash your whole subdivision into the Lake of Fire with a stream of lava."

Comingal felt trapped, no matter what he did. If the Black Angel was an Angel of Satan's sent to test him, joining would be disastrous, and Satan himself might unleash a stream of lava on the subdivision. If the Black Angel was telling the truth, it was still too early for political war. His entire group consisted of new arrivals that didn't have their feet on the ground. Still, if he didn't join the Black Angel right now, Comingal felt his group would be left out and might never have another chance to join. Comingal considered his options carefully. Finally, he said, "We'll join your club."

The Black Angel stood up, slapped his chest, and flapped his wings to shake some of the soot and grit off, and then smiled and offered his hand as he said, "I heard over the grapevine that you were an intelligent and dangerous man. That's why Satan put you in this subdivision perched so close to the Lake of Fire. I'll see you from time to time and bring you up on the events you can't be told of any other way." The Black Angel gave Comingal instructions for the use of the safe equipment and made his exit.

Bullman's invisible eavesdropping on the proceedings made him very edgy. He decided to remain invisible and make a visible approach to Comingal's domain at a later time. He realized the Black Angel and Comingal had given him either an enormous problem or a wonderful opportunity. He decided to stay in the building long enough to see how Comingal would handle the political challenge the Black Angel had dropped in his lap.

Comingal immediately called a closed-door caucus of his core advisors, including Patsy, Flim Flamm, Cornball, and the members of his Cabinet. He explained the opportunities and dangers of the Black Angel's offer and added, "We have to move very cautiously. No information about a revolt or any deviation from Satan's control of us must be discussed outside of this room. The two telephones, the fax machine, and the computer are in my office. They will be restricted to team use, and the only information sent out on them will be on my or the team's approval. We are too near the Lake of Fire to make a mistake, and either side can put us in it.

"I want Flim Flamm and Cornball to take charge of telephone contacts. We need a marriage of our very best public relations and legal procedures to protect ourselves from traitors in the other subdivisions. Xavier can cover the fax machine, and I will be responsible for the computer. Patsy will take care of the information going to Satan's phony communications system. We'll use the most trusted employees we have for Patsy's communications team, and every use of the equipment will be monitored—*as it is used*. The rest of the team will pre-plan the outgoing and sift the incoming communications to make sure none of us make a fatal error. Are there any questions or comments?"

Flim Flamm, who had just been elevated to the high position of conspiratorial telephone operator, gave his fellow coconspirators his vision statement. "As I see it, we must couch our words in the most benign language while seeking hard-core evidence of revolutionary intent from the other subdivisions. We must be affably probing, ever aware of our own delicate balance, while discovering the true feeling of our off-subdivision counterparts. We must effectively use invasive questioning to gain a definitive perception of their true revolutionary feelings, while maintaining our own posture of simple, friendly inquiry. Clandestine methods will afford us the greatest return of critical information while amplifying our own need for absolute security."

Cornball, the other half of the conspiratorial telephone team, blew his stack. "Damn it, Flim Flamm, if you talk to real people like that, none of them will know what the hell you said. There ain't no law offices in this place. Forget the lawyer talk and be more straightforward. We can be clever without being ridiculous."

Comingal broke in to bring some calm to the situation. "Flim Flamm is only saying that we have to get information from them without giving them any information about us. You do agree with that—don't you, Cornball?"

"Sure," admitted Cornball, "but sooner or later, we will have to ask some dangerous questions and make some dangerous admissions. The two telephones are supposed to be safe and connected to other revolutionaries. We aren't calling everyone in Hell. I say we should tell who we are to those we talk to on the safe telephones, and ask who they are. The longer a revolution is in the planning stages, the easier it is to fail. We got to get on with it."

Bullman listened from his invisible perch. He wanted to straddle the fence for a while before choosing which side to jump on. Bullman didn't know when he wanted to take over, even if he did jump onto the revolutionaries' side. He didn't know how they would plan it; but, since the Democrats had already planned one revolution that might have worked, he would temporarily bow to their expertise in revolutionary matters.

He wanted them to continue their operation, but he feared Cornball had a big mouth; and Cornball didn't understand the dangers the revolution might cause for Bullman. He feared Cornball would turn it into the Charge of the Light Brigade before he, Bullman, decided on a personal course of action.

After a quick, personal judgment of Cornball's propensity for screwing things up, Bullman decided to take Cornball out of the picture until there was more of a certainty for revolutionary success, or it became an obvious failure. Bullman thought the best course of action was to put a curse on Cornball's speech. A cursed Cornball would be able to understand his own words and the words of others, but he wouldn't know why the others couldn't understand him. After cursing Cornball, Bullman thought the revolutionaries couldn't get into any serious trouble for a while. He left to make a personal in-depth assessment of the other revolutionary subdivisions.

"Until I give the order," ordered Comingal, "we follow Flim Flamm's plan and concentrate on what we can get from our counterparts. We give only the most obvious information about ourselves, and information the others already know or can easily guess. Will you go along with that, Cornball?"

"Ouy named lewl terteb bielve ti (You damned well better believe it)," replied Cornball, "hatst twati natwed ni eth sirft eclap (that's what I wanted to do in the first place)."

Harve Crik, Comingal's pre-bubble and present chief of staff, exclaimed, "What did he say? Did anybody understand what Cornball said? Say it again, Cornball."

"Tondi wche ym conab wicte (I don't chew my bacon twice)," warned Cornball, "eancl hte opopatteos tou fo royu reas (clean the potatoes out of your ears)."

Comingal put his hand on his forehead and rubbed it gently as Cornball prattled on in his personal language. He thought for a moment and then said, "Cornball seems to have gone ape on us when we need him most. Harve, you take over the telephone with Flim Flamm, at least until we can get Cornball back to normal. Xavier, take him into the other room and have a bunch of the women talk to him. He always enjoys it when he can find women to talk to. Maybe they can talk him back from whatever has happened to him.

"All right," announced Comingal, "we have work to do. That dirt-covered Angel gave me a list of numbers and web sites for the other subdivisions. Harve, you and Flim Flamm get on the phones and see who answers. The gritty angel didn't give me a list of names with the phone numbers. Maybe you can contact someone who has been here a long time. You know, maybe some old Romans or

Huns and get a few names to go with the numbers. Their subdivisions should be operating full steam.

"Xavier, your fax machine won't be needed for a while. Take a look around the main room for a really good-looking girl who is a computer nerd. I'll supervise her work on the web sites—and while you're there, see how Cornball is doing."

Xavier sallied forth and spied a few girls at one of the computers. All of them were a little grimy from the volcanic pumice floating everywhere, but true beauty can't be hidden by grime. He tapped the most beautiful one on the shoulder and asked her to report to Comingal's office.

Xavier took a slow view of the room in search of Cornball and discovered him in a corner surrounded by several men and women who seemed to be enthralled with his gibberish. Everyone was seated except Cornball, who was addressing the woman sitting in the most forward place in the group.

"Teg oury taf sas tou fo ym raich (Get your fat ass out of my chair)," ordered Cornball.

The lady in Cornball's chair effused, "How profound, and James is speaking directly to me."

Another added, "We will all be thrilled with his brilliant words of wisdom when we can understand him better."

One of the men exclaimed, "If we can't teach him our language, we'll learn his. A mind like James's must not be lost to posterity."

Several of the Cornball admirers nodded their approval of the last remark. Cornball's newly acquired command of gibberish made him the center of attention for those with the need to express their approval of what insiders say—whether it makes sense or not.

Xavier returned to Comingal's office to find everyone busy. The telephones were in full swing. Comingal, encouraged by his undying worm, tried to put his arm around Nadine Crumpet while he attempted to explain the computer to her. His new computer nerd knew more about the computer than Comingal did. The Virtues of Hell kept Nadine's waist and bottom in pristine condition. Comingal's arm and hand remained just out of reach. Comingal didn't understand his Virtues yet, so he tried several more moves in Nadine's direction before he gave up the chase. His worm couldn't move fast enough to grasp the warmth from Nadine Crumpet.

Comingal's office was terrible, and he always preferred comfort and style. He had no hope for style, but since Xavier didn't seem to be busy, he could take over the comfort part of the project. "Xavier, see if you can find something we can see through to put in the holes this place has instead of windows. The hot air from the bubbles breaking over the Lake of Fire keeps squirting smoke through the windows. We want to see out but we can do without the damn smoke."

Flim Flamm added, "And see if you can find some different chairs and desks. Everything in here is made of volcanic cement. It's rough as hell to sit on the chairs, and it's impossible to write on the desks. Maybe you can find some cushions somewhere if you can't find decent furniture."

Harve Crik suggested, "See if you can locate covers for the telephones. My ears are getting numb from whatever gritty stuff Satan turned into telephones."

Xavier retorted, "I'm not running a fool's errand to search for non-existent comforts. If you want something different than what you already have, find it yourselves. I'll man a phone while you're gone."

None of them had enough confidence in the project to accept Xavier's offer. Everything was made of the same dark stone, and none of it was soft, smooth, or clear enough to see through. Comingal admitted defeat for his hope of putting something akin to comfort in his office, and he agreed with Xavier, "We have what we have, and our only hope for change is to beat Satan at his own game. When we beat Satan, we move as far as we can get from this Lake of Fire to the best place we can find."

Flim Flamm remarked, "Everyone I've had conversations with on the phone speaks English. How can we all speak the same language? I don't believe English-speaking people are the only ones in Hell. I expected to run into a language barrier most of the time."

Harve suggested, "Maybe everyone in Hell speaks the same language and it just sounds like English to us. A German might think everyone speaks German. The revolution will be less trouble if we all speak the same language—so, so much the better."

Cornball came into the room with one of his admirers in tow. Cornball was in a dither, pointing toward the outside of the building while he shoved his admirer close to Comingal. Comingal asked, "Do you know what Cornball wants?"

The admirer answered, "I don't know what he is saying, but Judge Bullman is walking toward us, and Cornball is pointing at him to warn you he is coming."

The subdivision activities stopped immediately. Comingal remarked, "I figured he and Clause would be spreading their wings and rolling around Heaven. I wonder why and how he happens to be here."

Bullman entered the office to find everyone staring at the door he entered. He said, "I'm glad to find you at home. I was afraid you might be out to dinner or enjoying one of the many night clubs in the area."

No one laughed at his sorry excuse for a joke. Comingal, in the wrong mood to be polite, asked, "What brings an illustrious Heavenly judge to this balmy climate?"

"I came to see how you are doing and offer my help if there is anything I can do for you as one of the friendly, and more privileged, of your fellow inmates," replied Bullman. "I know your circumstances are terrible, and the ecology of this place is nearly unlivable, even for Hell. I thought it would be a good time to tell you a few things you don't know, and some things that might possibly help you with your revolution."

Comingal advised, "We are perched on a volcano slope between the Lake of Fire and the mouth of the volcano. Our problem isn't how to start a revolution, it's keeping out of the Lake of Fire. We have no means and no desire to revolt. "

"I'll explain a few things about Hell for you," Bullman remarked. "You haven't been here long enough to understand most of it. You're always thirsty, but there is nothing to drink. You're always hungry, but there is nothing to eat. You're always tired, but you can't rest. You're always horny, but you can't have sex. Some of those in Hell would like to die, but they can't die. If you were in the Lake of Fire, it would make you more uncomfortable, but you wouldn't die. No one in Hell can die. Our bodies are completed for lives in Hell, but nothing can kill us. Satan didn't cause any of that. God caused it when he created Hell. Satan had nothing to do with it.

"Your ambition for power will never be satisfied. If you rule everything in Hell, it won't be enough to satisfy your desire for more power. God didn't put anyone in charge of Hell, not Satan and not you. Satan was thrown in here just like you, me, and everyone else, but Satan is smarter than we are, and he has more knowledge of how Hell works than any of us. He uses his knowledge to manipulate the inmates to his advantage, and his hellish manipulations give him the veneer of power he projects to us 'minor' intellects.

"Satan's greatest fear is that some of the other inmates will learn as much about Hell as he knows. If he can keep the rest of us ignorant, he can stay in the top position for eternity. If a revolution succeeds in removing Satan as Hell's leading inmate, Satan would be reduced to being just another unlucky inmate.

"Satan wants Hell locked down and in his control. He thinks he must keep all of the human inmates in fear of him. He intends to regulate every movement every inmate makes. Satan wants the fraud of his invincibility to remain intact forever. I have a very good position here, considering the ecology of this place, but I don't want to spend any more of my eternity in Hell under the thumb of Satan than I absolutely have to.

"I know about the revolution, about the re-connected communication system, and the revolutionaries in the other subdivisions. I would have brought a few hundred of Satan's Gray Angels with me to throw all of you into the Lake of Fire if I intended to spill the beans. I have a plan of my own for the revolution, and unless you want to test your tolerance for pain in the Lake of Fire, this revolution is going to go *my way*."

Comingal asked, with a certain amount of justifiable fear, "What about the renegade Black Angels? They think they are in charge of the revolution. If you have a way to control them, we do not. Will you share your means of controlling them with us so we can follow your orders instead of theirs?"

"Controlling them is only a minor problem to my plans," stated Bullman, "and they have the same general plan I have. The difference is in who is on top when the revolution is won. Follow their orders to the letter until I tell you different. In the final hours, when I see the revolution has made me the winner, I'll share the secret method I have of controlling the Black Angels.

"You and I will be in charge when it's over. I'll need the expert political abilities of yourself and your associates to clinch my control of Hell. If you fail me, I'll punch a hole in your volcano that will blast you and your entire organization into the Lake of Fire."

A worried Bullman departed the Democrat subdivision and headed for his appointment with Satan. Bullman had to keep Satan satisfied that Bullman was still on Satan's side as a first-line team player. If Bullman lost that battle, he was afraid it would be a hotter time in the hot town every night.

Comingal recognized that he needed a closed team meeting to sort out the difficulties with Bullman's new threat against the Democrats' revolution. While concentrating on the problem Bullman had given him, Comingal thoughtlessly reached over to pat Nadine Crumpet on the butt before asking her to leave. Somehow, his hand didn't quite make it all of the way to Nadine's butt. With that startling failure, he decided she already knew too much, and it would be just the same if she stayed. He began his meeting with all the major revolutionary culprits,, and Nadine Crumpet in attendance.

Comingal studied the complicated infrastructure of the revolution to assess the disaster or success equation before he remarked, "We may be at the bottom of the geographic totem pole, but we are on the top on the revolutionary totem pole. Two major contenders for power want us on their side in the battle. Neither of them has given us a plan of battle, only threats if we don't remain on their side. I don't think they have a plan. They must be waiting for us to come up with a plan they can claim as their own. What do you think, Harve?"

"I think we should use our communications expertise to get all of the information we can about this place," replied Harve. "We have no map and no idea of how Hell is arranged demographically. We need to know where we are and where everyone else is to form a plan of our own."

Flim Flamm added, "If our revolutionary expertise is required to form the master plan, our political vision should be employed to put us in control of Hell. The plan we formulate within our Progressive's framework, political expertise, and our enlightened guidance of the other inmates must, of a certainty, insure that our actions will be formed to put us at the very top of the revolutionary totem pole. A lesser effort will be detrimental to our future wellbeing. In these dangerous and complicated times, we must never cease our endeavors to place ourselves in the leading positions of power. Not to do so would compromise our abilities to guide ourselves, and our associates, to the epitome of service to the entire spectrum of our new society. "

Nadine commented, "This place is so ugly. Why would anyone want to be in charge?"

"There are two kinds of people," Xavier responded. "Those who are in charge and those who are not. The ones in charge get the best deals, and it doesn't matter if they are in Hell or not. In this case, it's a matter of whether you want to live on a cliff over the Lake of Fire or in a less dangerous location. There is also the problem of getting thrown into the Lake of Fire; would you rather be the thrower or the thrown?"

Nadine gave Xavier her sweetest smile and answered, "I don't want to be either, but if I must choose one or the other, I choose to be the thrower."

"Nadine, you have made the right choice," remarked Comingal. "We'll make the plan, and we'll be the ones who profit from it. We have two telephones and one computer to use as a throwers' do-it-yourself-kit, and we'll begin putting the kit together now."

The small team kept the phones smoking with revolutionary intent. They found it wouldn't be easy to organize Hell in their own image. The Democrat subdivision was filled with the newest arrivals, and they were in the most dangerous position nearest the Lake of Fire. The other political revolutionaries, with more than the average disrespect for newcomers, considered them down-and-outers trying to horn in on the leadership of the revolution.

The Democrats had an advantage the others did not. They were a like-minded group who shared a similar expertise and would hang together in difficult circumstances. The other political subdivisions had gathered their populations slowly from people of many nations and times. The older subdivisions were filled with a larger variety of crooked political types who could be counted on to stick together only as long as things were going well for those in charge.

Comingal wracked his mind and the minds of his advisors to find a cohesive ideology to hold the large variety of revolutionary elements together under his umbrella. There didn't seem to be anything in Hell that one person, or one group, could offer to a large population. He couldn't offer better food or drink; there wasn't any of either. He couldn't say Satan would take their social security or medical care away from them; none of them had either, and no one became poorer or sicker than they were when they arrived. He couldn't play on their sympathy for children; there were no children to be sympathetic about. They couldn't attach themselves to someone else's rule of law; the Virtues were the only rules, and the few who knew about them didn't understand them. The only other rule of law in Hell was Satan's threats, and Satan's rule of law was obeyed with fear and hatred.

"We need a master scheme to replace Satan with something better than

Satan," Comingal advised his advisors. "To remove Satan from power, we need a way to convince the people in Hell that they will be in control. Most of our political counterparts lean toward a monarchy with themselves and their handpicked lieutenants in control. Our biggest problem is this: we are so poorly aligned with the politics of the other political subdivisions that we can't get past their leadership to see how many in the non-political subdivisions will join our revolution.

"If we publicly begin this revolution with what we have, and by some chance get the other political leaders to join with us, we'll still end up in the Lake of Fire. All of us put together aren't strong enough to oppose Satan. We need a general uprising that will strengthen our democracy and assure us of winning."

Harve Crik lamented, "We have no media system to help us build our consensus. The information we send out is received and controlled by the revolutionaries the Black Angels trusted to support them. If we can find a way to contact and get the help of the Democrats who deserted us for their own individual defenses, and were also kicked into Hell with us, we might be able to float the democracy card."

"That always makes people think they will be in charge," Xavier agreed. "If anyone wants to know what *democracy means*, we can tell them it means majority rule. No one ever asks how the rulers are ruled by the majority or how the rulers know what the majority actually wants."

"I like the idea," admitted Comingal, "but we can't get past the other political leaders. Each of them will insist on being the one who leads the majority in ruling. The democracy ploy won't work unless we can sell the idea to Bullman and the Black Angels. It won't matter what anyone else thinks of it if Bullman and the Black Angels like the idea. They have the means to spread the idea to the ordinary inmates in the non-political subdivisions. The ordinary inmates won't care who the leaders are, as long as they think they are in charge of the leaders."

Nadine asked, "Why don't we ask VP Patsy what he thinks? He's supervising our inputs to Satan's network. Maybe he knows something that will help."

"That's a good suggestion, Nadine," Comingal encouraged. "As a reward, you can sit on my lap."

"You're too hot!" Nadine insisted. "I've barely gotten this gritty chair cooled down enough to sit on."

Comingal faced another sexual failure with the calm of a man whose lively worm doesn't believe in final defeat. He shrugged and asked Harve to bring Patsy in for consultation.

Patsy explained his operation. "We have asked every kind of question any of us can think of. The return is always the same whether we fax, telephone, or use the computers. We receive some kind of form letter as an answer, and there is always an additional questionnaire to fill out. The questionnaire is twenty-five questions asking us what we like about Hell and what we want done to improve it. We have received several different questionnaires, but they all amount to the same thing.

"There is only one question we ask that has an interesting answer. When we ask about water, we are told there is a frozen ocean somewhere in the far reaches of Hell. The information about how to get there is not available, and we think the frozen ocean is one of Satan's frauds. They say it's kept in an ecologically pure condition to prevent it from being contaminated, and no one is allowed near it except the experts who maintain its purity. Whoever is on the other end of the conversations tells us, 'At some time in the future, the ice will melt and provide Hell with a better climate and an abundant water supply.'"

"Everyone else must know about it if Satan told us," Nadine exclaimed. "We think it's a fraud, but does everyone else think it's a fraud?"

Comingal jumped on the idea. "Harve, you and Xavier get on the phones and find out what the others know about ice water in Hell. Ask them if they believe it really exists. Tell them to query Satan's network for information. I don't want them to think we dreamed this up to throw lava in their faces if they haven't heard about the frozen water. This could be the selling point for our democracy. We can promise *ice water in Hell*.

"Patsy, I want you to find a way to use Satan's communications network to take a poll. I need to know how many people in Hell believe there is an ocean of ice. I know I may be asking you to do the impossible, but if you can find a way to take a poll for me, I think I have a plan."

The Ice Water in Hell Plan

The phones and the computers began, once again, to smoke from the heat of activity instead of the heat of the Lake of Fire. Harve and Xavier discovered that Hell's other revolutionaries knew about the ocean of ice story. The others were as disbelieving as the Democrats. Every last one of them thought Satan fielded the story himself. They thought he kept the lie alive to give the less intellectually gifted inmates a false sense of hope in the future, and their hope would help him control Hell.

Patsy's clever machinations produced a bonanza of information from Satan's phony communications system. He found it wasn't totally phony if he pushed the right buttons. For instance, when he stopped asking questions about Hell and asked, instead, to speak to people by name, he could be connected to those people by telephone.

He asked for "Big" Sam Pilfrey first; Patsy thought Sam was the most likely of the deserters to have remained in Hell, and he was lucky enough to get him on the phone. Patsy began asking to be connected to others whose names he could remember, and he was able to speak with all of them.

With a max effort by his team, he located many of the deserters who were in the Court and found none had escaped the sentence of Hell. All of the Democrats he spoke with had heard of the ocean of ice and were as unbelieving as he was.

VP Patsy returned to Comingal in his safe equipment office, and exuberantly reported his clever use of Satan's phony communication system. Comingal listened to Patsy's report with mixed feelings. On one hand, everyone knew about the ocean of ice, and that was good. On the other hand, no one believed it was real, and that was bad. But, if he had a third hand, the fact that he could get information in and out of the Democrat subdivision using Satan's communication system was good. Two out of three on the good side was a definite improvement over the past. Comingal decided to be pleased with the results. He felt his idea of taking a poll was a success.

Xavier asked, "Did any of them tell you how they are doing or what kind of place they are in?"

"They are all better off than we are," replied Patsy. "Most of them are so far away they don't know where our Lake of Fire is, but there are smaller ones spread around. Many of them have been threatened with being thrown into one of the Lakes of Fire, but the threats come from people around them, not Satan. Some of them said they were fairly comfortable. None of them have trees, grass, or anything growing around them, but the soil isn't all volcanic."

"Did any of them say they were ever cold?" asked Comingal.

"Not a one," replied Patsy, "but there seems to be a temperature difference between them and us. They aren't as hot as we are, but that could be because they aren't as close to one of the Lakes of Fire."

"Did any of them say anything about sex?" Nadine interjected curiously.

"None of them mentioned sex," Patsy responded. "If you want sex, there are plenty of men here. None of us would reject your pretty little body. Grab whoever you like and have sex."

"You're all so hot," Nadine lamented, "I want to have sex but I don't want to be toasted at the same time. I'm too toasty already."

Comingal gave Nadine a dirty look before he announced, "Here's the plan. Patsy, I want you to make up some talking points and get them to everyone you have contacted. The talking points must include the following: the ocean of ice is real, we are working on a way to melt some of it and turn it into water, we Democrats are the only ones able to distribute it fairly to all of the inhabitants of Hell. We are attempting to establish a democratic government that is big enough, intelligent enough, and honest enough to redistribute the ice water in the name of the people.

"No one will be left out, *period*. Supporters and non-supporters of the new government will receive their fair share of the ice and the water, *period*. Be assured that people who have ice water will be able to keep it for themselves, *period*. No one will be forced to take more ice water than is wanted, *period*.

"You will have to use the differences in our temperature and theirs to convince them the ice really exists. If you are asked what happens after the ocean is melted, tell them we will redistribute the ice water as fairly as we distribute the ice. You'll need to call the people you contact back at regular intervals to see how the story is going over. We may have to fatten up the talking points if they don't believe us at first.

"I want you to build a list of the names of people known to those we call. I think we can build a computer database of everyone in Hell if we play our cards right.

"Harve, You and Flim Flamm get on your phones and contact the revolutionary leaders. See if you can convince them that we've discovered the ocean of ice that is real ice, not just one of Satan's dirty tricks. Nadine and I will be looking for a map of Hell on a website somewhere. The map must exist in the Black Angels' computer system somewhere, and we'll find it. When we find the map, we will pin point the farthest most likely place for an ocean of ice. I think we can win the top spot on the political totem pole if we can keep the Black Angels and Bullman off our backs long enough to pump up this ocean of ice thing."

Nadine asked, "What will we do when people find out there isn't any ice?"

"I haven't gotten that far in the plan yet," Comingal replied. "First things first. We'll take care of the naysayers when they start naysaying."

The nascent plan was put into operation. The Democrats were busy as Hell.

Patsy's Democrat telephone operators waited in lines at the telephones to make their calls. Computer operators—who really knew how to build a database—were typing as fast as they could, and the list of names grew beyond anyone's expectations.

There were many anti-democracy naysayers naysaying, but there was also a large interest in the Democrats democracy ploy. The pluses looked good for a beginning operation.

It was good timing on his part when the gritty Black Angel returned to check on their progress. He was shocked by the high level of activity. The Black Angel didn't know if it was a good sign or bad. He hurried to Comingal's semi-private office to be certain it was a bad sign before he threatened to blow the volcano and dump them into the Lake of Fire.

Comingal's plan had progressed far enough to be ready for inspection, and he treated the grit-covered unfortunate like a cousin coming to repay borrowed money. "I've been hoping you would drop by," the smiling Comingal assured the dirty angel. "Your operation is going better than we hoped. I think you can look forward to being the new landlord of Hell.

"We are, however, having a few minor problems. We need a map of Hell showing the location of the ocean of ice. The map is essential to our future operation. Also, my people are finding it increasingly difficult to work in the smoke and the heat coming from the Lake of Fire. If you can arrange for your team to move to a more work-friendly location, your revolution can be expedited to an even higher level of efficiency. I'm sure someone of your magnificent stature can arrange these small matters with ease."

The dirty Angel ignored Comingal's request but anxiously asked, "Have you changed sides? Have others been here and convinced you to help them instead of us? You seem to have gotten further along than my associates and I thought possible. Are you receiving help I don't know about?"

"Not a soul," Comingal lied. "We are very familiar with government processes, and my team has found a way to bypass Satan's communication blocks. We're also using your safe telephones and your computer to your best advantage. Without your leadership, we have no chance of success. We thank...well, we thank whoever is responsible for your confidence in us. With your leadership, the help you've been so far, and I'm sure will continue to be in the future, I believe we have a winning team."

The Black Angel shook some of the grit and pumice off of his wings before he said, "I'm glad our plan is going so well, but if you let Satan get even a slight suspicion of what we're doing, he'll be on us like a lake of fire. Getting around his communications block is one thing; getting around it without Satan knowing about it is slick by any definition. I think you and your team may have been successful; your volcano isn't blowing its top."

After some careful consideration, the grit-covered angel returned to Comingal's absurd environmental requests. "Finding a more work-friendly location is very difficult. Satan has every square inch of real estate in his control, but I'll give it a try. As for the map—there is no map, and the stupid ocean of ice is one more Satanic lie." The trust-challenged gritty angel remained with them for a long time, checking the database and listening to telephone conversations.

A more satisfied Black Angel finally left after a few more shakes of his gritty wings. He was satisfied enough with the abundant progress from Comingal's group that he apparently decided to leave the Democrat volcano alone. He hurried around the Lake of Fire to acquaint his fellow angelic conspirators of Comingal's progress and his own worries about Comingal's loyalty to the cause. He had a long way to go, and he had to walk. Flying requires air to fill the wings, and there are no air currents near the Lake Of Fire. It probably has something to do with the ground temperature being the same as the air temperature and the fact that the heat from the Lake of Fire permeates everything around it instead of rising.

The Black Angel's long walk brought him to the Hall of Angels, which wasn't really a hall. The Black Angels had hollowed a large, roofless square out of the side of a volcano to establish their base of operations. Their Hall wasn't in a subdivision, and few in Hell knew anything about them except that they occasionally showed up and demanded some favor to be done. They made their demands with belligerent threats. They were received with fearful respect around the Lake of Fire.

At the front of the Hall of Angels stood a statue of a Black Angel pushing Satan's broken trident into the ground. Satan's trident is supposed to be unbreakable, and its tines are supposed to be depicted pointing upward. The downward-pointing, broken trident served as a symbol of their hatred for Satan.

The Black Angel leader addressed his fellow Black Angels gathered inside the Hall. "Comingal may be with us or against us. It's too difficult to tell for certain. His Democrats appear to have made too much progress to be working alone, but Comingal's bunch are very clever, and they may have discovered the weak spots in Satan's communications system by themselves. You who are monitoring the other subdivisions must be especially alert to discover Comingal's confederates. He and his crew are too clever to make a slip that will tell us if he has turned traitor or is partnering with someone else.

"He's trying to form a type of government called a democracy. To pull it off, he's using the old lie about the ocean of ice. We don't care what he's forming or how he forms it as long as we can control it. Are there any questions or suggestions?"

A Black Angel in the center of the crowd asked, "How can we control Comingal and his Democrats if they come out on top? The Democrats are using their own plan, and we didn't help them make it. We don't know how it works."

The leader of the Black Angels replied, "We are, by far, the most powerful group around the Lake of Fire. Add to that, none of the Earth-born inmates can escape from their subdivision. If Comingal finds a way to unseat Satan, and it appears Comingal isn't going to cooperate with us, we can threaten to toss him and his whole crew into the Lake of Fire. Faced with that painful prospect, he will cooperate."

Another Black Angel asked, "How can we speed up the revolution? I'm tired of sitting around with nothing to do but shake this infernal grit off of my wings."

"We can move between all of the subdivisions," the leading Black Angel stated, "and no one else can do that. We'll go though the subdivisions and spread the news that a real ocean of ice has been found and that Comingal is the one with the best plan to distribute it. We need to build what Comingal called a consensus. That means something everyone believes, or maybe it's just something they can't keep from going along with. I'm not certain how they intend to use this consensus."

Another Black Angel recommended, "We need more of us working in the political subdivisions. Politicians say one thing while they do the opposite. We need more monitors to be certain they can't lie to us and get away with it. I suggest we form large enough squads to cover every inch of the revolution."

"Good idea," agreed the leading Black Angel. "You're in charge of getting it done. I will personally handle the Comingal camp. I want him pushed in the direction he's going, not frightened into doing something else."

The Black Angel meeting broke up on a hopeful note. The Black Angels entered a time of intense activity to cure their boredom. They had all of the bases covered and felt they were in control of the revolution. Their future escape from the Lake of Fire seemed a certainty, and they believed Comingal and his Democrats could not escape their grasp.

As things moved along in the political arena of Hell, Comingal's phony democracy won many friends. It also generated frothy-mouthed opposition from the older political leaders. Most of the older political leaders around the Lake of Fire wanted to form monarchies. The problem was making a decision about which of them would become the monarchs, or how monarchs could be installed over the objections of a political spectrum that would probably be divided between monarchists and democracy supporters in the non-political subdivisions.

In an attempt to cover the entire political spectrum with enough power to control everyone, the revolutionary leaders duked it out among themselves and, pressured by Comingal's Ice Water Democracy, decided on an empire.

The emperor would be chosen by the leaders of the political subdivisions in a free election, but not a free election by all of the people. Whichever, among the hopeful emperors was freely elected by the others, would become the Imperial monarch. The newly elected Emperor would be required to make kings of the other hopefuls that had just elected him the Emperor.

They all knew an emperor should have the power to remove and replace the kings, so they limited the imperial activities to benefit the kings. If the emperor wanted to remove a king, he would need the vote of all of the kings to do it, and at the time of the royal removal, there would be a mandatory vote for emperor. In other words, the emperor couldn't remove a king without risking his throne in the bargain; a very clever move on the part of the lesser kings. None of them thought it was important to make rules for the ordinary people in their hoped-for empire. They could make the rules for everyone else as the rules were needed.

The democracy supporters were generally found in the outlying subdivisions that weren't politically active. No one defined what a democracy was for them, but they already had a Prince of Hell running the place. Very few of them were happy about that. Most of them thought democracy meant they could do anything they wanted. What they wanted to do in a place with nothing to do was a problem none of them bothered to face. The richness of being able to suck on a piece of redistributed ice, or have a cold drink of water, was the greatest personal bonanza any of them could look forward to with some hope. The ice, and the cold water, as far as the leading politicians on both sides knew, was a fraud.

Comingal wished he had kept the method of bypassing Satan's communications block to himself. He began receiving opposition from all over Hell after the first surge of praise for his democracy. The other political subdivisions were as busy as his, and there were more Monarchists than he could deal with. The Monarchists stole Comingal's lie about the ocean of ice, which Comingal had stolen from Satan. The Monarchists told the lie to more people more often than the Democrats did. They knew the game of revolution would end in either Comingal's democracy or a Monarchist empire. They didn't intend for their empire to come under the thumb of one wily Democrat.

Fortunately for Comingal and his Ice Water in Hell Democracy, he had a powerful friend in Bullman. Bullman's entrance into the Democrat subdivision was welcomed as a solution to Comingal's many problems, but Comingal had to convince Bullman of his loyalty to Bullman's cause. Comingal explained his various problems in communication and location to Bullman and assured the great man of his undying devotion to Bullman's plan to take over Hell for himself.

Bullman was very happy with Comingal's progress. He thought, *Due to the carte blanche Satan has given me, I can handle these Democrats with ease. I can solve Comingal's public relations problems, and the problem he thinks he has with the Black Angels.* In an effort to prove his value to Comingal, Bullman stated, "I can move you to a nice location in a valley between two volcanoes. You'll have less smoke, less heat, and more comfort in your new surroundings.

You will also be farther from the Lake of Fire. I think I may be able to find a way to transfer the Democrats you need from the other areas to your new location. Your new area will have a larger communications complex. You'll have more room to maneuver, and you'll have more people to help you keep the consensus out of reach of the Monarchists. Using the Black Angels' paltry communications system no longer matters since you've bypassed Satan's communications block.

"The Black Angels won't be a problem for you anymore. If they come around, treat them as you have in the past. They are not very powerful. They have no credibility with Satan. They can't blow up volcanoes, and they must walk everywhere they go; that's why you don't see them very often.

"Satan has a map of Hell, and I'll bring it to you after you're in your new location. It will have the location of the ocean of ice marked on it. I'll make certain the location is shown in some far reach of Hell where no one can go, and I'll clear it with Satan so you can put the map on the computer network. The map can be the proof you need to convince the inmates of your democratic abilities to get things done.

"You haven't kept a low profile and Satan noticed your campaign activities. I've told him I'm letting you continue to keep you busy, but you must not—at any time in the future—mention your activities as a revolution. Satan is going along with this because he thinks it's in his interests to keep all of the inmates as busy as possible. He wants to use your campaign to keep their minds off of their terrible living conditions. He even thinks your activities are going to help him keep Hell under his control. He and his Gray Angels will come down on us like Hell itself if he decides we're trying to take over Hell.

"There is one more thing. It occurred to me as I recently considered your activities. You might be thinking of pushing me out along with Satan, and taking over yourself. I would advise you against the attempt. I am keeping myself in a very friendly position with Satan. I am also friendly with other political elements that must remain nameless. Should you attempt a lonely coup to make yourself the boss, I will expose you as a usurper of power to Satan, a lying charlatan to the other inmates, and I will have my nameless associates help me push you into the Lake of Fire."

The Lake of Fire threat was becoming old hat to Comingal. The only thing anyone could do to anyone in Hell that was less comfortable than what they were already suffering was push them into the Lake of Fire. It was the only threat that seemed to impress anyone, so it was the most impressive threat used. Comingal still needed Bullman's help, so he ignored the threat and reassured Bullman, "I have considered your welfare in every move I've made. I have no plan to take over Hell myself, and in truth, I don't think I could manage it alone. I, myself, need an experienced manager such as you to keep me from making the terrible mistakes I would make alone. You may be assured; I'm helping you take over as the top man, and I see myself in the servants roll.

"Our big problem is the Monarchists. Forming your democracy will be a walk in the park if you can find a way to take the Monarchists entirely out of the political picture."

Bullman knew the name of the game was power, and he wasn't willing to share his part of it. Bullman didn't he think he dared to try to stop the machinations of his nameless associates until the game was over. "That's why you are being given a new location and a larger work force," stated Bullman. "It's your job to beat the Monarchists. Use your superior intellect and your ability to build a consensus. The Monarchists will weaken and disappear from the big picture as you build your consensus."

'I wonder," asked Comingal, "if you can do anything to get James Cornball back in operation? He's the best we have to attack our enemies. We can use him right now, and we'll need him badly in the near future. The way he is now, I can't understand a word he says, and the people I've assigned to learn his language are stymied. The most formidable accuser I have ever known talk's gibberish."

"Satan himself put the curse on Cornball," Bullman lied, knowing he had put the curse on Cornball. "I can't take it off, but I can approach Satan and, very cautiously, inquire about having it removed. Maybe he will, maybe not. I'll take it as far as I can without endangering myself." Bullman was no longer worried about Cornball exposing the operation, but he wanted to straddle the political fence a while longer. Cornball's expertise might tilt the game in favor of Comingal before Bullman decided which side of that fence he wanted to jump to, but he was beginning to favor the democracy side. His real worry was Comingal's ability to switch things around so they favored Comingal. Bullman wanted to keep all the revolutionary perks in his own pocket.

Ice Water in Hell Democracy, or Ice Water in Hell Monarchy

The new location had certain comfort advantages. There was no smoke blown inside when the bubbles from the Lake of Fire burst. There were no lava bubbles to burst. The outside walls were no longer being splattered by the occasional gobs of hot lava from the exploding bubbles. There was much more room. The new subdivision was close to but not so precariously close to the other political subdivisions surrounding the Lake of Fire. The communications were more abundant, and the telephones, computers, and furniture weren't quite as gritty. Nadine Crumpet supplied the biggest personal plus for Comingal.

Nadine exclaimed, "I think my chair is cooler. Maybe the men will be cooler too. I'm glad President Comingal forced Mr. Bullman to move us. Mr. President, if there is anything I can do for you, anything at all, don't just ask me; order me!"

Comingal leaned over to give Nadine an appreciative kiss on the cheek, but Nadine, for some inexplicable reason, wasn't where the kiss was. Comingal chalked it up to his error and stored Nadine's offer for a later time with better planning. He and his crew had work to do, and they needed to make up for the time lost in the move to the new subdivision.

Pravus Maximus, the hopeful emperor elect, and Comingal's chief enemy among the Monarchists, spread the word that Comingal was a secret agent of Satan and was arranging the democracy to cheat the inmates out of their share of ice.

Attila the Red, another king in the making, accused Comingal of being the engineer of destruction for the democratic state he had been president of just before he drowned. Attila swore on the Lake of Fire that Comingal had secretly been a closet Republican falsely made president as a Democrat to destroy his nation's democracy.

Comingal's spinmeisters worked at full speed to counter the accusations, but none of them could compare to the gibberish-speaking Cornball for ferocity and ingenuity. Cornball had no equal when he was at full throat. Hot political rhetoric began to equal the heat of Hell itself, even with the Democrats' best spinmeister speaking unintelligible nonsense to adoring Democrats.

The other political subdivisions were becoming increasingly active, and they all understood the game of beating an enemy down with accusations. The accusations and counter accusations were expected by both sides and, so far, didn't bother the opposing politicians. Their job was to become the master accusers, and that takes hot rhetoric backed by cool heads, not stress in the ranks.

The outlying subdivisions were something else. The means of bypassing Satan's communications block had been given to the Monarchists, and they were using their new knowledge to inform all others of their coldness to the democratic ice plan. Internal strife in the non-political subdivisions grew with each passing moment. The inmates supporting the monarchy threatened to throw the inmates supporting the democracy into the Lake of Fire, and vice versa.

Modified riots were in full swing in some subdivisions. The men couldn't push the women, and the women couldn't push the men. The Virtues of Hell prevented activities that might become a measure of sexual pleasure, but the inmates kept busy with same-sex pushing around to their hearts content as long as the pushing didn't become too aggressive. If that happened, the virtues of Hell kicked in, and it was into the Lake of fire for the aggressor.

Comingal began to worry about the mini wars going on in the subdivisions. He felt sure Satan would notice and begin a cleanup action, starting with throwing the principle antagonists in the Lake of Fire. He tried fruitlessly to telephone Bullman for advice, but Bullman apparently had an unlisted personality. Comingal had a few phone numbers, but for most of the calls, he had to know the name of the person he was calling or there was no call made. Most of the contacts were on an as-the-person-is-available basis. If the called person wasn't available, he was expected to call back. In a place with almost nothing to do, a call back was almost a dead certainty.

In desperation to get in touch with Bullman, Comingal ordered VP Patsy, "Put a few lookouts around the complex. If Bullman is seen in the area, have him come into my office. I need to talk with him as soon as possible. Have the lookouts keep their eyes peeled for the Gray Angels. They are Satan's Storm Troopers. I want to know it when Satan's Gray Angels are seen flying near us."

"Sure, Chief, I'll get right on it, but what do Gray Angels look like, except they are gray?" Patsy asked.

"The Black Angel covered with grit would look like a Gray Angel if he wasn't covered with grit," Comingal replied. "They all look the same when they're clean."

Bad news interrupted the useless conversation between Comingal and Patsy. Nadine had just unearthed the latest disaster threatening to reverse the forward thrust of the Ice Water in Hell Democracy. The monarchists were busily sending Comingal's Map of Hell that showed the phony position for the Ocean of Ice to computers throughout Hell.

The Monarchists claimed their Royal Surveyors had discovered the Ocean of Ice. Comingal was furious. "Those dirty liars know we had the map first. They don't give a damn for the truth. We have got to get Cornball back in action to push those lying Monarchists out of the picture.

"I want the telephones jumping with this reply to their absurd claim. Call everyone we have a name for and tell them the Royalists have no surveyors, and if they did, the surveyors couldn't leave their subdivisions to do the surveying. Further, the ocean of ice is so far away they couldn't have found it to survey it.

That should settle that claim."

The revolution-straddling Bullman appeared as if from nowhere to the beleaguered Comingal, who immediately drew him to a quiet corner. "We are losing ground," reported Comingal. "The Monarchists have stolen our map idea and they are lying about its origin. The unrest in the subdivisions is increasing by the hour, and Satan is sure to notice. I think our revolution is in grave danger of defeat, either at the hands of the Monarchists or Satan."

"Don't worry about Satan," assured Bullman. "He and his Gray Angels are in his castle on the top of a big hill. He told me his communication center has been reporting to him from the beginning, and he doesn't give a damn if the people in Hell are stupid enough to fight over a non-existent ocean of ice. Satan said he doesn't care how many or what kind of treacheries either side uses to win. Satan promised special status and special living locations to the winners. That is, if the battle over ice water in Hell doesn't drag on for the rest of eternity. He hasn't a clue we want to take his power away from him, and that little fact is in our favor.

"If you need something to counter the Monarchists' use of the map, use this: One of Satan's angels, a closet lover of democracy, told you that the position of the ocean of ice as the map shows it is wrong. The ocean of ice is really much closer. If I were you, I would pick a location somewhere in the mountains behind Satan's castle. You can say Satan put his castle there because it is cooler there than anywhere else. Everyone will believe that, and the Monarchists won't be able to say their surveyors found it again. No one in Hell will believe they would have the guts to pass Satan's castle to find it.

"I spoke to him about Cornball, and Satan will lift the curse on him at any moment. Satan told me Cornball understands everything going on around him. He will be up to date and ready to accuse anyone in Hell of whatever they need to be accused so you can win.

"I'll keep tabs on the Monarchists and stop any unfair practices against your democracy. With Satan ignoring the situation, I may be able to control their actions, but it will be a tough battle. I don't want them worried enough to try bringing Satan in on their side. That's the real danger. We have to play hard and fast with them to keep them busy. That's your job. There is a light at the end of the tunnel, but it's still too dim to see victory."

The Roving Ocean of Ice

Comingal studied the map and found several places he could claim as leading-edge sites for an ocean of ice with Satan's castle near enough to scare off surveyors. He picked the most likely spot and instructed his crew of Democrats to renew their efforts for building consensus. The work went well. Cornball was back on the phone like a demon from Hell accusing all enemies of Comingal's democracy.

The most difficult phone conversations fell to the expert Cornball with increasing frequency as he became more familiar with the Monarchists' personalities. His full-throated savagery quickly dented the Monarchists' attempts to destroy the Democrats' efforts to create an Ice Water in Hell Democracy.

Comingal was appreciative of the new effort, but it wasn't good enough. They needed something more to cause the general uprising that would insure Satan's fall from power. Comingal ordered his staff to caucus. "We need a message that will get all of the inmates who are still sitting on their butts off of them and on our side," remarked Comingal. "We need an easy-to-remember slogan or a buzzword that will build consensus in our favor. We need something that is good enough to excite the ordinary inmates and bowl over the Monarchists."

Trusty Cornball came to the rescue. "Let's use the old 'chicken in every pot slogan.'"

Xavier Xanker burst out, "We don't have any chickens, and no one will believe we have any chickens. We can't use that."

"Damn it, Xavier," retorted Cornball, "use your imagination; I'm not talking about real chickens."

"Then what the hell are you talking about?" demanded Flim Flamm.

"I'm talking about a slogan like 'a chicken in every pot,'" growled Cornball. "Don't any of you have an imagination? I mean like 'an ice cube in every mouth.' Something like that will do the job."

Comingal breathed his relief. "Cornball, you've hit the nail right on the head. Our new slogan is 'An Ice Cube in Every Mouth.' I want that on every phone going to everyone in Hell. The Monarchists will never come up with anything that good. We can repeat the slogan to everyone we contact. We can build our consensus on the one common desire that is shared by all of us; people in Hell want ice water. I think Cornball's slogan will be the brightest light at the end of our tunnel."

The meeting adjourned, and the crew smoked the phones with constant repetitions of Cornball's slogan. Cornball felt a surge of power after his success in the staff meeting. Cornball's accusations peaked to full flower. "Them Monarchists don't know anything. They don't even know where the ocean of ice is. They wouldn't give their own mothers an ice cube. If you support the Monarchists, there won't be any ice because they'll be going in the wrong direction to get it."

One woman on the other end of Cornball's tirade insisted, "If you know so much about geography, send a copy of your map to me. I'm sitting at a computer, but it doesn't have the map."

Cornball's map hadn't been updated with the new location, but he thought he knew just where Comingal would put the ocean of ice. He quickly inserted the location, pressed the send button, and updated her computer to his file. Cornball repeated the Ice Cube in Every Mouth slogan to her a couple of times while she looked at the map.

Cornball kept his accusations alive with the next caller. "Pravus, that no good Monarchist, is nothing but a pervert. Attila the Red is called Red because he killed so many people, and he didn't care who they were. That royal nincompoop, Grossious the Insane, was a general who lost every battle because of his insane desire to become king. He caused more deaths than Attila the Red, but it was always his own troops that died. None of those Monarchists were kings, but they are all trying to be. They'll take your ice away from you. Stick with us, and you'll be sucking on ice cubes and drinking ice water till it comes out of your ears."

VP Patsy sat listening to Cornball's spiel with interest until one of his computer nerds told him someone wanted a copy of the map with the location of the ocean of ice on it. Patsy had forgotten to update his copy of the map, as per Comingal's instructions, but he thought he remembered where Comingal wanted the ocean to be located. He didn't want to go back to Comingal and admit he forgot, so he put what he thought was the right location for the ice on his map and sent it out. Patsy's location wasn't precisely the same as Comingal's or Cornball's, but it was close to the other two locations.

Comingal had been sending his map, as interest demanded, to anyone who asked. Cornball sent many copies of his map, and Patsy's computer people were busily sending Patsy's map. Patsy and Cornball didn't think the location was very important because the ice didn't exist anyway. Only Comingal thought the location was important.

Patsy returned from his map-sending duties to listen to Cornball spew vitriolic invective at the Monarchists. Cornball was doing really well until one of his callers began speaking about other things. She was really down in the dumps, and close to tears. She said she knew it wasn't right for her to be in Hell, and wanted to know what the Democrats were going to do about it. If they could find ice water in Hell, who knows to what heights they might ascend; they might even know a way to get her out of Hell.

Cornball didn't want to lose a good Ice Water In Hell Democracy supporter, and he truly enjoyed using his considerable talents to help women in distress.

Cornball began one of his most compassionate explanations of the situation to the lady in distress, "You poor, sweet thing, you are probably here for the same reason we are. There was some kind of bureaucratic error or something. None of us are supposed to be here, but we couldn't get God to review our case. He sent a rabid Republican named Clause to make sure we all ended up in Hell. God made a mistake, but we couldn't get him to admit it. He was judgmental. He was unfair to us. We deserved another chance. God didn't have any right to put us in this summer home for demented Republicans."

Suddenly, Cornball just disappeared. VP Patsy had been watching Cornball closely. Patsy hoped to get a few pointers as an aid to his hoped-for rise to rhetorical perfection in power politics. VP Patsy was astounded by Cornball's sudden disappearance.

Patsy went immediately to Comingal's semi-private office and reported Cornball's untimely disappearance. Comingal hung his head in disappointment for a few moments before he said, "Things were going so well. We were beginning to turn the corner on our consensus-building project. Now my best man is gone, and you don't know how or where he went. Keep putting our message out as fast as you can. Maybe we can win without Cornball's personal touch. I'll get with Bullman the first chance I have. Bullman may have some way of finding him."

Cornball's disappearance made Comingal tense, and his disappointment drove him to distraction. Every time he saw the light getting brighter at the end of the tunnel, something happened to dim it. He needed some kind of very special diversion to relax him, just a quick vacation from the many misfortunes of political life. In a place with no pleasant diversions, he naturally thought of Nadine and her inviting offer to do anything for him: "Anything at all."

Comingal realized his intentions for Nadine might possibly be a violation of the Virtues of Hell, but he was in no mood for virtue or for the Virtues. He decided to go for broke. He ordered everyone out of his semi-private office except Nadine. Comingal viewed the beautiful Nadine as she quietly worked at her computer for a moment, and then said, "Nadine, sweet, sweet, Nadine, stand up and take off your clothes, and that's an order!"

"It's so hot in here," Nadine replied. "I don't mind if I do." She rose slowly from her not-quite-so-hot chair, shook her hair loose around her shoulders, and gave Comingal a sexy smile. Nadine slowly began to unbutton her blouse.

Comingal stood up and came close as she began unbuttoning her blouse. When she had unbuttoned the third button, Comingal reached out to put his hand inside her loosened blouse. His hand didn't quite fondle the breast it was aimed at. He disappeared from his office and found himself teetering on the cliff overlooking the Lake of Fire. His breast-grasping hand was still extended. Comingal could feel his hand, stretched out above the Lake of Fire, absorbing the heat from the cauldron of hot lava. One of the boiling bubbles of lava spurted from the Lake close enough to engulf his extended hand. He lunged backward to avoid the hot, gooey bubble and landed on the volcanic rock at the edge of the cliff.

Comingal hadn't bothered to look into the Lake of Fire while he was living on its edge. He had been afraid of the danger if he got too close. Since he had inadvertently gotten close, and thought Nadine might be in the lake, he thought it would be a good idea to look. He would shout some encouraging words if he saw Nadine. His quick glimpse, while he was teetering on the edge of the cliff above it, had shown him nothing of Nadine or the fury of the Lake. He twisted around to draw himself to the edge, cautiously extended his head over the cauldron, and took a long look down. He saw a large number of people in the lava, but Nadine wasn't in sight.

Most of the unfortunates in the Lake were too busy, trying to reach the edge of the cliffs where they could climb out, to be making noises about being there. Writhing in the lava, just a short distance from where Comingal had been looking for the lovely Nadine Crumpet, was Cornball, yelling, "You got to get me out of here, Comingal. This damn stuff is hotter than Hell; see if you can find a rope somewhere. I'll wait here."

Nadine, by her willingness to help Comingal's worm crawl a little faster or maybe a little farther, had also violated the Virtues, but not as much as Comingal. Nadine also disappeared from the Democrat office at the same time as Comingal. Unfortunately, Nadine reappeared standing with her blouse half opened in the office of, and directly in front of, Pravus Maximus, the maximum pervert and hopeful emperor of the Monarchists.

There were girls stationed on the outside of Pravus's office, but not in it. The guard girls' job was to keep other girls out of Pravus's office. Pravus Maximus had little to no sexual control of himself, and the guard girls' job was to prevent their pervert leader's many trips to the Lake of Fire for his mindless sexual attacks against female inmates, especially during the Monarchists' heated campaign against the Democrats. Pravus's worm was much faster then Comingal's, so it made it to the Lake of Fire quicker and more often than Comingal's.

Nadine's sudden appearance with her boobs nearly exposed blew the self control Pravus might have had under other circumstances. He sat in stunned, eye-bulging disbelief for a few seconds before his perverted mind shifted into high gear. It dawned on him that the most delectable and enticing stack of feminine curves he had ever seen actually stood within his grasp. Pravus leaped to his feet, vaulted over his desk, raced across the office, lunged forward with arms outstretched to grab Nadine, puckered his lips, and kissed Cornball in the lake of Fire.

Cornball saw Pravus's pucker coming at him full speed, and felt Pravus's arms bringing him to Pravus's unavoidable pucker. Cornball dodged, but Pravus still laid a smeary kiss on cornball's cheek. Cornball screamed like a mashed cat, "Get the hell away from me, you crazy bastard. Ain't no place safe?"

Pravus, with the heat of his ardor cooled by the Lake of Fire, tried to explain himself. "I was trying to kiss a very beautiful girl, but..."

"I ain't a girl," screamed Cornball, "and anyone who'd try to kiss a girl in the Lake of Fire is crazy. Get your crazy hands off of me."

Pravus took his hands away from Cornball's face and gave Cornball a shove to show he wasn't a crazy bastard. Cornball took the shove as an unacceptable response to his rejection of the crazy bastard's intentions for a Lake of Fire romance. Cornball swung his fist over the lava and punched Pravus in the nose, which was a violation of the Virtue of Unacceptable Aggression. They were both already suffering the worst-case treatment for Virtue violators, so the punch only separated the two a few feet. Hell's reaction to Cornball's Virtue violation moved Cornball toward the cliff and Pravus toward the center of the lake.

Pravus's barbarian guard girls heard the noise caused by Pravus's attempted molestation of Nadine. They entered their dear leader's office and found the partially exposed Nadine with Pravus nowhere in sight. They didn't need to be really smart to figure out where Pravus could be found. The biggest guard girl backed Nadine into a corner and demanded, "Who are you and where are you from? You aren't from our subdivision!"

Nadine, not knowing she was speaking to the archenemies of the Democrats, replied, "I'm from the Democrat subdivision. I don't know how I got here or where here is."

"It's none of your business where here is," replied the Amazonian guard. "What are you Democrats doing that would bring you here?"

"I don't know," answered Nadine. "I was in President Comingal's office alone with the President. Mr. Cornball is missing, and the President was upset; now I'm here. What do you people do here? Maybe we Democrats can help you. We love to help people. President Comingal is forming a democratic government for all of the people in Hell. We know where Satan hid an ocean of ice, and we are trying to give it to everybody."

One of the shorter female guards said, "She's a spy. She came here to put Pravus in the Lake of Fire so the Democrats can take over Hell. They think we're so stupid we don't know there is no ice. We better get rid of her before Pravus returns. You know him, if he sees her again, the Democrats might succeed."

Those unfortunate enough to be in the Lake of Fire weren't there permanently. They were able to move in the hot lava and, with some effort, and depending on how close each is to the center of the Lake, work their way to the edge of the Lake, climb the surrounding cliffs, and get out.

Cornball's temper finally cooled enough for him to look around. He was pretty close to the cliff Comingal had peered over while he witnessed the bitterly contested romance between Cornball and Pravus Maximus. Cornball could see the rough texture of the cliff, and he discovered a place he thought he could climb to the top not too far from Comingal. Cornball worked his arms and body against the lava, and with great effort, arrived at his chosen place to climb the cliff.

Pravus's guard girls, wanting Nadine to be gone before Pravus returned for a repeat performance, gave her directions to return to her own subdivision. The beautiful Nadine's passage around the Lake of Fire was easy to follow by the volume of her attackers popping into the Lake of Fire as she passed by. The volume of new entrants into the Lake of Fire slowed a little after she buttoned her blouse, but they didn't stop flipping into the lake until she finished her trip.

Comingal had no way of helping Cornball out of the Lake of Fire. There are no ropes in Hell, and Cornball was too hot to touch, but Cornball did manage to get to the top of the cliff by himself. During their post Lake of Fire conversation, Comingal figured out why Cornball was tossed into the Lake of Fire. Comingal didn't mention the reason for his own near disaster in the same lake, but he told Cornball to watch his mouth and never talk to anyone about being sent to Hell. Cornball's mouth was about as uncontrollable as Pravus's perversions, so Comingal decided to have Patsy keep an eye on Cornball to keep him in operation.

The Democrat subdivision was in turmoil when Comingal and Cornball returned. Things had gotten so bad there was no round of congratulations for Cornball's escape from the Lake of Fire. The Monarchists had discovered the Democrats' three different locations for the ocean of ice. The Monarchists' lucky discovery gave them the ammunition they needed to beat back the Democrats' gains in forging their consensus for the Ice Water in Hell Democracy. The terms *liars* and *frauds* were prominent in the Monarchist's denunciation of the Democrat claim of three oceans of ice.

Grossious the Insane fielded the most sarcastic comment. "With three oceans of ice surrounding his castle, Lucifer must be getting pretty cold up there. The first project for our empire will be to take some of our excess lava to his freezing castle to warm him up."

The Monarchists didn't mention the lies they told, or their own scam about the existence of an ocean of ice, but that was just part of the game. The Monarchists did try to float the lie that their original map was the only true map. They also told all and hellish sundry that the Democrats' three different maps were proof of Democrat lies.

The Democrats didn't do so badly either. They, in their usual post-disaster caucus, decided the best defense was to blame the Monarchists for the three locations. They spread the word that making it appear there were three different locations was necessary to keep the Monarchists from knowing where the ice was really located. If the Monarchists knew where the ice really was, they would send crews of workers to it, steal as much of it as they could, put guards around what they couldn't steal, and cheat all of the people in Hell out of their share of the ice.

The new lie worked as well as could be expected in an essentially perverse population. However, the Monarchists developed a counter plan after Pravus Maximus, who had been in the Lake of Fire many times, managed a quick escape.

On Pravus's return, he was told the beautiful Nadine was a spy sent by the Democrats to spread ruin in the Monarchist's camp. Pravus racked his faulty brain for a means of revenge, but he didn't know how to fight an idea like democracy. He finally had to admit he didn't understand it. He had lower his exalted opinion of his majestic intellect and ask for help. After a quick search, discovered among his associates was a man from Greece who claimed he knew what a democracy was supposed to be. The Greek explained to Pravus that a real democracy would put the majority of people in Hell in charge of everything all of the time. Pravus instinctively knew tyrants like his opponents weren't going to let loose of any power they could keep. Pravus Maximus formed his plan!

The real coup in Pravus's plan was in his use of the communication system. He moved all of his telephones close together, and that allowed him to make a speech that reached one hundred prospective constituents, give or take a few, at the same time. The one hundred listeners included as many people on each of the listeners' phones who could hear most of what was said. Pravus's operators could only call one person at a time, so the listener gathering process was lengthy, but still a big improvement. The phone handlers would bring the gathered phones to Pravus as soon as everything was ready. Pravus could speak to all of the listeners using the entire collection of phones. The time it took to accomplish this new use of modern technology didn't bother the people of Hell. People in Hell are very bored, and no one minds being on hold for a long time. Any phone call is an interesting diversion, especially a call filled with the certainty of some enjoyable skullduggery.

The operators finally informed the listeners that Pravus Maximus, the great leader and pioneer of the Monarchist cause, had an important message for them. The phones were ready, and Pravus boomed his loudest in a way Cornball would admire, "This is Pravus Maximus speaking. I have the unfortunate duty to report to you that there are vipers in our midst, vipers planning to steal your future of cooling comfort. They are using fraud and deceit that is unheard of in the history of Hell. The lying vipers present themselves to you as builders of a democracy. They would have you believe they will put you, their victims, in charge of Hell if they become the leaders—but here you must take warning. Democracy has no real leaders. Democracy gives supreme power to the majority of the people, and that means all of the people in Hell, not just the majority of Democrats.

"The viperous frauds have no way of knowing what the majority of people will decide. The people of Hell have no means of informing them, except by telephone, and there aren't enough democrats to make or take that many telephone calls. Even more, democracy has no rule of law except laws made by you. The laws of a voiceless majority who are not consulted can be twisted into anything the Democrats want it to be. The vipers are planning to be your dictators, not your benefactors."

Pravus paused a moment for his words to sink in, but not long enough for anyone to think he was finished and hang up on him. He began again in a more conciliatory tone, "We Monarchists are the arch enemies of the deceit and fraud the Democrats are using to crush your hopes. We will share our benevolent rule of law and our royal management with all equally. To support the Monarchist cause for equality and justice is to end the reign of viperous terror seeking the ruin of your hopes for a cool, relaxing future. We are leaders who take advice from our subjects, and turn that advice into the worthwhile fulfillment of their hopes and dreams of future comfort.

"The Democrats have nothing to offer except their many lies about the location of the ice they hope will make them masters of Hell. They have no hope of a success for the people of Hell, only hopes of cheating each of you out of your long-awaited comfort.

"We have discovered the true location of the ocean of ice. Our agents have, moments before I called you, brought the location of your common bonanza of comfort to me. You may view that on the computer screens in your subdivisions if you will be patient for only a few more moments. I wish all of you good fortune in your royal future. This is Pravus Maximus, your friend, wishing you a cooler journey through eternity. Good-bye."

"Pravus, we don't have a new location for that ice," exclaimed one of the operators.

"We do too," growled Pravus, pointing to the Democrat's map on the computer "It's right there." Pravus's pointing finger decided the ocean's new location was to the left of the Democrat's three locations, making the fourth Ocean of Ice look like one more ornament on Satan's castle. For some strange reason, all of Hell's mapmakers seemed to think oceans are round.

Pravus erased the Democrat locations for the Democrats' three oceans of ice and fielded the Monarchists' map as having the only true ocean of Ice. He remained on his new phone system for many hours to give his Pravus Maximus speech its maximum public exposure.

The Democrats eventually discovered Pravus's newest effort to cheat them out of their opportunity to rule Hell. Countering Pravus's Cornball imitation, his new map, his new method of using the phones, and the fact that the Democrats had a public-relations problem became their first priorities. The new caucus in

Comingal's office was tense. Comingal asked, "Does anyone have a plan?"

Cornball, with no plan, opened the meeting. "Those dirty liars said we don't have a rule of law. We had a rule of law."

"Is that right?" asked Harve Crik. "What was our rule of law?"

"We Democrats had a constitutional rule of law in the USA," defended Cornball.

Flim Flamm gave Cornball a disgusted look and then said, "The rule of law we Democrats had in the United States was the Constitutional law of the Republic of the United States. We Democrats had no rule of law of our own. Do you want to start a Republic in Hell? A republic must have a rule of law, but a democracy does not. No one in Hell obeys rules except the Virtues of Hell, and no one knows exactly what they are. We have to stick to our democracy and majority rule. We don't need to start a different argument with the with the Monarchists about who has the best rule of law."

Comingal interjected, "Our major publicity problems are the accusations of no discernible leaders, no rule of law for our democracy, and three locations for our ocean of ice. We must settle those problems or go down to defeat. We can use the phones the way Pravus does, but those three things are hitting us right in the butt. I want to hear present solutions—not discussions about what we didn't have in the past."

Harve Crik remarked, "Our rule of law must be binding on everyone else but seem to be binding on us. I think we can pull it off by insisting on our own democratic distribution system for the cubes of ice. We'll say our distribution system keeps the people from being cheated by the Monarchists. We don't need to mention that our bureaucrats will be the ones employed in the distribution system. We must allow a few others in on it so we can say it is a non-partisan system. As long as we Democrats control the flow of ice, we control the power of government."

Flim Flamm added, "Our good leadership can be included as the only reasonable choice, necessitated by the need to control the bureaucracy engaged in the distribution of the ice cubes, and also in the manner in which the masses receive the ice cubes. Our control of every cube of ice must appear to be regulated by the majority. Regulation by the majority can be sold as superior to a rule of law. Our regulation of the total efforts of the many who desire the ice must appear as a necessity of majority rule to insure equal treatment. Our leadership must be presented as the only means to guarantee a process for our Progressive distribution of the abundant ice supply to all for eternity.

"At this early time in the establishment of our caring bureaucracy, it would be a mistake to mention the collection of taxes before the masses receive the ice cubes. If we introduce our democracy in small doses, it will be easier to sell."

"I don't understand what the hell you said, Flim Flamm, but the

Monarchists shouldn't get any ice," Cornball railed. "They have lied about us from the beginning. We shouldn't help our enemies become prosperous."

"I like what Harve and Flim Flamm have put together," commented Comingal, "but we can't freeze the Monarchists out of the ice. We can make it difficult for them to get their share, but we have to give them some ice. We can accuse them of being rich Monarchists, and put a bigger tax on their ice after things are running smoothly, but we don't want to appear unfair in the beginning."

Cornball howled, "We're talking about the damn ice as though it really exists. Remember, there ain't no damn ice."

Comingal ignored Cornball's untimely revelation and said, "Harve, you and Flim begin working up some kind of a document we can use. We'll need some easy to understand talking points for the telephone operators. Patsy, you and Cornball put as many phones together as you can possibly get in a small space. I'll spring our rule of law on our constituents, and I'll answer the leadership accusation. I already have an explanation for the three locations of the ice. I want to talk to as many people as I can, so be creative and get as many phones as you can in the smallest space. Get that done as soon as possible."

Comingal's substitute for a rule of law was written. It outlined the responsibilities of the democratic leaders. The phones were put together just as Comingal had asked. Comingal began his opposing diatribe to the Monarchists' diatribe in a quiet dignified voice. "We, the people of Hell, are establishing a democracy to insure that each of you will have an equal share in the surplus of ice. Our democracy will be your guarantee that your government will work quickly and efficiently on your behalf. The Monarchists would have you believe we have no rule of law, and even worse, no leadership to accomplish this great task of distributing the bounty, which as I speak, is speeding its way into your future. The Monarchists have proven they know nothing of democracy and nothing of our leadership. I am here to disprove the misguided, unfair, and uninformed rumors spread by their poorly equipped and ignorant leaders.

"The rule of democracy is as ancient as the isles of Greece. *Democracy* means the majority rules, rule by the ruled. Those fortunate people of Hell who are privileged to become citizens in a democracy are, in reality, the dictators of the democracy—a dictatorship of the people.

"Our democracy has been wronged by those with royal ambitions and would seem to those denizens of fraud to have no leadership. We cannot expect royal pretenders to non-existent thrones to understand why the citizens in a democracy are in total control of their leaders. We cannot expect Monarchists to understand how the supreme power of a democracy rises up from its citizens, nor why it cannot, cannot, descend from its leaders to become a yoke of political power on its citizens. Monarchists cannot be expected to understand that the authority of government, descending from its leadership to its citizens, is not democracy but tyranny.

"Pravus Maximus has told you there are no leaders in the democratic cause. He lied—I am a leader in that cause. My associates and advisors are leaders in that cause. Our coworkers are leaders in that cause. You, the pain-filled citizens seeking our expert and honest leadership, are leaders in that cause. We! The democratic leaders are putting the people of Hell in charge of our democracy. We are bringing you the bounty of our concern for your future welfare. The bounty of the cooling ocean of ice is so close it can virtually be seen just over your horizon.

"You may ask, *How much is included in the duty of these wonderful leaders needed so desperately to protect you from the pirates of your future comfort?* I will answer your question from the wealth of my experiences as a leader of my proud democratic nation. It is our duty to establish democracy, equality, and social justice for the citizens of this eternity. It is our duty to secure the ocean of ice for your benefit. It is our duty to redistribute the bounty of the ocean to each of you equally. It is our duty to keep supply lines open so a continual supply of ice can be delivered to every person and community. It is our duty to listen to your counsel in making every decision we must make as leaders. It is our duty to protect you and the supply of ice from Hell's many predators who would bring you and your future to ruin. If others who are less qualified, and without our expertise in democracy, are allowed to expend their calamitous efforts on this project, we cannot be responsible for the chaos and misery it will cause. They will take the ice from the poor and give it to the rich.

"We are democratic leaders, and we are at your command. The Monarchists are leaders who will command you. You and I must fight this desperate battle for a comfortable future together. I have worked so hard for your success. Now, I must ask all of you who will share in the cool bounty of the future to work just as hard for your own success. To succeed, you must become our supporters. You must support our efforts to secure a fair and prosperous future for you. Together, tomorrow is ours. Divided, tomorrow is lost. Your future and the future of our democracy are in your hard-working hands.

"I must also address our purposeful and necessary deception of our Monarchist enemies concerning the position of the peoples' ocean of ice. We could not allow the real location of your ocean of ice to fall into the Monarchists' unclean hands. We deceived them to protect your interests and to force them to give you their false location of your property. We, of course, know the real location of the virtually eternal supply of ice.

"If our methods were confusing, they were calculated to confuse your enemies, the Monarchists, and to protect your property. Please remain with we who are fighting in your battle for equality and social justice. Allow us to protect your future from the tyranny of the Monarchists. I, President Comingal, the chief protector of your future comfort, bid you good day."

Comingal, like Pravus, kept the phones hot for many hours repeating his message. Finally, the individual operators, supplied with the democrat talking points, began using the phones in their more personal manner. The returns from Comingal's speech were good, and once again, the democrats began to gain the high ground in the battle for political supremacy in Hell.

Unfortunately, one of the phone calls made during Comingal's personally massaged message was inadvertently made to Pravus Maximus's office. Pravus was livid with rage. "Comingal is the slickest enemy I've ever had. He told everyone how he intends to control them and the ice supply, and he made it sound like he's doing everyone in Hell the biggest favor of their lives."

Forgetting for the moment that the ice was as much of a Monarchist fraud as it was a Democrat fraud, he shouted, "That's our ice! Comingal and his crew of liars are not taking it from us. We will not allow a democrat empire to rise above ours. Comingal's lies and insults will not go unpunished. I want a meeting of the Council of Kings, Attila the Red, and all of the others. We have some planning to do."

The Council of Kings assembled very slowly. Each of the future kings felt Satan would throw him into the Lake of Fire, if he were discovered leaving his subdivision. Personal safety requires cautious travel. The future kings passed slowly and carefully through the subdivisions they had to cross to get to Pravus Maximus's meeting. They cautiously arranged for friendly lookouts to protect them as they sneaked around the Lake of Fire.

Attila the Red did not attend just any Council of Kings meeting. He only attended if the situation was desperate. For this meeting, Attila was especially careful. He had been in the Lake of Fire almost as many times as Pravus, but not for attacking women. Attila the Red attacked, with malice aforethought, and deadly force, anyone who got in his way, whether they were male or female. Actually, he ended up in the Lake of Fire an instant before each attack, but he would have been attacking with deadly force and malice aforethought if he could have managed to get it done. He didn't learn a lesson from his many trips into the Lake of Fire. Attila, with no understanding of the Virtues of Hell, thought it was just his bad luck for Satan or one of his Gray Angels to be watching when he got mad.

While Pravus nervously waited for help from his future staff, Comingal's democrats gained ground. Comingal's speech and the democrat talking points were going over like free beer at Friday Night Bowling. Pravus's fraudulent monarchy seemed doomed to be defeated by the climbing popularity of Comingal's phony democracy. If he couldn't come up with a new and more impressive plan, Pravus felt the battle was lost.

Pravus was at his wits' end. He couldn't come up with a plan of his own, and none of his advisors were of any help. His hatred for the democrats grew with each disappointing report from his telephone operators. His only hope was in the successful plotting that might be accomplished during the meeting of the Council of Kings.

The Best Fraud Battle

Attila the Red was the last to arrive for Pravus's meeting. He brought three bodyguards with him to insure his safe arrival. The three bodyguards were not for Attila's personal safety; their job was to keep Attila from assaulting anyone. If Attila assaulted someone he didn't like—and he didn't like anyone—it would draw Satan's angels to the area to throw Attila into the Lake of Fire, or so Attila thought. His cautionary measures to avoid Satan or his Gray Angels made his journey to the meeting a slow process.

Pravus opened the meeting; "You have all seen the results of Comingal's latest deceptions to cheat us and our empire out of taking over Hell from Satan. Comingal's plan is a good one, and we must come up with something even better to defeat him. What we come up with at this meeting will decide whether we, or Comingal, runs Hell. I need your ideas. Who has one?" Pravus scanned the quiet room for responses until his eyes rested on Ilene Bogus.

Ilene was the only female in the king business, and Pravus's attendants seated her on the opposite side of the table from Pravus. If he dived for her, the other kings would either protect Ilene from Pravus's advances or Pravus from the Lake of Fire, depending on which of the two ideas they liked best. Pravus wasn't staring at Ilene because he thought she would be the one with the idea, but Ilene thought he was.

Ilene Bogus's stare-inspired idea was a credible one. "Comingal has entirely ignored the women of Hell. His democracy gives political power to men only, and we women are never mentioned. Half of the inmates are women, and we deserve as much power as you men. Why should women have ice cubes doled out to them by men?" Ilene was on a roll, and she continued, "And further more, why in Hell must they be cubes? An ice cube, if my memory still works, is a small piece of ice. Why aren't they talking about blocks of ice or slabs of ice instead of cubes? Why aren't they talking about huge rivers of ice water coming into the subdivisions like a torrent of comfort to cool the Lake of Fire instead of a mouthful of ice whenever one of their bureaucrats decides to let us have it?" With a few passion-filled words, Ilene summed up her feelings, "We women will not put up with this Democrat travesty. We women demand leadership that will bring comfort to us without bowing and scraping to some stupid bureaucrat. Our imperial leadership is the only acceptable leadership for the job."

Ilene blew Pravus's mind. He had never thought of women in any way except in his own sexually perverted way. He was so happy with Ilene's idea that, for a moment, he forgot she was a female. Pravus exclaimed, "That's it! You've given us the fatal counter punch to Comingal's democracy. We can play on the women's feelings and the men's at the same time. No one wants their ice handed out to them in little pieces by a bunch of bureaucrats. We'll promise equality to women and rivers of ice to everyone. We'll promise to cool the Lake of Fire."

Attila the Red and Grossious the Insane didn't like Ilene's plan. They had teamed together before the meeting and hatched a plan of their own. They wanted to scrap Ilene's plan in favor of a frontal assault on the Democrat subdivision. Attila expounded, "This back and forth political crap will be the death of us. We come up with a plan; then they come up with a plan. Then we come up with a better plan; then they come up with an even better plan. It will never end. We'll be here until Hell freezes over with nothing to show for the time we're losing but plans and more plans.

"Grossious and I can field enough warriors to take the Democrats in an hour. All they have is a bunch of bureaucrats who couldn't fight their way into the Lake of Fire. Grossious and I checked every subdivision on our way here. Satan and his Gray Angels haven't been seen since the beginning of this political do-nothing exercise. Now is the time to strike—before Satan notices where we are and what we're doing. Grossious is with me all the way on this, and so is everyone else in our subdivisions."

Pravus Maximus didn't like the assault plan. It wasn't that he objected to the violence of it; Pravus was afraid the other contenders for kings would choose Attila for emperor if it worked. Keeping in mind his fear of a successful assault, Pravus lied, "I think your assault plan is very good, but it is premature. I would back it personally if Ilene's idea didn't have such a sure-fire way to win. Comingal can't possibly come up with a better idea. With Ilene's plan, the people will see a trickle of ice coming from Comingal and his Democrats, but the trickle will become a torrent of ice coming from us Monarchists.

"We have him beat, but to prove it, the warriors among us must be patient for a while longer. If Ilene's plan fails, we will attack just as you and Grossious suggested, and all of us will join in the attack. If we all attack, the Democrats will be in the Lake of Fire in minutes."

The ersatz kings voted, and Ilene's plan, backed by Pravus's illustrious leadership, won the vote. The kings left for their own subdivisions to wait for the success or failure of Ilene's plan. The amount of time each would wait depended on how bloodthirsty he was.

Pravus reassembled his telephone network and brought out the new Monarchists' Party platform. "Dear friends in Hell, the Democrats would have you believe their distribution network will bring cooling prosperity to all of you. Nothing could be further from the truth. They offer small cubes of ice from a vast ocean to slake your thirst for brief moments before you must return to them for more; and, at what cost? We Monarchists offer rivers of ice water coursing through each of your thirsty subdivisions, icebergs as big as ships bringing you cargoes of cooling refreshment.

"In contrast to the sexually desolate Democrats, we offer it to all of the citizens of Hell, not just the men. Ladies, with the Monarchist plan, it won't be necessary for you to enlist the aid of men to secure your share of ice in this crude, rude place. Unlike the Democrats, we Monarchists offer the ice to both sexes freely. There may be some slight charge for overhead, but we Monarchists are a non-profit monarchy. What we have, we give freely to all women and men. The Democrats' ice-rationing system is nothing more than a method of profiteering by unsavory politicians who care nothing for your welfare. Queen Ilene Bogus guarantees with her personal word that all women will be given equal shares of ice with the men.

"My dear friends of the Monarchy do not be confused or fearful of the tyrants who spew their verbal vomit from only one subdivision. They are only Hell's varmints, and they are too few and too weak for the monumental task that must be performed. The Democrats are not strong enough to bring the long-awaited cool comfort to us all. We Monarchists have many subdivisions, some filled with strong, friendly warriors like Ilene Bogus, Attila the Red, and Grossious the Insane to protect and serve you. Their peaceful help and our non-profit monarchy will insure all of us the large work force and organization necessary to free the ice from its vast ocean and bring its endless comfort to your waiting hands. To complete this act of philanthropy, we must have your support to overcome the deceit and profiteering of our Democratic opponents. Convince your friends and inspire your neighbors to support your great cause. This is Pravus Maximus, your obedient servant, saying good-bye and wishing you cool fortune in your future."

Pravus didn't make the mistake of using one of his phones to alert his opponents as the Democrats had done. The Democrats realized something was up when their huge consensus began falling lower and lower. Trouble in the non-political subdivisions often exceeded the pushing and shoving stage, and many occupants blamed Satan for throwing them into the Lake of Fire. Few of the inmates knew what a Virtue violation was or realized a serious Virtue violation caused a trip to the Lake of Fire. Their ignorance of that fact was one of Satan's most impressive weapons.

The Democrats pieced Pravus's message together from the friendly reports and nasty accusations they received from constituents and opponents. They finally realized what the problem was and, of course, caucused to cure it. Comingal invited the usual band of his seasoned advisors, but this time they were joined by Bullman.

Comingal summarized the problems. "We are weak, and that criticism is true. We need to make—or fake—some allies, and it's difficult to fake them. I'll take care of the criticism about not inviting women; that's a piece of cake. Our biggest problem is their promise of a river of ice and blocks of ice floating down the river to the subdivisions. Our 'Ice Cube in Every Mouth' slogan was good, but the Monarchists destroyed it when they promised blocks of ice. The Monarchists' non-profit monarchy is hogwash, but we have to handle it. Who has the ideas?"

Cornball was nervously moving around in quick little steps while Comingal spoke. In his outraged condition, Cornball couldn't manage the wait for a real idea, so he just burst forth, "Those Monarchists are a bunch of dirty sons-of-bitches. They can't produce anything they said. There ain't no ice. We should tell the people the truth and find some other way to rule Hell. We don't need a bunch of subdivisions to do that. The fewer people ruling, the better it is. The Monarchists don't have a plan; they just wait for us to say something and then they think up a bigger lie. The first liar doesn't have a chance!"

Comingal aimed the mean side of his mouth at Cornball. "Cornball, shut up! I want ideas, not another broadside of meaningless accusations. Anyone have any *ideas*?"

Bullman pulled their melting irons out of the hot fire of having no allies. "I've been talking to the Black Angels, and they want to come in with us. They are willing to settle for a new location after we beat Satan, if the new location is far enough from the Lake of Fire. The Black Angels are the strongest allies we can get. Attila the Red and Grossious the Insane know that all of their warriors thrown together can't beat the Black Angels.

"Since there is no ice and there won't be any work involved, the Black Angels have agreed to let us say they are willing to help with the work of distributing the ice. They agree for us to use their names any way we want to, and that should solve both our rivers of ice water and blocks of ice problems."

Patsy added, "We can invite everyone in Hell to help us free the ice from the ocean. That should settle their worries about not being included in its distribution. We can make a big thing of inviting women to work beside the men."

Comingal was satisfied. "We'll do it just like before. Put the phones together and make up some talking points for the phone operators. Patsy, tell John Caughess and Bill Presser to come into my office. I want them to write my speech. This is too important to wing it. I want a hammer speech that will put the last nail in the coffin of the Monarchists' lies."

The speech-writing experts finished the last-nail-in-the-coffin speech, and Comingal stepped up to the phones. Hell's inmates were well aware of the nature of the battle, and some of them had become convinced the ice really existed. No inmate hung up his phone. The phone holding inmates of Hell waited in eager anticipation for the next absurd promise to be made by the leader of the newcomers to Hell.

Comingal began in his usual dignified manner. "Dear friends, we share your pain caused by the constant setbacks to our hard work for the greater good of us all. We have been unjustly accused of cheating you, and especially our women supporters, of an abundant share in the bounty of the ocean of ice waiting to be freed for your use. It is tragic that the lying Monarchists could not understand our truthful message. They have traded the truth for visions of self-promoting grandeur.

"Our former message to our dear friends did not specify the difference between men and women for excellent reasons. Our former message was gender perfect and would have lost its gender perfect quality if we had recognized one gender above the others. All seven genders are as welcome as the flowers of spring by us Democrats. Our friends in all seven of the perfect genders are invited to help us free the ice and bring good fortune to the communities throughout the broadest regions of Hell.

"We Democrats have been accused of being too few for this great task. We are accused of being without allies to protect the cooling supplies from predators. We are accused of being without the numerical strength to manage the distribution of the magnificent store of ice in a fair manner. We have been accused of being too weak to free the ice from its oceanic repository. All of the accusations are Monarchist lies. We could easily do everything alone with the enormous number of Democrats we have in our personal subdivision.

"We, because of our love of everyone in Hell, have accepted an alliance with the kindly Black Angels. These champions of the weak have promised to guard the workers in the ice fields. They have volunteered to use their great strength for the difficult task of breaking the ice into manageable proportions for all of us. The Black Angels will risk the toughness of their great wings to dig the canals that must be used to bring the ice to the subdivisions. Finally, they have promised to keep the subdivisions safe from attacking predators such as Attila the Red, Grossious the Insane, Ilene Bogus, and all of the other Monarchists' warriors of doom to your future prosperity.

"Our allies and supporters in the outlying subdivisions are real and powerful. They include all seven of the perfect genders. The Monarchists have no allies. The Monarchists have only themselves, and most of them are of imperfect gender. Our gender-perfect message would, of course, be unacceptable to those whose gender is uncertain. The Monarchists rail at us for offering the tantalizing hope of an ice cube in every mouth and assume an ocean would provide nothing more. Our original plans were made to supply Hell with a new order of comfort that is beyond anything the gender-imperfect personalities of the Monarchists could comprehend.

"Our original plan has not changed. I hope the fleshing out of its abundance has put to death the accusation of meagerness and, indeed, brought out the imperfect nature of its accusers. Those of you who support our democracy will prosper with all of the other gender-perfect inmates of Hell, and all of us are gender perfect, except within the Monarchist's subdivisions. Those who do not support us will remain in heated poverty, trapped among the imperfect natures of our accusers. Show your perfection; support our democracy. We welcome all of you as dear friends and coworkers on the cooling ocean of ice. All of the gender perfect people of Hell will be working at our side as we free the endless abundance of comforting ice for your benefit.

"I am your willing servant, Clint Comingal, wishing you cooling health during your eternal future. Good-bye!"

James Cornball was the first to question the wisdom of Comingal's speech. "What's all this gender stuff about, Comingal? I can only think of four. What will I tell people who want to know what the other three are?"

Comingal knew in his heart that he had made a good speech, and he didn't want to hear it criticized from his own camp. "Damn it, Cornball, you're the spinmeister. Make up three more genders and stop bothering me. I need to concentrate on the feedback from the field. I think we've got the Monarchists cold. They came here so long ago they won't know what *gender* means. We'll gain enough ground to beat them while they try to figure it out.

Comingal's speech played well in the hot, grimy regions of Hell. Most of the inmates had no idea what the word *gender* meant, but the word promised each a sort of perfection for whichever of the seven genders each happened to be, even if he couldn't figure out which of the perfect genders he was.

As welcome as modern-verbal disinformation was to most, it found little sympathy among the Monarchists. They were incensed by the ease with which the Comingal turned their best effort for a coup de grace into a cup of ash.

The Monarchists' pretenders for non-existent thrones began sneaking their way toward a meeting with Pravus Maximus even before he called for a meeting. Pravus Maximus, in fear that their unannounced disappearances from their subdivisions might mean they were coming to vent their disappointment on him, put extra guards around his perverted person for self protection. Pravus dispatched lookouts to the most favored routes of entry into his subdivision with instructions to inform him of any dangerous attitudes among his incoming royal associates.

The pretenders arrived with Attila the Red, as usual, being the last and most cautious. Pravus explained his extra guards by blaming a feared attack by the Democrats and Black Angels on the meeting of kings. The pretenders to the non-existent thrones, not knowing of Pravus's fear of them, applauded Pravus's foresight in protecting himself and them from the possible attack by Democrats and Black Angels. Pravus, realizing he had pulled it off one more time, resumed his imperial directorship of the Council of Kings with no more fear of being attacked by disappointed pseudo kings.

Ilene Bogus, whose plan was gendered out of business by Comingal and his two speechwriters, asked for an explanation of gender. She turned her gaze to each of the royal monuments to the king business, but only received their several blank stares in return.

Pravus Maximus felt it was his duty as the prospective emperor to start the ball rolling. "We can forget the perfect part of gender and settle for seven different kinds of people. The Democrats have categorized the seven kinds of inmates and invited each kind into their plan. We know two of the genders, male and female, but we don't know what the other five are. If any of you have an idea about how to figure this gender mess out, now is the time to speak."

Grossious the Insane interjected his own misunderstanding into the gender search. "Gender has nothing to do with male and female; that's sex, and there are only two. It has to do with the type of crimes people came to Hell for committing. The Democrats have found seven types they think are perfect. They want those perfect criminals on their team. They are scamming everyone else to make them think they are perfect. The Democrats have most of the inmates believing each of them is included on the gender-perfect Democrat team."

Attila the Red brought the ice scam problems back to a point somewhere near reality. "I'm tired of these lies about the stupid ice. We don't have any ice. We are not going to have any ice. The ice doesn't exist, and we have to stop treating our problems as though they will be solved by the next biggest lie about ice. The only problem is which of us is going to run Hell, and how we can take that leadership from the Democrats. I say we mount an assault and throw their stinking butts into the Lake of Fire. That will settle who the rulers of Hell are— once and for all."

Pravus wanted to avoid Attila's offer, but he had already promised Attila and Grossious an attack if Ilene's plan failed. There were eleven subdivisions in the Monarchists' circle around the Lake of Fire. Everyone in those eleven subdivisions knew both sides were lying about the ice, and most were beginning to tire of the lies and word games coming from the liars on both icy sides. A political revolt in the Monarchist subdivisions was looming. Pravus felt the pressure of that looming revolt on his shaky position as leader. He had to sanction the attack or be left behind, and being left behind was unthinkable for a hopeful but uncertain emperor. Pravus said, "If we are going to attack the Democrats, we need a tricky plan."

Attila the Red presented the plan he and Grossious the Insane had plotted before the meeting. "The only weapons we have are pieces of lava we've made into swords and knives. They aren't very good, but the Democrats don't have weapons of any kind. Seeing our weapons will fill them with fear. The fear may drive them to surrender without a fight. We don't want them to surrender before we push them into the Lake of Fire. We need to prove to everyone that we are the winners. Grossious and I have planned a way to lull them into thinking they can win.

"We'll make them think Ilene Bogus and her women warriors are the only ones attacking; even Democrats will think they can beat girls."

"You want me to be the general in charge of the attack and lead our troops to victory?" Ilene asked.

"Of course not," replied Attila. "We want you to *act* like you're in charge so the Democrats will fight. You're a woman; you can't be in charge. You and your troop of girls will act like you are the only ones attacking. Our real warriors will be far enough behind you so the Democrats won't see us. Your attack will make the Democrats think the attacked is only by a few women. After you begin your attack, and get the Democrats to fight, you and your girls will make a quick retreat to get out of our way. Us men will take over the action and finish it the right way."

Ilene was incensed; she knew her women were some of the bloodiest women fighters who ever lived. Attila the Red had just insulted all of Ilene's girl warriors. Ilene had no immediate response to the insult, but getting even for it was a no brainer. Ilene decided to act as though she was going along with Attila's plan, but she knew, in the certainty of her climbing anger, that her women warriors wouldn't be in the first line of attack against the Democrats.

Grossious the Insane, unaware of the certain doom of the Monarchists' battle plan, was so proud of his weaponry that he wanted to share his technical expertise with the other blood-seeking Monarchists about to launch their attack. "We have found a way to cool the lava thrown around the Lake of Fire when the bubbles burst. The stuff cools so slowly it can be hammered into swords and knives, and they can be made pretty sharp. Our weapons are far superior to those the rest of you have, and I'm willing to share my method of producing them with all of you before we attack. You'll be surprised at the quality of the armament we have been stockpiling for just such an emergency as this."

Grossious's magnanimous offer was a little late, but everyone acted surprised. Attila, Ilene, Pravus, and the rest of the king hopefuls had been using the same weapons and making process with the hot lava, but they hadn't told each other about it; friends don't tell friends everything, so Grossious had to be given sole credit for the discovery of a new technology.

The Monarchists male warriors' only battle plan was simplicity itself. Ilene and her women warriors would be on the front line of the attack. They would, with predictable feminine fears, retreat at the first sign of battle. Attila the Red and Grossious the Insane, with well-armed warriors, would lunge forward with malevolent intent immediately after Ilene's retreat. They would carry the battle to its natural masculine conclusion by defeating the Democrats and throwing the whole bunch into the Lake of Fire.

The kings from the other subdivisions would be behind Attila and Grossious with Pravus Maximus's troops bringing up the rear guard, just in case something went wrong and the Democrats found a way to fight all eleven subdivisions.

Pravus's private plan was to advance or retreat depending on how well the

Democrats were doing in their defense. If, as expected, the Democrats were easily beaten, Pravus would work his way to the head of the battle and take credit for the win. If the Black Angel's actually helped, and the Democrats won, Pravus would beat a hasty retreat to insure the safety of his unsavory person. Pravus, emphatically, believed that a bold plan must insure the safety of the bold planner.

The ersatz kingly warriors thought their biggest problem was getting to the battle without alerting Satan to the battle plan. They felt Satan was the wild card in the battle, but none of them knew how to plan around his unwelcome appearance. Their hope was that he would continue to remain absent from the conflict, and they were strengthened by the fact that none of them had seen him or his Gray Angels since it began.

The Monarchists' preparations around the Lake of Fire were something to behold. All political activities went on hold while the combatants concentrated on making swords and knives out of hot lava. Every bubble bursting over the Lake of Fire was farmed for its supply of lava thrown over the cliffs out of the Lake. The hot lava was picked up with tools made from previous pieces of cooled lava blown over the cliffs. The newly regurgitated lava was then quickly moved inside and under the cover of the subdivision buildings. Once hidden from Satan's prying eyes, the hot lava was pounded into something more useful to the war effort than a piece of soft, hot stuff. The amount of armament grew beyond anyone's needs, but old warriors are always wary of not having enough arms, and the Lake of Fire always had a generous supply of bursting bubbles of lava.

Queen Ilene Bogus brought her nearly unmanageable temper to the meeting of her formidable clan of lady warriors. The meeting had been called so Ilene could vent her dissatisfaction with her masculine royal partners. Her outraged expressions of hatred weren't the epitome of femininity, but they were direct. "Those filth- mouthed mongrel dogs calling themselves kings want us to act like we're going to fight the Democrats and then run away like we're scared. We can beat the Democrats without the lousy help of a bunch of phony kings, and we can beat the phony kings just as easily.

"Attila the Red and Grossious the Insane think the Democrats can beat us in the battle, and they are anxious to prove they can beat the Democrats. That cowardly Pravus will be so far behind everyone else he won't even be in the battle. We are not going to have our superior battle tactics insulted by those bragging, ignorant, useless men. We are not going to put ourselves below all of the other subdivisions by running from an easy fight. You and I will not be looked down upon by the inferior fighters in the ranks of a bunch of screwed up male perverts trying to become kings. We are the best of the best, and we are going to prove it.

"We all know this long-winded crap about an ocean of ice is being used to set up a power base for whoever runs Hell. There will be no democracy when it's finished, and there won't be a monarchy either. One group will be in control; the other will not. I suggest we change sides. We will throw our fighting abilities on the side of the Democrats. The Democrats have the Black Angels on their side. With us on the side of the Democrats, the Monarchists can't win. We will insist on keeping our own power structure in place, and become equal partners with the Democrats in running Hell."

A cheer went up from Ilene's ladies in arms, and the plan was set. Ilene left with a few of her girls to contact the Democrats and tell them of the Monarchists' battle plan. The other lady warriors followed in small groups, sneaking quietly through the Monarchists' subdivisions until Ilene's entire clan was brought slowly into the Democrat compound. The Monarchists didn't trip to Ilene's defection, and the feminist warriors' slow passage through their subdivisions didn't alarm the other royal aspirants.

Ilene and a few of her lady warriors, lacking in feminine beauty, but well endowed with weapons, entered the Democrat subdivision without incident and approached Comingal with their offer. Ilene stated the case. "We have split with the rotten collection of filth called Monarchists and have decided to join you Democrats in repelling their invasion of your subdivision. Naturally, there are some demands you have to meet, if you want our help. First, we will be equal partners in your democracy. We intend to share equally in the spoils of victory. Second, I remain in charge of my subdivision, and if you try interfering with us, we will put you the same place we are going to put the Monarchists. Third, we want to be in the front line of your troops when the filthy-dog Monarchist horde attacks you. We have a score to settle with them, and we intend to teach them that women fight better than men. Fourth, we know the ocean of ice is phony, and we are not helping in any public works programs you may have dreamed up—canal digging or anything else—while you try to convince everyone it's real.

My women are on their way here now, and they are armed to the teeth. If you accept my offer, they will fight on your side. If you don't accept my offer, we will stand and watch until the battle is over and then kick the winners into the Lake of Fire."

Comingal had no problem with one more equal partner who wanted nothing to do with his democracy. His plan didn't actually include a democracy, so that was never a problem. Like the democracy, he had no plan to share any of his future authority. Promising to share his authority was no more of a problem than sharing the democracy. He had some misgivings about a large number of well-armed women entering his subdivision. Comingal decided the armed females were to his advantage after Ilene's heated speech convinced him they really were pissed off with Pravus Maximus and the Monarchists.

Comingal was glad for Ilene's help, and his acceptance speech reflected his appreciation. "We, in our democracy, gladly accept your conditions. I am especially appreciative of your discovery of the true nature of the Monarchist scoundrels. They have never understood or appreciated the strength of ladies of quality, and you and your ladies certainly are of the highest quality."

Ilene interrupted him and asked, "Which of the perfect genders are my warriors, and what are the other six?"

Comingal was disconcerted by the question he had assigned Cornball to come up with an answer for, and couldn't himself. He could see she was a female through the grit covering her, but he felt uneasy about giving Ilene an answer for the other six genders. "You need to talk to James Cornball about that," replied Comingal. "James is in charge of the gender determination committee. He is very busy right now, but I will have him make a determination in the near future and inform you after it is done.

"The most important thing to do right now is for us to meet your lady warriors, make sure they know we are their friends, and place them in the best positions for the coming war." Ilene left Comingal to do as he suggested. Ilene didn't know that she would be even less informed after Cornball managed to think up three more genders.

Cornball had become almost euphoric with his telephone successes. The Monarchists had deserted the field of political battle, leaving the Democrats' propaganda effort running wild. Cornball reported, "The resistance to our democracy would be dying on the vine if there was a vine for it to die on. Our success is getting bigger in every subdivision we're talking to, and we are talking to all of them except the Monarchists. We could win an election if there was any way to vote. I think it's time for us to confront Satan with our reorganization of Hell."

"There is still the problem of the armed Monarchists coming at us," reminded Comingal, "and we don't know when they'll be here. We have to confront them first. We have Ilene's warriors here, but the Black Angels haven't shown. Without the Black Angels, we could lose."

Bullman reassured them, "The attack is doomed no matter how many of our allies are here or how many Monarchists there are in the attack. We have to wait until the attack is over to be rid of the Monarchists once and for all. Ilene is lucky she brought her women here, or they would suffer the same fate as the rest of the Monarchists. When the attack is over, we'll confront Satan."

The long wait for the expected attack began. Comingal's telephone operators restricted themselves to only received phone calls. They had consolidated their victory, and further propaganda efforts would prove to be counterproductive. However, people were still calling for information about the Ice Water in Hell Democracy, and those calls had to be taken to keep the victory stable.

Ilene positioned her women warriors around the perimeter of the Democrat subdivision to make certain the Monarchists' attack would be met with fatal female force fueled by feminine fury. Bullman, who seemed to be sure of the future, and had nothing else to do, stared at Nadine's breasts while entertaining himself with futile imaginings of a future with her. Comingal, in deep thought, anticipated his future meeting with Satan. Cornball was in the midst of a rare time of quiet for himself; his lies had all been told, and he had no one left to insult.

The loud, grinding, earth ripping sound and the terrible shaking of a massive earthquake tore Bullman's eyes and heated thoughts from Nadine's breasts. He' said, "The Monarchists' attack is over. We can go to the Lake of Fire and see what happened."

A short walk brought the Democrats and Ilene's warriors to the Lake of Fire, which had gotten much larger. Ten Monarchists' subdivisions had collapsed into the Lake of Fire just moments before the Monarchists would have left to begin their attack on the Democrats. Ilene's subdivision jutted into the Lake of Fire like a big boat dock surrounded by lava. The earthquake hadn't shaken it loose with the others. The Monarchists still stood in their subdivisions as the land beneath them and the buildings around them slowly melted into the Lake of Fire. The greatest of Hell's warrior politicians sank slowly into the Lake, their weapons melting into the hot lava they were formed from.

Ilene watched the sinking of her erstwhile royal pretenders with dismay. She knew Satan had nothing to do with the monumental collapse around the Lake of Fire. Ilene asked, of no one in particular, "How can something like this happen? It seems impossible for the whole area to collapse at the same time."

Bullman tried to explain the process to her. "Ignoring the Virtues of Heaven put us all in Hell. Ignoring the Virtues of Hell put the Monarchists in the Lake of Fire. We didn't bother to understand the Virtues of Heaven while we were alive, and none of us understand the Virtues of Hell now. We know the Virtues exist, but we discover what our personal Virtues are the hard way. The Monarchists have discovered, the hard way, the Virtue against making war in Hell."

Ilene took her ornately formed sword and threw it into the Lake of Fire it came from. Her Ladies of Hell Warriors followed her lead, and all of their weapons arced back to their beginnings in the Lake of Fire. There would be no more wars in Hell. Many might be contemplated, but none carried out. The Virtues of Hell canceled all plans for physical conquest.

They watched the Monarchist buildings melt into the slithering lava. No one was happy at the sight. Comingal offered, "There but for the power of the Virtues of Hell stand all of us." Cornball couldn't think of a single insult to throw at the door of the Monarchists, and for the moment, he was too terrified of the Virtues of Hell to open his mouth and utter one.

Bullman remarked, "It's time for us to visit Satan."

Bullman, Comingal, Cornball, Ilene Bogus, and the Black Angel who originally met with the Democrats approached Satan's castle with a certain amount of fear. Satan had at no time entered the political fray. He had left the field of political battle to the other inmates during the turmoil. Satan had left all credit for the successful rise of the Ice Water in Hell Democracy to the Democrats and their associates. They felt they had beaten Satan politically, but they knew he had lost none of his personal powers. All of them still feared him. Their moment to enforce their victory, and Satan's loss of supremacy in Hell, could be dangerous. The five of them had prepared to exhaustion for this moment, and the only rule they could come up with was as common as dirt; do not add insult to injury.

Satan's castle covered a hilltop far from, but overlooking, the deep basin the political subdivisions of Hell occupied. As castles go, it wasn't much of a castle. Low walls protecting its perimeter surrounded the castle's broad area covering the hilltop. Nothing stood more than one story high, and there were no roofs atop the walled areas used as rooms. Bullman explained the castle's strange appearance. "Nearly everything in Hell was constructed before any of the occupants arrived. There are many multi-storied buildings like the ones in the basin, and they stay together because of a process of construction that we cannot duplicate.

"Anyone can build a house or any other type of building he chooses. The problem is finding equipment and building materials to use for the construction. We have only our hands. We can use stones to form walls in an upright position, but we have no water to mix materials with. We have nothing with which to make cement, mortar, rebar, grout, or the other materials needed to keep the stones from falling down again."

"Why can't we use lava for mortar?" asked Comingal.

Bullman dredged up a little of his sorry abundance of patience for the ignorant question, and shared the simple logic with Comingal. "First, no one is going to pick up the hot lava with their hands and carry it to the place he wants to build something. Second, the temperature of Hell is very hot, and the lava cools very slowly. Everything in Hell is uphill from our Lake of Fire, or one of the other Lakes of Fire, and the molten lava eventually flows back to the Lake of Fire from wherever it spewed out.

"Satan has no more building materials than the rest of us, but he has a large work force of Gray Angles. The Gray Angels built his castle, and they keep its crumbling walls repaired. Satan couldn't build a high castle, so he built a wide castle."

Cornball, never quiet for long, added his shaky wisdom to the situation. "Satan ain't got no power at all. He was kicked out of Heaven. He can't even put a roof over his head. We should walk in, throw him out of his castle, and take over. He can't stop us. We should have done that at the beginning. We could have saved ourselves a lot of trouble."

Ice Water in Hell Democracy by Marvin E. Fox

Bullman didn't like Cornball. He thought Cornball was more trouble than he was worth, but Comingal couldn't seem to do without him, and Bullman needed Comingal for an undetermined amount of time in the future. Bullman advised Cornball, "There are no roofs because the earthquakes bring them down on whoever is under them.

"Satan has plenty of power. If you insult him or try to take one personal action against him, you'll find out how much power. You keep your mouth shut while we are with him. He can put all of us in the same boat with you if he chooses, and he may be waiting for us with his anger ready to explode."

They entered the castle and were shown to Satan's large, roofless great hall by Herkimer, his Gray Angel butler. Satan's furniture was made of the stones from his hilltop but polished smooth to give a nicer look—in a hellish sort of way. Comingal and Cornball looked around the room for an impressive Satan with large wings, long tail, red horns coming out of his head, and a trident in his hand, but the only one in sight was Mr. Clause.

Satan said, "Welcome to my home. I thought Mr. Comingal and Mr. Cornball would feel more at home if I appeared in the less-impressive form of Mr. Clause. They are more familiar with Mr. Clause than the form I sometimes use to frighten the more ignorant inmates of Hell. Proper dress is important for important businessmen, and our business, I hope, will be of mutual benefit to all of us.

"I'm delighted that your democracy won the battle for supremacy in Hell. Empires are so difficult to deal with, and a democracy is so easy to control. With your combined abilities to exercise that control, your lives would be a bed of roses, except for your one little problem. You promised all of the inmates in Hell an ice cube in every mouth.

"I enjoyed watching you Democrats battle it out with the Monarchists, lie for lie, fraud for fraud, neither giving an inch, both of you fighting your desperate battles to the last ounce of your strength. Each of you recovered from the onslaught of the other's vitriolic accusations with admiral ingenuity, inventing a new lie for each new situation. I must admit that, in the beginning, I couldn't tell who would win the ridiculous battle for supremacy.

"When the Monarchist leaders decided to make war on the Democrats in angry retaliation for your superb gender attack on their character, and received the approval and help of their entire subdivisions, I knew it was all over. The attack was a massive violation of the Virtues of Hell, and all of their subdivisions fell into the Lake of fire. That was the moment you won.

"I'm glad to see Ilene Bogus and the leader of my old associates among the Black Angels are with you. I was touched by Ilene's change of sides at the last moment. What blind luck on her part, and all because she was insulted by her fellow conspirators. I would have welcomed the Black Angels back into my fold any time, but they are even harder headed than the Monarchists. The poor, angry Black Angels blame me personally for their fall from Heaven. All of them have been dedicated to the moment of my fall from power from their first moments here. All of you richly deserve your prize for outmaneuvering me.

Due to your masterful handling of the Monarchists and winning the final disaster, I have decided to ignore Mr. Bullman's personal treachery to me. I will ignore Mr. Comingal's personal treachery to all of his associates, and to every other person in Hell. I will even ignore Mr. Cornball's rotten accusations against my own benevolent person and everyone else he dislikes. I shall take no personal action, whatever, against any of you.

"I promised the winners of the democracy fraud and magnificent political fiasco a prize. I, Lucifer, am always good for my word; everyone knows that. The prize I am offering you is the most astounding thing any of you could wish for. It is so unbelievable that I think you will want to see it for yourselves. I'm glad my main antagonists are here to receive my magnificent gift. Gentlemen and lady, for beating the Monarchists at their game and me, Lucifer, at my game, I wish to inform you that the ocean of ice is real and that I will tell you where it is. You may view it at your leisure. Your very own ocean of ice is only a short walk from here.

"It isn't really an ocean; it's more like a mammoth glacier that has been creeping quietly to its present position for eons. Its source is somewhere inside the Gulf that surrounds Hell or, perhaps, on the other side of the Gulf; I don't know which. It has been stable in its present position for a very long time, probably waiting for some enterprising souls like you to offer it to the inmates.

"There is a caveat you should be aware of. If that tremendous glacier of ice moves any closer to the Lake of Fire basin or just begins to melt on its own, the political basin will fill up with cool glacial water. However, the water may not remain cool. The intense heat of the Lake of Fire might possibly heat the water to the usual temperature of the Lake of Fire. That will take a very long time. Don't worry yourselves about it.

"Your ocean of ice will keep you in control until the entire population of the political basin can enjoy your triumph, and properly share their adulation for your wonderful gift to them. I think your Ice Water in Hell Democracy will keep you in pretty good shape for a long time to come.

"You may reach your gift by going down the pathway at the rear of my palace. Follow the pathway between the mountains until you reach it. It isn't very far. If you encounter a small problem or two after you reach it, please return to my palace, and I'll help you find the most workable solution."

They followed Satan's instructions, and after what seemed to be days, the path turned into a deep canyon. Sure enough, ice blocked the other end of the canyon from the top to the bottom. They couldn't see anything of the ocean of ice except that one tantalizing sliver that intruded into the narrow canyon. They decided to climb the mountain with the ice canyon at its bottom and view the entire glacier or ocean—whichever the case may be.

As they climbed, Comingal remarked, "Satan appeared so happy about being beaten that I thought he was lying about the ice. I thought he might be putting us in a trap—but I guess I was wrong. We can make a success of our democracy with just the ice we've seen. We can keep it going forever if the glacier is as big as Satan said it is."

"I don't like it," Bullman disagreed. "He was too polite. When he's polite, he has something really bad up his sleeve, and I don't like it."

"You're nothing but another naysayer," Cornball accused. "We have wealth more precious than gold in that ice. We can have everyone in Hell working for us if we play our cards right, and we know how to play those cards. Satan knows he's whipped, and he's bowing out gracefully to keep himself on our good side."

They reached the top of the mountain and were rewarded with a breathtaking view of the ice. It stretched as far as the eye could see and became wider as it extended farther toward the Gulf of Hell. They could see no end to it. "How far is the Gulf from here?" Comingal asked.

"Satan is the only one who has been there—well, he and some of his Gray Angels," Bullman answered. "He once told me he had a glimmering of a way to break out of Hell. He may have a plan to tunnel through the ice and go through the Gulf instead of around it."

The enthused Cornball became the winner's planner. "We need to get crews up here to make the ice cubes and redistribute the ice. We'll bring our Democrats, Ilene's warriors, and the Black Angels. They can make pretty large cubes of ice; we don't need to skimp. We can regulate the workers by making them sign work permits and pay them in ice to do the work. We can tax the inmates so many hours of labor for so much ice.

"As soon as they all get a taste of the ice, we can begin some public works projects. I want a castle farther back in the mountains where it is cooler, and there ain't no Lake of Fire. My castle will be near our air-conditioned headquarters. We can make the inmates build canals and then melt some of the ice and use the canals to carry ice-cold water to our constituents. We can force everyone in Hell to pay taxes to support our ice water projects. They won't mind; they don't have anything else to do; we'll be doing them a big favor."

After listening to Cornball's stupid plans and no objections from Comingal, Bullman wished he had stayed with Satan. Bullman was afraid there might be something wrong with the ice. They were all close enough to see it, but he could feel no coolness from the ice. The others hadn't noticed that small problem. He didn't want Cornball calling him a naysayer again, so he decided to let the impossibility of Cornball's plans take care of not getting any of them done if he was right about the ice.

All five of them stared at the ice for a long time. They were transfixed by the endless expanse of something they'd thought was impossible. The massiveness of the huge ocean of ice caused Bullman to forget about his misgivings and join the others in awestruck appreciation. As their awe diminished, they began to think of the wealth and political possibilities of what seemed an infinite supply of power that had just dropped into their hands. After they had appreciated the bonanza for a time, it occurred to them, that they should be tasting it. After all, they had to do the hard work of bringing the good news of their success to their constituents. Taking a well-deserved drink of the ice water would make the work much easier.

The leading edge of the ice stuck out of the canyon like the prow of a giant ship. From their lofty position, they could look toward their Lake of Fire and see what had survived of the political subdivisions. The entire lake was clearly visible.

A direct route from the top of the mountain and nearer to the ice was closer to their subdivisions than Satan's mountain-skirting route. They decided to leave Satan to his own miserable devices, take the short route down the mountain, and grab a bite of the ice at the same time. The descent was easy, but it brought them far from the large ice cliff on the leading edge of the ice.

They five of them walked for a while before Cornball announced, "I think I hear running water. It sounds good. Let's hurry up and see what it looks like." Just around the last outcropping of rock, and falling from the top of the ice, was a small waterfall, just a trickle, drifting down form high above them. The falling splashes of water were slowly filling a large, shallow basin in front of the ice. It would take time for the basin to fill, but if the water kept flowing, it would eventually fill and overflow the basin to form a river that would work its way through the valley to the Lake of Fire.

Bullman and Comingal, deeply involved in calculating the power and profit they could extract from the inmates when they taxed them for the ice, held back instead of rushing to the pool of ice water. Cornball, who was ecstatic with the discovery, raced ahead of the others, plunged his hand into the water, and tried to raise the water to his lips. The ice water in his hand turned to steam before he could bring it to his lips and drink. He tried several more times but had to give up on drinking the water because it kept turning to steam.

Cornball turned to the massive cliff of ice. He and the Black Angel walked to the leading edge of the protruding glacier of ice. While Cornball and the Black Angel were studying the ice, Ilene tried her luck at drinking the cool water the way Cornball had failed to do. She was no more successful than Cornball, even though she tried to cool her hand by leaving it in the water for a while. The water turned to steam in her hands no matter how long she kept her hand in the water or how quickly she brought it to her lips.

The Black Angel reached up as high as he could and broke off a hanging icicle, but his hand melted it with steaming ferocity before he could bring it to his mouth. Cornball picked up a rock and knocked off a sizable chunk of ice. The ice chunk began steaming in his hand as he brought it toward his mouth. He quickly crammed the last melting sliver of ice between his waiting lips. A long narrow blast of steam came out before he could close his mouth. Cornball, in confusion, stood silently inspecting his dry hands for the moisture he thought should remain from the ice.

Comingal and Bullman, after finishing their tax calculations, joined the other three in the desperate attempts to drink the ice water or suck on a piece of ice. None of the new rulers of the Ice Water in Hell Democracy could find a way to do either. Bullman and Comingal, stunned by the fact that none of them could drink the water, or suck on a piece of ice, sat down, looked each to the other, and said, "Oh, shit." Bullman remarked, hopelessly, "We need to talk to Satan."

Comingal stood up and stared at Cornball, who was again trying to drink the ice water. After many more tries, he still had only steam in his hands. Comingal said, "Come on, Cornball, we have a long walk."

Ilene Bogus and the Black Angel refused to make the long walk and listen to Satan, even if it was necessary. They decided to take the shortcut back to the subdivisions, but they agreed to keep quiet about the uselessness of the ice. Bullman, Comingal, and Cornball still had a vague hope of finding a way to get Satan to tell them how to save the future of their Ice Water in Hell Democracy.

Each step of their return to Satan's castle was taken in the depths of despair. They had enjoyed their escape from Satan's power for only a brief moment before they realized they hadn't escaped at all. Satan knew every move they made, and he let them continue making the moves because they were all wrong. Knowing something is wrong can be helpful, but only when the wrongdoers can figure out how to right the wrong. Bullman, Comingal, and Cornball knew they had screwed up. They didn't have a clue about the right way to unscrew their mistakes.

Satan's butler, Herkimer, was waiting for them when they reached Satan's back gate. He announced, with a smile, "Lucifer anticipated your return. Follow me."

They entered Satan's great hall and found Satan in an especially good mood. Satan, in feigned concern for their welfare, asked, "Was your view of the ocean all you expected it to be? Or was there an unexpected problem or two I may help you solve?"

Comingal, the wise campaigner, who realized he had been had, asked in return, "All right, what's your price? You knew the ice was impossible to use, and now we know it too. We'll cut you in any way you want. We have all of the subdivisions, and you have no power. What's your price to even things out between us?"

Satan seemed wounded. "Price! I have no price. What is it you think I may do to help you? Ask, and if I can do it, it will be done."

Bullman suggested, "Make the ice drinkable or usable."

"The reasons you can't drink or use the ice has nothing to do with me," cried Satan. "Your bodies neither require nor will they tolerate water, frozen or piping hot. You don't eat or drink because your bodies neither require nor will they permit you to use food and drink. You are dead people; you don't have stomachs, kidneys, bowels, or anything else requiring something you don't already have for your lives in Hell. You are here, but your earthly bodies are not. I can't help you with the problem you think you have, but should have recognized is not a problem. It is a natural advantage shared by each person in Hell."

Cornball was not to be denied. He said, "You knew the ice was already melting. You probably started it melting to get even with us. You have to freeze the water and keep it from flowing into the subdivision. Pretty soon there will be an ocean of water flowing into the subdivisions, and the subdivisions will be under water if you don't stop it. You surely don't want everyone in Hell to drown?"

Satan smiled broadly at Cornball and said, "The ice dripped its first drop of water when you let your ignorant motor mouth loose, blaming God because you are in Hell. Getting slammed into the Lake of Fire wasn't enough for breaking that Virtue. All of you were trying to gain control of Hell. You wanted the personal power that control would give to you, and you convinced your associates to join you in that deception. Your stupid actions violated a whole list of the Virtues that govern us all.

"I kept myself and my Gray Angels completely away from you while you were carrying out your miserable fraud. I wanted to remain free of the affects of your Virtue violations while you were screwing up. I didn't start the ice melting, and I can't stop it from melting. I have feared that ice for a very long time. I knew everyone in Hell would blame me if it melted. Fortunately for me, you came along making yourselves the cause, and you will take the blame for its happening.

"You won't drown from the cold water. It will immediately heat up to the temperature of the Lake of Fire. However, you will certainly be in trouble with all of the unfortunate souls who expected an ice cube in every mouth. Your political enemies, the Monarchists you have treated with such loving respect, may not like living in hot water any more than you will. They, like you, will come to understand that Hell is not as hot as their own bodies. The only thing hotter than your own bodies is the Lake of Fire. Your Ice Water in Hell Democracy will bring the heat of the Lake of Fire to every political misfit in the basin.

"You used my excellent communications system to speak with many of the subdivisions, but you don't know where the majority, no pun intended, of the subdivisions are. None of the other subdivisions in Hell will be under your ice-cold water, and they will all be told how lucky they are that I was able to save them from sharing your fate. I'll point the bony finger of scorn at you to make sure they put the blame for your self-generated misery on you instead of me.

I'm sure the telephones, computers, and fax machines connecting the subdivisions will work wet, but it is something of a mystery how you will use them. Besides that, my central control operators might not be so easy to fool the next time you try. If I were you, I wouldn't answer the phones after the cool, refreshing water begins pouring into the Lake of Fire. The disappointed ice cube recipients on the other ends of the telephones will make Cornball, your master accuser, sound like a warm-hearted Sunday school teacher."

Satan's sarcasm even exceeded Cornball's accusations at full flower, but Comingal still wanted help if there was a way to get it. "Will you help the political subdivisions resettle at a higher elevation?" Comingal asked. "Maybe we can salvage something if we move."

"I didn't build the subdivisions," Satan replied. "They were here when I arrived. I made the rule about not leaving them, but I lied about the punishment. I've never thrown anyone into the Lake of Fire. The inmates who violated the Virtues found themselves in the Lake of Fire and believed I threw them there—so the lie worked. Lies are not a violation of the Virtues, or we would all be living in the Lake of Fire. If you want to leave your subdivision, take all of those who are willing to leave and see what happens. You won't have a problem with me if you go, but who knows what other Virtuous calamities your exodus might cause. I'm so *terribly* sorry, but I can't help you. I hope at least one of the problems you've caused for yourselves will be something that will allow me to prove what a wonderful friend I really am."

Bullman knew Satan had his own plan for what was about to happen, and he wanted to know what the plan was. Satan was crowing so loud with his 'I would help you, but I can't' act that Bullman thought he might tell them about it to prove his superior intellect. "What's your plan for all of this? You were controlling Hell, and now, at least for the time being, you are not. How does a superior intellect like yours deal with a problem you refused to help make, can't cure, but intend to profit from?"

Satan gazed contentedly through his open roof at the small portion of the Gulf of Hell he could see directly overhead. He entwined his fingers and cracked his knuckles. Satan looked at Bullman as though Bullman had just given him a precious gift; then he crowed again, "You three bone-brains gave me the only interlude of interest I have had since my arrival. For that great favor, you deserve an explanation.

"I have been trying for eons to gain control of Hell without violating the Virtues. You handed me control with absolutely no effort on my part and without my coming close to violating a Virtue. You, yourselves, violated all of the Virtues, and what a magnificent job of it you did.

"I think this is what is happening, and I will, of course, come out on top. The water will cover your subdivision, and the Monarchist rabble that are, as we speak, waiting patiently in the Lake of Fire. The cold glacial water will become as hot as the Lake of Fire itself. It will do that because of your expertise in engineering the most massive Virtue violations Hell has ever experienced. I know all of the extra heat, and living under a big bubble of hot water is an untended result of your expert political actions, but politics is filled with unintended results, like the bubble of water that brought you here. You will tell everyone you worked so hard for them, but alas, things went wrong, and the unintended results just aren't your fault.

"You and all of the other revolutionaries will try, but none of you will be able to get out of hot water until each has served his time for his individual violations, and the time will be different for each inmate. All will exit slowly in a manageable stream to become a member of your Ice Water In Hell Democracy. You three, the eleven tin-pot psychos trying to become kings, and the traitorous Black Angels will be the last to escape.

"As the other inmates escape, they will turn to me for help because they will believe I am the only one who can help. I will extend my humble hands to them as help from a caring leader. They will form a deep trust in me in return for my benevolent guidance. I will help them find new homes far from the Lake of Fire and nearer to the Gulf of Hell—where the temperature at least has the appearance of being somewhat cooler.

"I will explain your treachery, your greed, and your bone-brained stupidity to them—in my own way, of course. I will perfect my own democratic credentials while your mouths are still stopped up with hot water. From that moment on, I will be the top dog in Hell, and you slow-brained political has-beens will be nothing. I will have won big, and you will have lost big. You can't win. You're no match for an intellectual giant like me.

"Your magnificent fraud, which I wisely kept myself and my Gray Angels completely out of, is the greatest favor anyone has done for me. I will benefit eternally from your hard work. You convinced the people of Hell that democracy puts them in charge, and I will put your democracy to them in your style. I will not define democracy for them. I will only tell them what it does for them. I will convince them that only a good Democrat, like myself, could possible manage the rule of such a large majority for the majority's benefit.

"I and my Gray Angels will be their only source of information, and we will tell them, as you would have, what the majority of them want. We will carefully spin the facts, as you would have done, to guide them along the pathway of their eternity. Each of them in the phony majority will have no way to check with enough of the others to prove my spin is not the majority's will.

"Democracy is such a powerful tool for my new government that I intend to keep it going forever. It will make everyone so much easier for me to manage. You Democrats have given me a way to control Hell that I would never have dared to try myself. Since you have gratuitously put it in place for me, I can use it without violating a single Virtue.

"I have secured the help of one of your better-known associates, whom you didn't seem to notice was missing from your group. He was lonely and feeling left out of your activities, so he came to me. After I explained the situation to him, we became good friends. Mr. Fringe has offered to share his political expertise to benefit all of us in the new government. Also, a new arrival I have waited patiently for will be Mr. Bullman's replacement. Mr. Sulaman DePresske is now my man, and he is a very good lawyer. He and Mr. Fringe were good friends in their former lives. He tells me he knew Mr. Cornball in pre-bubble days. What a team the three of us will make! We will bring democracy to Hell, and I won't need any of your useless meddling."

Cornball could take no more; he busted a gusset. "You dirty lying rat. You ain't nothing but a petty thief. You're stealing our democracy and leaving us with nothing. You can't run a democracy! You're just a troublemaker who thinks he can. Running a real democracy takes real Democrats, like us. You ain't no real democrat, and your two traitors can't make you any better."

Satan raised his eyes to the Gulf of Hell, smiled his secret smile, cracked his knuckles once again, and then declared, "Cornball, the democracy was never yours; it only seemed to be yours." He raised his face to the hated Gulf, smiled through his hatred of it, at some sweet inner thought, looked into Cornball's eyes, and jeered, "You must surely understand by now; the Devil was in the details."

Satan looked at his three main antagonists for a moment before he remarked, "While you are under your new bubble of water, I hope you three will make plans to take the Hot Water Democracy, you created just for me, out of the hands of a good, warm hearted, successful Democrat like myself, and restore it to failures such as yourselves. I need continual exercise for my mind, and you three are the most interesting exercise I can look forward to during the coming eternity."

They listened to Satan's blowhard act patiently to keep from angering him further, but finally, Satan ran out of blow. They left Satan's castle knowing they had exhausted the only avenue of personal recovery from their political failure. Bullman, Comingal, and Cornball marched toward the Democrat subdivision with only two things on their minds: what method to use to escape blame for the failure of the Ice Water in Hell Democracy, and how to get even with Satan.

Comingal already had a plan cooking. He was still working on the *escape blame* part of the plan, which was the really tough part. Getting even with Satan consumed his attention. "While we're in that hot water, let's find a way to take care of Satan once and for all. We can tell a few lies to make friends with the Monarchists and the Black Angels. They'll be in the hot water as long as we are, and none of them like Satan. We can tell them Satan knew we couldn't use the ice, so he melted it to get even with all of us who tried to get rid of him. They won't know the difference, and they won't believe anything Satan says about it.

"We can find a way to make Satan violate the Virtues of Hell instead of us real Democrats—if we all work together. With Satan in the Lake of Fire, Hell will become our private domain."

After a moment of silence, Comingal added his only pleasant thought about the disaster to his Ice Water in Hell Democracy, and his Democrat Party's stay under the Virtue of Hell bubble of water. "Nadine will look great in a wet blouse."

THE END

Ice Water in Hell Democracy by Marvin E. Fox

www.ingramcontent.com/pod-product-compliance
Lightning Source LLC
Chambersburg PA
CBHW080902120626
46555CB00008B/2911